EMMA

AND THE

Vampires

JANE AUSTEN

AND

WAYNE JOSEPHSON

sourcebooks
landmark

Published by Sourcebooks Landmark, an imprint of Sourcebooks, Inc.
P.O. Box 4410, Naperville, Illinois 60567-4410
(630) 961-3900
FAX: (630) 961-2168
www.sourcebooks.com

Library of Congress Cataloging-in-Publication Data

Josephson, Wayne.
  Emma and the vampires / Jane Austen and Wayne Josephson.
    p. cm.
  1. Austen, Jane, 1775-1817—Parodies, imitations, etc. 2. Vampires—Fiction. 3. Fathers and daughters—Fiction. 4. Female friendship—Fiction. 5. Mate selection—Fiction. 6. Young women—England—Fiction. 7. England—Fiction. I. Austen, Jane, 1775-1817. Emma. II. Title.
  PS3610.O6785E46 2010
  813'.6—dc22
                              2010010125

Printed and bound in the United States of America
VP 10 9 8 7 6 5 4 3 2 1

To Peggy

CHAPTER 1

EMMA WOODHOUSE—HANDSOME, CLEVER, and rich, with a comfortable home and happy disposition—had lived nearly twenty-one years in the world with very little to distress her. Until the vampire attacks began.

Emma resided with her affectionate, indulgent father at their estate, Hartfield, in the village of Highbury. She had been the mistress of the house ever since her sister Isabella's marriage seven years past. Her mother had died too long ago for Emma to have had more than a vague remembrance of her caresses. In her mother's place, an excellent woman named Miss Taylor had served as governess.

Miss Taylor was less a governess than a friend—their relationship had more the intimacy of sisters. Miss Taylor imposed hardly any restraints on Emma, living together as mutual friends, and Emma doing just what she liked.

The real evils, indeed, of Emma's situation were the power of getting too much her own way and a disposition to think a bit too well of herself.

These were disadvantages that would lead to dangers which were presently unperceived—everyone in Emma's village was pale, this being England, so the vampire gentlemen of Highbury blended in quite nicely. Emma was blithely unaware when she found herself in their presence. And especially when she found herself attracted to them.

A gentle sorrow came when Miss Taylor married. The wedding had every promise of happiness for Emma's former governess. Her new husband, Mr. Weston, was a vampire of exceptional character, easy fortune, appealing scent, and eternally suitable age. He had the pale blue-coloured eyes of a vegan who feasted only on animal blood. Emma thought it slightly odd that Mr. Weston requested the wedding be held at midnight. The guests struggled to stay awake, but since Mr. Weston never slept, he was quite alert throughout the ceremony.

How was Emma to bear the loss of Miss Taylor? With whom would she now share an intimate acquaintance?

She dearly loved her father, but he was no companion for her. He could not equal her in conversation, and the disparity in their ages was much increased by his having been a hypochondriac all his life. And with the recent vampire attacks, he was quite fearful of leaving home.

Emma's sister Isabella, being settled in London sixteen miles off, was much too distant for daily contact. Many a long October and November evening must be endured at Hartfield before Christmas brought the next visit from Isabella, her husband, and their little children to fill the house and give her pleasant company again.

Highbury, the large and populous village in which Hartfield was located, afforded Emma no possibility of new friends. The Woodhouses were the grandest family in town. All looked up to them. She had many acquaintances, but not one among them who could be considered a replacement for Miss Taylor.

It was a melancholy change losing Miss Taylor, and Emma could only sigh over it. But she needed to act cheerful for her father. He was a nervous man, easily depressed, hating change of every kind. He was still not reconciled to his daughter Isabella's marrying, when he now had to part with Miss Taylor too.

"Poor Miss Taylor! I wish she were here again."

"But Papa, Mr. Weston is such a good-humoured, pleasant, and excellent man that he thoroughly deserves a good wife. We shall often visit with them. We must pay a dinner visit very soon."

"But—"

"What is it, Papa?"

"My dear, you know how I dread leaving the gates of Hartfield. I just heard of another young lady, a boarder at Mrs. Goddard's school, being murdered by a vampire as she walked home from the village, her blood sucked completely dry."

"Yes, Papa, that was tragic indeed. I hope in my heart she was not pretty—it would have been such a waste! That makes the third attack in just a few months. It seems no one is safe in Highbury any more. But we would take the carriage to visit the Westons. That would relieve your worry, would it not?"

"Yes, but—"

"What is it now, Papa?"

"It is just that Mr. Weston—he never eats. We shall arrive at dinner and there will be no food to sustain us."

Emma nodded at her father's wisdom. "Perhaps we ought to visit for tea."

Her father smiled, and Emma hoped that a game of backgammon might help him through the evening.

The backgammon table was set up, but before they could commence, Mr. George Knightley paid a call.

Mr. Knightley was a strikingly handsome vampire who claimed to be thirty-seven but was actually two hundred thirty-seven, with alabaster skin and thick brown hair combed back off his high aristocratic forehead. He had deep purple circles under his eyes from never sleeping.

A traditional vampire who favoured human blood, Mr. Knightley had not feasted for a great while and thus his eyes were black from need of sustenance. Being a gentleman, of course, he would never consider roaming about at night attacking young ladies to whom he had not been properly introduced.

Mr. Knightley was not only an intimate friend of the Woodhouse family but an in-law as well—his younger brother John Knightley was married to Emma's sister Isabella.

He lived about a mile from Highbury at his estate, Donwell Abbey. Mr. Knightley was a frequent visitor and always welcome at Hartfield—tonight more welcome than usual, having come directly from John and Isabella's house in London to say that everyone was well there.

His visit this evening cheered Mr. Woodhouse for some time. Mr. Knightley had a reserved but pleasant manner which always did him good. And since his eyes never blinked, he flattered everyone with an uninterrupted gaze.

Mr. Woodhouse gratefully observed, "It is very kind of you, Mr. Knightley, to come out at this late hour to call upon us. I am afraid you must have had a shocking walk, with so much danger lurking about."

"Not at all, sir. It is my favourite time of day—a beautiful moonlit night. I now find myself so warm that I must draw back from your great fire." Lest, he thought, I should spontaneously combust into flames.

"But you must have found your walk very damp. I wish you may not catch cold."

"Damp, sir!" exclaimed Mr. Knightley. "I thrive in the dampness and cold. The sun quite disagrees with me. And by the by, I have not wished you joy about the wedding. I trust it all went off well. How did you all behave? Who cried the most?"

"Ah! Poor Miss Taylor!" said Mr. Woodhouse.

"I should think she would indeed be crying on her nuptial night," said Mr. Knightley, "from the anticipation of the coldness of her new husband's—uh, skin. Well, at any rate, Miss Taylor has been accustomed to having two persons to please, sir—you and Emma. She will now have but one—her husband. It must be better to have only one to please than two."

"Especially when one of us is such a fanciful, troublesome creature!" said Emma playfully. "That is what you have in your head, I know. Mr. Knightley loves to find fault with me, Papa—it is all a joke. We always say what we like to one another."

Mr. Knightley was one of the few people who could see faults in Emma Woodhouse. In fact, he seemed to possess a strange ability to look into her mind and discern what she was thinking. He was the only one who ever told Emma of her faults. This was not agreeable to Emma—she wanted to be thought of as perfect by everybody.

"Emma knows I never flatter her," said Mr. Knightley. But she also knew how much he cared. On his advice, Emma now carried a wooden stake under her skirt, tied to her leg with a fashionable pink ribbon. Moreover, he instructed her in its proper use, all the while on tenterhooks that she should ever have occasion to employ the weapon against him.

"I know that Emma will miss such a companion as Miss Taylor," continued Mr. Knightley, "but she knows how much joy the marriage brings to her former governess."

"And you have forgotten the considerable joy to me," said Emma. "I made the match myself, you know, four years ago; and to have it take place, when so many people said Mr. Weston would never marry again, may comfort me through anything."

Mr. Knightley shook his head at her. His piercing eyes stared at her, and he drew back, becoming paler even still, employing his special power to know that Emma embellished the truth.

Her father fondly replied, "Ah! My dear, I wish you would not make matches. Pray do not make any more matches."

"I promise to make none for myself, Papa. But I must, indeed, for other people. It is the greatest amusement in the world! And after such success! Everybody said that Mr. Weston, who had been a widower so long, would never marry again. When I have had such success, dear Papa, you cannot think that I shall leave off matchmaking."

"I do not understand what you mean by success," said Mr. Knightley. "I rather imagine your saying to yourself one idle day, 'I think it would be nice if Mr. Weston were to marry Miss Taylor.' You made a lucky guess, and that is all that can be said."

"A lucky guess is never merely luck," said Emma. "There is always some talent in it. If I had not promoted Mr. Weston's visits here, and given many little encouragements, it might not have come to anything after all."

"My dear," replied Mr. Knightley, "a straightforward man like Weston"—whose heart never beats and lungs never breathe, he thought—"and a rational, unaffected woman like Miss Taylor may be safely left to manage their own concerns. You are more likely to have done harm than good by interfering."

"Emma never thinks of herself if she can do good to others," rejoined Mr. Woodhouse, understanding only part of what he had just heard. "But, my dear, pray do not make any more matches—they are silly things."

"Only one more, Papa. Only for Mr. Elton, our dear vicar. Poor, pale Mr. Elton! I must look about for a wife for him. He has been here two whole years and has fitted up his house so comfortably—though his black curtains are curiously always drawn against the light of day. He must be very sad to live alone. It would be a shame to have him single any longer. I thought when he officiated the wedding ceremony last night for Miss Taylor and Mr. Weston, he looked so very much as if he would like to have a wedding for himself!"

"Mr. Elton is a very handsome young man, to be sure," said her father. "I have a great regard for him. On Sunday mornings, when he touches my hand at communion, a shock like lightning courses through my body, which must be the Lord himself working his miracles. I do find it curious that he never ventures near the holy water or symbols of the cross. Quite strange behaviour indeed for a man of God. Nevertheless, my dear, if you want to show him any attention, ask him to come and dine with us someday. That will be a much better thing."

"I agree with you entirely, sir," said Mr. Knightley, although, he thought, considering the blackness of Mr. Elton's eyes, I would imagine his hunger lies in something other than the repast you will offer. "Invite him to dinner, Emma, but leave him to choose his own wife. Depend upon it, any man who appears to be twenty-seven and never seems to age can take care of himself."

CHAPTER 2

M R. WESTON WAS A native of Highbury, born into a respectable family of vegan vampires which, for the past two or three hundred years, had risen into gentility and property. He had received a good education and, after inheriting early in life a small fortune, had entered into the military.

Young Captain Weston was a general favourite, much admired for his good looks, great strength, and amazing speed. Then he met a Miss Churchill, of a great and wealthy Yorkshire family. Nobody was surprised when they fell in love except her brother, who, having never seen Captain Weston, objected strongly.

Miss Churchill, however, would not be dissuaded from the marriage. Thus the wedding took place, to the infinite mortification of her brother and sister-in-law, Mr. and Mrs. Churchill, who promptly disowned her.

Mrs. Weston loved her husband, but her extravagance caused them to live well beyond their means. She wanted to be both the wife of Captain Weston *and* the grand Miss Churchill of her family's estate, Enscombe.

Captain Weston had refrained from feasting on his wife, in order that she could bear children. After three years of marriage, Mrs. Weston succeeded in giving birth to a son named Frank. Sadly, however, Mrs. Weston died in childbirth.

Captain Weston was now a widower with no fortune and a child to raise. But he was soon relieved when the boy's aunt and uncle Mr. and Mrs. Churchill, having no children of their own, offered to take charge of little Frank.

With some reluctance on the part of Captain Weston, the child with pallid skin and pale blue-coloured eyes like his father's was given up to the care and wealth of the Churchills. They gave the child everything, including many pets—cats, dogs, and guinea pigs—all of which died mysteriously one after the other, their blood sucked dry.

For Captain Weston, a complete change of life became necessary. He quit the military and engaged in business with his brothers, who were already established in London. He still had a small house in Highbury, where he spent most of his leisure days, feasting on small animals in the forest; and between his useful occupation and the pleasures of society, the next eighteen or twenty years of his life passed cheerfully away.

He had, by that time, built up a satisfactory fortune; he was able to afford the purchase of a little estate near Highbury, called Randalls, which he had always longed for. He also had enough money to marry Miss Taylor, despite her small dowry.

As for his little son Frank, the adoption by the boy's uncle and aunt resulted in his assuming the name of Churchill on coming of age and becoming heir to the great family fortune.

Mr. Weston saw Frank every year in London and was proud of his strong, swift, handsome son. He was not quite so pleased, however, that Frank had taken to human blood, partaking of young ladies at various parties in London and at seaside resorts in the summer. Mr. Weston missed gazing into his son's pale blue eyes, for now they were black or, after every feasting, blood red.

Nonetheless, Mr. Weston's fond reports of Frank as a very fine young man had made Highbury feel a sort of pride in him. Everyone was curious to finally see Mr. Frank Churchill. His coming to visit his father had been often talked of but never achieved. Now, upon his father's marriage, it was generally assumed that the visit would take place.

It was indeed time for Mr. Frank Churchill to meet them all, and the hope greatly strengthened when he wrote a letter to his new stepmother. Everyone in Highbury mentioned the handsome letter Mrs. Weston had received.

"I suppose you have heard of the handsome letter Mr. Frank Churchill has written to Mrs. Weston?" said the ladies and gentlemen of Highbury to each other. "Mr. Woodhouse saw the letter, and he says he never saw such a handsome letter in his life," they said.

Mrs. Weston had formed a very favourable opinion of young Frank and greatly anticipated his visit. She felt herself a most fortunate woman, whose only regret was the separation from Emma and Mr. Woodhouse.

Mrs. Weston knew that Emma missed her terribly. But dear Emma was no feeble character—she had sense, energy, and spirit that would bear her well. And Mrs. Weston knew that Emma had an extensive collection of fashionable ribbons with which to secure a wooden stake beneath her skirt—although she was confident that Emma would never have to use her lethal weapon against any members of their social circle.

CHAPTER 3

M R. WOODHOUSE WAS ECCENTRIC. He liked very much to have his close friends come and visit him, but he had little intercourse with any families beyond that circle. His horror of late hours, large dinner parties, and attacks by bloodthirsty supernatural beings made him unfit for any acquaintances except those who would visit him on his own terms.

Fortunately for him, his closest friends all lived near by—the Westons of Randalls, Mr. George Knightley of Donwell Abbey, and occasionally Mr. Elton, the young vicar living alone without liking it.

Occasionally, through Emma's persuasion, his chosen circle dined with him at evening parties. He was quite terrified of the evils of food and, therefore, quite pleased that his friends, for the most part, consumed nary a morsel themselves. Mr. Woodhouse could not help wondering, though, what exactly his friends did eat.

Besides his inner circle, there came a second group, among the most come-at-able of whom were the elderly Mrs. Bates, her spinster daughter Miss Bates, and Mrs. Goddard, three ladies almost always eager to accept an invitation from the Woodhouses at Hartfield.

Mrs. Bates, the widow of a former vicar of Highbury, was a very old lady, almost past everything but tea and French square dancing. She lived with her daughter in a very small house and was regarded with the respect which a harmless old lady can excite.

Her daughter Miss Bates, however, enjoyed a most uncommon degree of popularity for a woman who was neither young, handsome, rich, nor married. Miss Bates stood in the very worst predicament in the world for having such popularity—she had no intellectual superiority, she had never been guilty of either beauty or cleverness, her youth had passed without distinction, and her middle life was devoted to the care of a failing mother and the endeavour to make a small income go as far as possible.

And yet, she was a happy woman, and a woman whom no one mentioned without compliment. She loved everybody, was interested in everybody's happiness, and was attentive to everybody's best qualities. She thought herself a most fortunate creature and was a great talker upon little matters, which exactly suited Mr. Woodhouse, who himself was full of trivial communications and harmless gossip.

Mrs. Goddard was the mistress of the local boarding school—not an establishment which might turn young ladies to vanity at enormous expense, but a real, honest, old-fashioned boarding school, where a reasonable quantity of accomplishments were sold at a reasonable price. Here, wealthy girls might be sent to get them out of the way of their parents, and orphan girls might learn to be ladies through the generosity of the local charitable trust.

Mrs. Goddard's school was in high repute, and very deservedly. She had an ample house and garden, gave the girls plenty of wholesome food, let them run about a great deal in the summer, and, in winter, dressed their frostbite with her own hands.

It was no wonder that, as the train of twenty young ladies followed Mrs. Goddard to church every Sunday, the bloodlust of the young male vampires in attendance was sorely tempted. Might some of these same young fangs have been among the wild, vagrant vampires who had recently preyed on the poor virgins of Mrs. Goddard's school? All of Highbury speculated, but no one knew for certain.

Mrs. Goddard, Mrs. Bates, and Miss Bates, then, who would gather around Emma's father, were the same ladies whom Emma also found very often gathered around her. They were pleasant enough, though they were no remedy for the absence of Mrs. Weston. Emma was delighted to see her father look comfortable and was pleased with herself for organising things so well. But the quiet conversations of three such old women made her feel that these evenings were indeed the longest evenings of her life.

As she sat one morning, looking forward to exactly such an evening, a note was brought from Mrs. Goddard requesting, in most respectful terms, to be allowed to bring a Miss Harriet Smith with her—a most welcome request, for Miss Smith was a girl of seventeen whom Emma knew very well by sight, and Emma had long felt an interest in meeting her on account of Miss Smith's beauty. And thus, the evening was no longer to be dreaded by the fair mistress of the mansion.

Harriet Smith was the natural daughter of Somebody whom nobody knew. This Somebody had placed her, several years back, at Mrs. Goddard's school. This was all that was generally known of her history. She had no visible friends besides those acquired at the school, other than a family in the country with whom she had spent two months in the summer—unbeknownst to her, a family of vampires.

Harriet was a very pretty girl, and her beauty happened to be of a sort which Emma particularly admired. She was short, plump, and fair, with a fine bosom, blue eyes, light hair, regular features, and a look of great sweetness. The male vampires in Highbury drooled over her, contemplating vile thoughts about sinking their fangs into her plumpness. And Emma herself felt a vague sense of foreboding that Miss Harriet Smith was just the sort of delicacy who might appeal to the dreaded vampire attackers who skulked about the countryside.

That evening, at the dinner party, Emma was introduced to Miss Harriet Smith. She was not struck by anything remarkably clever in Miss Smith's conversation, but she found her altogether very engaging and not too shy. More commendably, Harriet seemed so pleasantly grateful for being invited to Hartfield and so impressed by everything that was superior in style to what she had been accustomed that Emma decided that Harriet must have good sense and deserved encouragement.

Emma concluded that Harriet's soft blue eyes and all those natural graces ought not be wasted on the inferior society of Highbury. The acquaintances Harriet had already formed were most unworthy of her. The friends whom she had visited last summer, good peasant farmers, were a family by the name of Martin, who rented a large farm from Mr. Knightley and resided in his parish of Donwell.

Emma knew that Mr. Knightley thought highly of the Martins—not realising, of course, that most vampires thought highly of each other—but Emma decided they were coarse, unpolished, and very unfit to be the close friends of a girl who needed only a little more polish and elegance to be quite perfect.

Yes, Emma would take her on. She would improve Harriet; she would detach her from her bad acquaintances and introduce her into good society. Emma would form Harriet's opinions and manners, and instruct her in the proper use of a wooden stake in case she was ever attacked at night. It would be an interesting and certainly a very kind undertaking, highly becoming to Emma's own situation in life, leisure, and powers.

Emma was so great a personage in Highbury that Harriet had as much panic as pleasure upon first meeting her hostess. But the humble, grateful little girl was delighted with the friendliness with which Emma had treated her all evening.

Emma was so busy admiring those soft blue eyes, talking and listening, and forming all these schemes in the in-betweens that the evening flew away at a very unusual rate.

As the perfect hostess, Emma eagerly did all the honours of the meal and recommended the minced chicken and scalloped oysters to the ladies present. Missing from the party were precisely the guests who would rather have had Emma's wooden stake driven through their hearts than partake of such disgusting victuals.

At these dinner parties, poor Mr. Woodhouse's feelings were always in sad warfare. He loved to have the table set, but his conviction of food being very unwholesome made him rather sorry to see anything put on it—in this respect, he would have made an excellent vampire.

While his hospitality welcomed his visitors to enjoy everything, his care and concern for their health made him grieve that they should consume a single taste.

A small bowl of thin porridge was all that he could recommend; though, while the ladies were comfortably eating nicer things, he would say, "Mrs. Bates, let me propose your venturing one of these soft boiled eggs," and "Miss Bates, let Emma help you to a little bit of tart—a very little bit," and "I do not advise the custard, Mrs. Goddard; what say you to a small half-glass of wine? I do not think it could disagree with you."

Emma allowed her father to talk while she supplied her guests in a much more satisfactory style, and on this evening she had particular pleasure in sending them away happy, especially Miss Harriet Smith.

At the conclusion of the party, Emma accompanied Harriet Smith and Mrs. Goddard outside the house, as they awaited the carriages to be brought round.

"A very lovely evening, Miss Woodhouse," said Mrs. Goddard. "And it is always such a pleasure to see Mr. Woodhouse again."

"Oh, yes," gushed Harriet Smith, "I so enjoyed meeting you, Miss Woodhouse, and trust that I did not bore you exceedingly with my prattle."

"Dear Harriet, I find you quite engaging and lovely. I trust that we shall become friends. You are quite a charming young—"

At that moment, the ladies heard a loud rustling in the shrubbery nearby. All were silent, then Mrs. Goddard spoke with great trepidation.

"Miss Woodhouse, was that the wind crackling the bushes?"

Emma wore an expression of concern. "I think not, Mrs. Goddard. The evening air is quite still and bushes do not normally crackle."

"I do wish the carriage would hurry," said Harriet, her plump face flushed with worry.

Suddenly, the tall bushes parted. The ladies gasped in unison and froze where they stood.

A hideous apparition emerged, male, his face and hands pale as snow; wearing a suit of rags that hung off his spare frame; hair black as night—long and unkempt; eyes even blacker, if that were possible; and his pale lips parted to reveal sharp, white fangs.

It was a wild vampire.

Harriet and Mrs. Goddard shrieked as Emma dashed into the house. In a blur of motion, the vampire was next to Harriet, grasping at her bosom, his fangs flashing ominously.

Screaming, Harriet beat at him with her fists, flailing about and keeping him at bay. Weakened as the vampire was from lack of sustenance, it was nevertheless clear that Harriet had only frantic moments to live before she would succumb to his vicious designs.

Mrs. Goddard fainted dead away and fell to the ground as Emma came running from the house, waving her father's old sabre in both hands.

With a single, clean swath of the sword, Emma severed the head of the vampire. It bounced on the ground and rolled a few feet, and then the body of the creature collapsed as well.

Emma then pulled her handy wooden stake from beneath her bombazine skirts which were, like everything else she wore, at the height of fashion, and drove it through the vampire's heart.

Emma stared speechless at the carnage then looked at Harriet, who was gaping at her, wide-eyed.

"Miss Woodhouse!" exclaimed Harriet. "Oh, dear Miss Woodhouse! You have saved my life!"

"Indeed, I suppose I have," Emma said, still shaken from the surreal experience. "Are you all right, Harriet?"

"Indeed I am, Miss Woodhouse. But are you? What possessed you to have the presence of mind, and the knowledge, to vanquish such a despicable foe?"

"I honestly do not know, Harriet. I suppose a well-bred young lady knows instinctively what to do in any circumstance. I knew I must help you."

"Indeed you did, Miss Woodhouse. Indeed you did! Oh, Miss Woodhouse, I shall be indebted to you for the rest of my life!"

Mrs. Goddard had now awakened, and the Bateses and Mr. Woodhouse had hurried out the front door after hearing the screams and commotion.

"Dear me!" squealed Miss Bates. "Upon my word! Is that a vampire? Dear Miss Woodhouse, have you just killed a vampire? I have never in my life seen anything equal to this moment! Mrs. Goddard, are you quite all right? May I help you up? Mr. Woodhouse, do you see that your precious young daughter has just killed a vampire and saved Miss Harriet Smith from certain death?"

Mr. Woodhouse could not find words to speak. His eyes were the size of Delft china saucers.

Old Mrs. Bates had not heard a word. "Eh? What was that? What did she say?" said she, cupping her hand to her ear.

Emma helped Mrs. Goddard to her feet. "Dear Miss Woodhouse, how can we ever repay your kindness? I have never seen such courage!"

Emma, still reeling in disbelief, pondered, "I wonder how this horrid vampire came to be here."

Harriet spoke up. "He must have followed Mrs. Goddard and myself from the school. Miss Woodhouse, surely you must have heard of the recent attacks on my fellow boarders."

"Yes, of course, that would explain it," said Emma. "Well, your carriage is waiting. Perhaps we should all hasten to the safety of our homes."

Mrs. Goddard and Harriet and Mrs. and Miss Bates stepped into their respective carriages and were rapidly conveyed out the gates of Hartfield.

Emma watched them silently as they left. Then, dragging her sabre along the ground, she walked slowly back into the house, her eyes in a daze.

Mr. Woodhouse stood in the doorway. "Emma, dear Emma. How did you—"

And at that moment, without further words, Mr. Woodhouse fainted.

CHAPTER 4

NEWS OF EMMA'S VANQUISHMENT of the wild vampire soon spread throughout Highbury, thanks to the dependably loquacious Miss Bates. All were astonished at Emma's courage—for they had always considered her quite frivolous—and she commanded a respect heretofore unknown by a young lady of such refinement.

Mr. George Knightley, upon hearing the news, felt a mixture of pride and horror—pride that his dear Emma demonstrated such bravery in the face of danger, and horror at the thought that a young lady for whom he cared so deeply came so close to being taken from him.

Harriet Smith's presence at Hartfield was soon a regular occurrence. Emma lost no time in inviting, encouraging, and telling her to come very often; and Harriet, for her part, was not only flattered that Miss Woodhouse would pay her such attentions but also full of undying gratitude that she had saved her life. Thus, as their acquaintance grew, so did their satisfaction with each other.

As a walking companion, Emma saw how useful Harriet might be. Mr. Woodhouse never went beyond the shrubbery, and since Mrs. Weston's marriage, Emma's exercise had been much too confined. She had once ventured alone to Randalls, but it was not pleasant—she sensed bloodthirsty creatures lurking behind the privet in the moonlight—and

Harriet Smith, therefore, one whom she could summon at any time to a walk, would be a valuable addition to her privileges.

And quite frankly, though Emma was now regarded by her social circle as the resident expert *par excellence* on the art of vampire killing, she continued to feel apprehensive at wandering about the countryside alone. A companion such as Harriet alleviated such anxiety.

On the other hand, Emma was fully aware that Harriet seemed to attract vampires like chutney attracted flies. To that end, Emma presented her plump friend with a gift of a wooden stake of her own and a yellow satin ribbon—a very long satin ribbon—with which to secure the weapon to Harriet's rather ample thigh. Thus armed, Emma felt that she and Harriet could stroll about freely without undue concern.

Harriet certainly was not clever, but she had a sweet, docile, grateful disposition and was not conceited. Emma was quite convinced of Harriet Smith's being exactly the young friend she wanted—a friend to whom she could be useful. For Mrs. Weston, there was nothing to be done; for Harriet, everything.

Meanwhile, Harriet's thoughts were a good deal occupied, not only with surviving the vampire menace but also, on a more pleasant note, by the Martins of Abbey Mill Farm. The two months she had spent with the vampire family had been very happy, and she now loved to talk of the pleasures of her visit and describe the many comforts and wonders of the place.

Emma encouraged her talkativeness, and learned such things as that Mrs. Martin had "two very good parlours, one of them quite as large as Mrs. Goddard's drawing room, an upstairs maid, eight cows, and a very handsome gazebo in her garden."

As Emma came to understand the Martin family better, she realised she had been mistaken in thinking it was a mother and daughter and a son and his wife who all lived together. When it appeared that Mr. Martin, whom Harriet always mentioned with praise for his great good nature, was a single man and that there was no wife named Mrs. Martin, Emma sensed danger to her poor little friend from all this hospitality and kindness.

Emma enticed Harriet to talk more of Mr. Martin. She was very ready to speak of their moonlight walks, the romantic gaze of his black eyes, and the chill that surged through her body when his cold hand touched hers.

His mother, Mrs. Martin, had told Harriet that it was impossible for anybody to be a better son, and whenever he married, he would make a good husband. Not that she wanted him to marry. She was in no hurry at all.

Well done, Mrs. Martin! thought Emma. Then she turned to Harriet and asked, "What sort of looking man is Mr. Martin?"

"Oh! Handsome, though I thought him very plain at first. Pale skin, of course, like his mother and sisters—he detests the sun, most unusual for a farmer, do you not agree? He works outside only on cloudy days. He possesses the most beautiful white teeth, almost like fangs, and his eyes are deep onyx. He is so strong—he can lift a cow over his head. Did you never see him? He is in Highbury every now and then."

"That may be, and I may have seen him fifty times, without having any idea of his name. A young peasant farmer," sniffed Emma, "is the very last sort of person to raise my curiosity. The yeomanry is precisely the order of people with whom I feel I can have nothing to do."

"But Mr. Martin knows you very well indeed—I mean by sight."

"What do you imagine his age to be?"

"He said his birthday was the eighth of June, but he did not mention the year of his birth. His mother said he has always been twenty-four as far as she was concerned."

"That is too young to settle down. His mother is perfectly right not to be in a hurry. Six years from now, if he could meet a good sort of young woman in the same social rank as his own, with a little money, it might be very desirable."

"Six years! Dear Miss Woodhouse, he would be thirty!"

"Well, and that is as early as most men can afford to marry, who are not born wealthy. With diligence and good luck, Mr. Martin may be rich in time, but it is next to impossible that he should have realised anything yet."

"To be sure, so it is," said Harriet, "though the Martins live very comfortably."

"My dear Harriet, the misfortune of your birth ought to make you particularly careful as to your associates. Though we have precious little knowledge of your ancestry, there can be no doubt of your being a gentleman's daughter, and you must support your claim to that station by everything within your power, or there will be plenty of people who would take pleasure in degrading you."

"Yes, to be sure, I suppose there are. But when I visit at Hartfield, you are so kind to me, Miss Woodhouse, I am not afraid of what anybody can do."

"I would have you firmly established in good society, Harriet. I want to see you permanently well connected, and to that end it will be advisable to have as few odd acquaintances as may be. And therefore, when Mr. Martin marries, I wish you not to be acquainted with his wife, who will probably be some mere farmer's daughter without education."

"To be sure. If he marries a very ignorant, vulgar woman, certainly I had better not visit her, if I can help it."

Emma watched Harriet during their conversation and saw no alarming symptoms of love. Mr. Martin had been her first admirer, and Emma felt that Harriet would not oppose a more suitable arrangement by Emma.

They met Mr. Martin the very next day as they were walking on the Donwell road. He was on foot and, after looking very respectfully at Emma, gazed with great satisfaction at Harriet.

Emma was glad to have such an opportunity to survey him; and walking a few yards behind, while Harriet and he talked together, her quick eye soon became acquainted with Mr. Robert Martin.

His appearance was very neat and quite strong. All in all, Mr. Martin looked like a sensible young man, but had no other advantage; and when compared with real gentlemen, Emma thought he must lose all ground. Harriet was sensible of manner; Mr. Martin looked as if he did not know what manner was.

Harriet and Mr. Martin remained just a few minutes together, so Emma would not be kept waiting. Harriet then came running back to Emma with a smiling face, in a flutter of spirits, which Emma hoped very soon to compose.

"Imagine our happening to meet him! It was quite by chance, he said. Well, Miss Woodhouse, is he like what you expected? What do you think of him? Do you think him so very plain?"

"He is very plain, but that is nothing compared with his lack of gentility. I had no right to expect much, but I had no idea that he could be so very clownish, so totally without air. And those fangs! When he smiles and his black eyes glow, I daresay I imagine he thinks of you as his supper."

"To be sure," said Harriet, in a mortified voice, "he is not so genteel as real gentlemen. And yet he expressed his horror upon hearing the news of the vampire attack upon us. He was quite pleased that I had recovered from the shock, and he complimented you on your courage in saving my life. Those kind words could only have come from a gentleman, could they not?"

"I think, Harriet, since your acquaintance with me, you have been repeatedly in the company of some very real gentlemen, so you must be struck with the difference in Mr. Martin. I should be surprised if, after seeing those very gentlemen, you could be in company with Mr. Martin again without perceiving him to be a very inferior creature—and wondering at yourself for having ever thought him at all agreeable before. Do you not begin to feel that now? I am sure you must have been struck by his awkward look and the uncouthness of a loud voice."

"Certainly he is not like Mr. Knightley. He has not such a fine air and way of walking as Mr. Knightley. And Mr. Knightley does not drool at a lady when he speaks. I see the difference plain enough. Mr. Knightley is so very fine a man!"

"Mr. Knightley's air is so remarkably good that it is not fair to compare Mr. Martin with him. You might not see one in a hundred with *gentleman* so plainly written as in Mr. Knightley. But he is not the only gentleman you have seen. What about Mr. Weston and Mr. Elton? Compare Mr. Martin with either of them."

"Oh, yes! There is a great difference. But Mr. Weston is almost an old man—forty or fifty."

"Yes, but he seems never to grow older, which makes his good manners all the more valuable. The older a person grows, Harriet, the more important it is that their manners should not be bad—what is passable in youth is detestable in later age."

"Would you think," said Harriet, "that Mr. Martin's ice-cold skin might grow warmer with age?"

Emma shook her head. "Mr. Martin is now awkward and abrupt; what will he be at Mr. Weston's time of life?"

"There is no saying, indeed," replied Harriet rather solemnly, "unless, as his mother says, he remains twenty-four."

"Unlikely. He will be a completely gross, vulgar farmer, totally inattentive to appearances, and thinking of nothing but profit and loss. I have no doubt that he will thrive and be a very rich man in time—and his being illiterate and coarse need not disturb us."

Emma paused a moment, then offered, "In one respect, perhaps, Mr. Elton's manners are superior to Mr. Knightley's or Mr. Weston's. They have more gentleness. Mr. Elton is good-humoured, cheerful, obliging, gentle, and electrifying. And he possesses Mr. Martin's ebony eyes. I do not know whether he has any desire to befriend either of us, and I have nary a clue what he does inside the darkened vicarage alone. But did I not tell you what he said about you the other day?"

Emma then repeated some warm personal praise which Harriet had drawn from Mr. Elton. Harriet blushed and smiled and said she had always thought Mr. Elton very agreeable. She then paused from her walk and, in a very ladylike and unobtrusive manner, adjusted the wooden stake beneath her skirt so that it would not rub a nasty callous between her thunderous thighs.

Mr. Elton then became the very person fixed on by Emma for driving the young farmer out of Harriet's head. She thought it would be an excellent match. It had entered her brain during the very first evening of Harriet's coming to Hartfield.

Mr. Elton's situation was most suitable, quite the gentleman himself, and he had no family that could object to the doubtful birth of Harriet. He had a comfortable home for her and, Emma imagined, a very sufficient income; for though the vicarage of Highbury was not large, he was known to have some independent property.

Emma had already satisfied herself that Mr. Elton thought Harriet a beautiful girl. And a girl who could be gratified by a Robert Martin's dripping fangs and arctic skin might very well be conquered by Mr. Elton's admiring black eyes with dark circles.

CHAPTER 5

"YOUR SKIN DOES NOT grow pale, Mrs. Weston, and your eyes do not turn red," said Mr. Knightley, with great concern. "You choose not to become one of us?"

"We hope some day to have a child, Mr. Knightley. And so Mr. Weston finds sustenance among the raccoons at Randalls. Might I be so bold as to ask when you will find sustenance?"

"My dear Mrs. Weston," he sniffed, "a gentleman feasts only on the blood of fellow aristocrats—they are much tastier than the common people. These wild, vagrant vampires who drift about the countryside like gypsies randomly attacking young women are not my brethren."

"I wish you all the best, then," smiled Mrs. Weston.

"How have you fared without the daily companionship of Miss Woodhouse?" he inquired.

"I miss Emma, of course, but since she has found her new friend—"

"I do not know what your opinion may be," interrupted Mr. Knightley, "of this great intimacy between Emma and Miss Harriet Smith, but I think it is a bad thing."

"A bad thing? Why?"

"I think neither of them will do the other any good—although I must say, it was indeed fortunate that Harriet was in the company of Emma when that vicious creature attacked her. This scourge, which heretofore has not affected our circle, is beginning to draw too close to home for my comfort. But I digress. All in all, I still maintain that Emma's acquaintance with Miss Harriet Smith will accrue no benefit whatsoever."

"You surprise me, Mr. Knightley! Emma will indeed do Harriet good. I have been watching their intimacy with the greatest pleasure. How very differently we feel! This will certainly be the beginning of one of our quarrels about Emma!"

"My hearing is acute, Mrs. Weston. There is no need to shout."

Mrs. Weston quieted her voice. "Mr. Knightley, you are so used to living alone that you do not know the value of a companion. And you have been without sustenance for so long that perhaps your mental clarity has been affected. No man can be a good judge of the comfort a woman feels in the company of her own sex. I can imagine your objection to Harriet Smith. She is not the superior young woman which a friend of Emma's ought to be. But on the other hand, as she wants to see Harriet better informed, it will be an inducement to Emma to read more books. They will read together."

"Emma has been meaning to read more books ever since she was twelve years old. She will never submit to anything requiring work and patience. Although I must admit she quite rose to the occasion with her slaying of that vampire. Nevertheless, when it comes to literary pursuits, where you failed to stimulate Emma as her governess, I may safely affirm that Harriet Smith will not stimulate her either."

Mr. Knightley continued with unblinking eyes. "Emma is spoiled by being the cleverest of her family. At ten years old, she was able to answer questions which puzzled her sister Isabella at seventeen. She was always quick and assured; Isabella was slow and shy. And ever since she was twelve, Emma has been mistress of the house. When her mother died, she lost the only person able to cope with her."

Mrs. Weston looked down. "I am sure you always thought me unfit as a governess for Emma."

"Yes," said he, smiling. "You are better placed here—very fit for a vampire's wife but not at all for a governess. At Hartfield, you were preparing yourself to be an excellent wife and receiving a very good education from Emma—submitting to her will, doing as you were bid—and if Mr. Weston had asked me to recommend him a wife, I should certainly have named you, Miss Taylor.

"But Harriet Smith—I am not half done with Harriet Smith. I think her the very worst sort of companion that Emma could possibly have. She knows nothing herself and looks upon Emma as knowing everything. I will venture to say that Harriet cannot gain by the acquaintance. She will grow just refined enough to be uncomfortable with her equals. On the whole, I regard Harriet Smith's value to Emma solely as a diversion for the bloodthirsty leeches that skulk about—better they prey on Miss Smith than on our fair Emma."

"Mr. Knightley, indeed! To hear you speak so! I have more faith in Emma's good sense than you do, for I cannot lament the acquaintance," said Mrs. Weston. She added, "How well Emma looked last night!"

"I shall not attempt to deny Emma's being pretty."

"Pretty! Say beautiful, rather. Can you imagine anything nearer perfect beauty than Emma altogether—face and figure?"

"I do not know what I could imagine, but I confess that I have seldom seen a face or figure more pleasing to me than hers. She excites my venom, to be sure."

"Oh! What a bloom of full health, and such a pretty height and size; such a firm and upright figure! Emma is loveliness itself, Mr. Knightley, is she not?"

"I have not a fault to find with her," he replied. "I love to look at her, and I think of her at night—all night, to be precise, since I never sleep. If I could breathe, she would make me breathless. If my heart could beat, she would cause it to beat rapidly."

"How poetic, Mr. Knightley!"

"And I shall add this praise—that I do not think she is vain. Considering how very beautiful she is, she appears to be little occupied with it. But, Mrs. Weston, I am not to be talked out of my dislike of Harriet Smith or my dread of their friendship doing them both harm."

"And I, Mr. Knightley, am equally stout in my confidence of it not doing them any harm. With all dear Emma's little faults, she is an excellent creature. Where shall we see a better daughter, or a kinder sister, a truer friend, or a more valiant vampire slayer? No, no, she has qualities which may be trusted. She will never lead anyone really wrong; she will make no lasting blunder. Where Emma errs once, she is in the right a hundred times."

"Very well," smiled Mr. Knightley. "I shall not plague you any more. Emma will be an angel, and I shall keep my spleen to myself till Christmas brings John and Isabella. John loves Emma with a reasonable, but not a blind, affection; and Isabella always thinks as he does. I am sure they will agree with me."

"Isabella might become unhappy if you bring the matter up about her sister."

"Be satisfied," said he, "I shall not raise any outcry. I shall keep my ill humour to myself. I have a very sincere interest in Emma." He paused a moment, then added, "I wonder what will become of her."

"So do I," said Mrs. Weston gently, "very much."

"She always declares," said he, "that she will never marry, which of course means nothing at all. But I think she has never seen a man she cared for. It would not be a bad thing for her to be in love with a proper vampire. I should like to see Emma in love. It would do her good. But there is nobody hereabouts she is attracted to."

"There does, indeed, seem to be little to tempt her to break her resolution," said Mrs. Weston. "I do not recommend matrimony at present to Emma, though I mean no slight to marriage, I assure you."

Part of her meaning was to conceal thoughts of her own and Mr. Weston's on the subject. They had some wishes respecting Emma's future, concerning Mr. Frank Churchill, but it was not desirable to reveal them. And the quiet way in which Mr. Knightley soon afterwards changed the subject to "I hope the rain continues" convinced her that he had nothing more to say about Emma.

CHAPTER 6

EMMA WAS PLEASED TO turn Harriet's attention towards Mr. Elton. Harriet thought the vicar, with his stunning black eyes, pallid complexion, black tunic, and white vicar's collar, created a remarkably handsome portrait in black and white. And Emma was quite convinced of Mr. Elton's being close to falling in love, if not in love already, with Harriet. He had praised her warmly and had noticed the striking improvement in Harriet's manner since her association with Emma.

"You have given Miss Smith all that she required," said Mr. Elton. "You have made her graceful and easy. She was a beautiful creature when she came to you but, in my opinion, the attractions you have added are infinitely superior to what she received from nature. And your recent valour in the presence of imminent death has preserved Miss Smith's plump bosom to breathe yet another day." And, he might have added, that bosom and fair neck remind me that my thirst greatly needs satisfying.

"You have a unique way of complimenting women, Mr. Elton," said Emma. "I am glad you think I have been useful to her; but Harriet only needed drawing out and receiving a few, very few, hints. She had all the natural grace of sweetness in herself. Great has been my pleasure in helping her."

"I have no doubt of it." And Mr. Elton spoke with a sort of sighing animation, which was remarkable considering he never seemed to take a breath of air.

Emma was pleased the next day when Mr. Elton agreed with Emma's wish to have Harriet's picture drawn.

"Did you ever have your likeness taken, Harriet?" asked Emma. "Did you ever sit for your picture?"

With a very interesting naïveté, Harriet exclaimed, "Oh dear! No, never." Then she quickly left the room.

No sooner was she out of sight than Emma exclaimed to Mr. Elton, "What an exquisite possession a good picture of Harriet would be! I almost long to attempt her likeness myself. You do not know this, I daresay, but two or three years ago I had a great passion for drawing likenesses. I attempted several of my friends—for some peculiar reason, the looking glass would not hold their pale reflections, so I thought they might be interested to see their aspects reflected on paper. But for one reason or another, I gave it up in disgust. But really, I could almost venture it, if Harriet would sit for me. It would be such a delight to draw her picture!"

"It would indeed be a delight!" cried Mr. Elton. "Let me beg you, Miss Woodhouse, to use your talent in favour of your friend. I know what your drawings are. Is this room not rich in examples of your landscapes and flowers?"

Yes, good man, thought Emma, but what has all that to do with portraits of real people? You know nothing of drawing. Do not pretend to be in raptures about my pictures. Save your cold raptures for Harriet.

"Well, if you give me such kind encouragement, Mr. Elton, I believe I shall try what I can. Harriet's features are very delicate, which make a likeness difficult; and yet there is a uniqueness in the shape of the eye and the lines about the mouth which one ought to catch."

"Exactly so—and fortunately, she lacks the dark circles under the eyes. I have not a doubt of your success. Pray, pray attempt it. It will indeed be an exquisite possession."

"But I am afraid, Mr. Elton, Harriet will not like to sit. She thinks so little of her own beauty. Did you not observe her manner of answering me—'Why should my picture be drawn?'"

"Oh, yes! It was not lost on me. But still I cannot imagine she could not be persuaded."

Harriet was soon back again, the proposal was made, and she could not object against the earnest pressing of her friends.

Emma wished to go to work directly and therefore produced the portfolio containing her various attempts at portraits—for not one of them had ever been finished—that they might decide together on the best size for Harriet.

Emma's many beginnings were displayed. Miniatures, half-lengths, whole-lengths, pencil, crayon, and watercolours had been all tried, but none completed.

They soon decided on the size and sort of picture. It was to be a full-length portrait in watercolours and was destined to hold a very honourable position over the mantelpiece.

The sitting began, and Harriet, smiling and blushing, presented a very sweet, youthful expression to the steady eyes of the artist.

But with Mr. Elton fidgeting behind Emma and watching every stroke of the brush, she gave him a spot in the room where he might gaze without bothering her.

Then it occurred to Emma to employ him in reading. If he would be so good as to read to Emma and Harriet, it would amuse away the difficulties of Emma's part and lessen the irksomeness of Harriet's.

Mr. Elton was only too happy. Harriet listened, and Emma drew in peace. She allowed him to still come and look at her progress, and he darted back and forth with such speed that the young ladies could barely see him move.

The sitting was very satisfactory, and Emma was quite enough pleased with the first day's sketch to wish to go on. She gave the figure a little more height and considerably more elegance and had great confidence of its being a pretty drawing at last, a memorial of the beauty of one, the skill of the other, and the friendship of both.

The whole progress of the picture was rapid and happy. Everybody who saw it was pleased, but Mr. Elton was in continual raptures, his fangs appearing to glisten for a taste of Harriet's fair neck.

When Mrs. Weston saw the picture, she observed, "Emma has given her friend the beauty she wanted but never had. The expression of the eyes is most correct, but Miss Smith has not those eyebrows and eyelashes. It is the fault of her face that she does not have them."

"Do you think so?" replied Mr. Elton. "I cannot agree with you. It appears to me a most perfect resemblance in every feature. I never saw such a likeness in my life. We must allow for the effect of shade, you know."

"You have made her too tall, Emma," said Mr. Knightley.

Emma knew that she had but would not admit it; and Mr. Elton warmly added, "Oh, no! Consider, she is sitting down, and the proportions must be preserved, you know."

"It is very pretty," said Mr. Woodhouse. "So prettily done! Just as your drawings always are, my dear. The only thing I do not thoroughly like is that she seems to be sitting out of doors, with only a little shawl over her shoulders—and it makes one think she must catch cold."

"But, my dear Papa, it is supposed to be summer—a warm day in summer. Look at the tree."

"But it is never safe to sit out of doors, my dear."

"Sir," cried Mr. Elton, "I regard the placing of Miss Smith out of doors under the clouds with no sun as most admirable! Her skin looks so white! I cannot keep my eyes from it. I never saw such a likeness."

The next order of business was to get the picture framed, and it must be done in London. Mr. Elton's gallantry was always on the alert. "Might I be trusted with the commission? What infinite pleasure I should have in executing it! I could ride to London at any time."

"But Mr. Elton," cautioned Emma, "would you not be in danger of being attacked by the fierce vampires that conceal themselves along the road? And in London, too, we hear tell of creatures rampaging the city."

"My dear Emma," he said, reassuringly, "I fear them not, so neither should you fear for my safety." They will of course, he thought, show me professional courtesy and allow me to proceed unharmed.

He was too good, thought Emma, and in a very few minutes settled the business. Mr. Elton was to take the drawing to London, choose the frame, and see it completed.

"What a precious treasure!" said he, receiving it.

This man is almost too gallant to be in love, thought Emma, but I suppose there may be a hundred different ways of being in love. He is an excellent young man and will suit Harriet exactly.

CHAPTER 7

THE VERY DAY OF Mr. Elton's going to London
produced a fresh occasion for Emma's services towards
her friend.

Harriet had visited Hartfield soon after breakfast, as usual.
After a while, she had gone home to Mrs. Goddard's for her
lessons but soon returned again to Hartfield with a nervous,
hurried look.

"Dear Miss Woodhouse! The most extraordinary thing
has happened! I thought I should have fainted! While at
Mrs. Goddard's, a postboy had arrived on his horse bearing
a letter. Or perhaps I should say the horse arrived carrying a
bloodied young man, barely alive! Oh, Miss Woodhouse! I
thought it would have been the death of me! The boy then
slid off his horse and collapsed to the ground, still holding the
precious letter in his hand."

"Dear Harriet! I am absolutely astonished! What
happened next?"

"Oh, Miss Woodhouse! Mrs. Goddard and myself and
the other boarders hurried out of the school, aghast at
the horrid sight, some screaming and others crying. Mrs.
Goddard promptly sent for the doctor, Mr. Perry, and in the
meanwhile brought the poor young victim inside to admin-
ister care. Dear Miss Woodhouse! I would rather have had
anything happen than that!

"His countenance was gaunt and white as snow. His eyes were sunken into their sockets! There were two small holes in his neck! With a feeble voice, he recounted his unspeakable misfortune. Riding along the road from Donwell parish, he said he was suddenly attacked by a band of hideous, ferocious vampires that seemed to appear out of thin air! Dear Miss Woodhouse, I was feeling dreadfully! Then he told us that with almost supernatural strength the creatures pulled him from his steed and held him down. One vampire sunk his fangs into the boy's neck and sucked his blood, then the others proceeded to feast on him as well! Then they vanished as quickly as they had appeared! Oh, Miss Woodhouse!

"But he was determined to complete his appointed duty, and so the postboy mounted his horse and rode to our boarding school! Dear Miss Woodhouse, he then presented the letter to Mrs. Goddard—and, oh! This is the worst part of all—he announced that the letter was for a Miss Harriet Smith! Then he breathed his last breath and died. Oh! Miss Woodhouse! Have you ever heard of anything so hideous!"

"Upon my word!" exclaimed Emma. "My dear Harriet, what a horrid experience it must have been for you! We must do something about this horrid vampire scourge. To think that a young man gave his life for your insignificant little letter is too ghastly to contemplate!"

"Yes, Miss Woodhouse, it was indeed terrifying. But then, something even more astonishing happened."

"Dear Harriet! There is more? What could possibly be more shocking than the tale you have just related?"

"The contents of the letter, Miss Woodhouse. It came from Mr. Robert Martin. It contained a direct proposal of marriage!"

"Upon my word, dear Harriet!"

"Indeed! Who could have thought it? I was so surprised that I did not know what to do! Yes, a proposal of marriage, and a very good letter at that. And he wrote as if he really loved me very much, and so I came as fast as I could to ask you, Miss Woodhouse, what I should do."

Emma was half-ashamed of her friend for seeming so pleased and so doubtful about refusing him.

"Upon my word," Emma cried, "the young man is certainly determined to marry well if he can."

"Will you read the letter?" cried Harriet. "Pray do."

Emma read and was surprised. The style of the letter was much above her expectation. It was not only devoid of grammatical errors but as a composition it also would not have disgraced a gentleman. The language, though plain, was strong and unaffected, and the sentiments it conveyed were very much to the credit of the writer. It was short but expressed good sense, warm attachment, propriety, and even delicacy of feeling.

She paused over it; Harriet anxiously watched for her opinion and finally asked, "Is it a good letter?"

"Yes, indeed, a very good letter," replied Emma rather slowly. "So good a letter, Harriet, that everything considered, I think one of his sisters must have helped him. I can hardly imagine the young man whom I saw talking with you the other day could express himself so well. Certainly, it is strong and concise." Emma returned the letter. "A better written letter, Harriet, than I had expected."

"Well?" said the still-waiting Harriet. "Well—and what shall I do?"

"But what are you in doubt of? You must answer it, of course, and speedily."

"Yes, but what shall I say? Dear Miss Woodhouse, do advise me."

"Oh, no, no! The letter had better be all your own. You will express yourself very properly, I am sure. Your meaning must show no doubts or demurs. You need not appear sorrowful for his disappointment."

"You think I ought to refuse him, then?" said Harriet, looking down.

"Ought to refuse him! My dear Harriet, what do you mean? Are you in any doubt as to that? I thought—but I beg your pardon, perhaps I have been under a mistake. I certainly have misunderstood you if you feel in doubt as to the intent of your answer. I had imagined you were consulting me only as to the wording of it."

Harriet was silent. With a little reserve, Emma said, "You mean to return a favourable answer, then, I assume?"

"No, I do not. That is, I do not mean—what shall I do? What would you advise me to do? Pray, dear Miss Woodhouse, tell me what I ought to do."

"I shall not give you any advice, Harriet. I shall have nothing to do with it. This is a point which you must settle with your own feelings."

"I had no notion that he liked me so very much," said Harriet, contemplating the letter. "Granted, his cold skin against mine in the moonlight and his mysteriously attractive scent gave me an excitable thrill, but this—"

For a little while Emma was silent, but soon she began to sense that the bewitching flattery of that letter might be too powerful.

"My dear Harriet, I lay it down as a general rule that if a woman doubts as to whether she should accept a man or not, then she certainly ought to refuse him. If she can hesitate as to *yes*, she ought to say *no* directly. It is not something to be entered into with half a heart. I thought it my duty as a friend, and as one older than yourself, to say as much to you. But do not imagine that I want to influence you."

"Oh, no! I am sure you are too kind to do that. But if you would just advise me what to do—no, no, one should not be hesitating. It will be safer to say *no,* perhaps. Do you think I had better say *no?*"

"Not for the world," said Emma, smiling graciously, "would I advise you either way. You must be the best judge of your own happiness. If you prefer Mr. Martin to every other person, if you think him the most agreeable man you have ever been in company with, if his white skin and black eyes and drooling fangs are everything you desire, if you do not care that he never sleeps, and that he would never seem to age while you grow old, grey, and wrinkled, and that if he stood too near the fireplace he would explode—why should you hesitate? You blush, Harriet. Does anybody else occur to you at this moment that fits the definition of agreeableness? Whom, dear Harriet, are you thinking of at this moment?"

Instead of answering, Harriet turned away, confused, and stood thoughtfully by the fire imagining her Mr. Martin in flames. And though the letter was still in her hand, it was curiously twisted about. Emma waited for the result with impatience but not without strong hopes.

At last, with some hesitation, Harriet said, "Miss Woodhouse, as you will not give me your opinion, I must do as well as I can by myself. And I have now quite determined to refuse Mr. Martin. Do you think I am right?"

"Perfectly, perfectly right, my dearest Harriet. You are doing just what you ought. While you were in suspense, I kept my feelings to myself, but now that you are so completely decided, I have no hesitation in approving. Dear Harriet, it would have grieved me to lose your acquaintance as a consequence of your marrying Mr. Martin. I could not have visited you as Mrs. Robert Martin of Abbey Mill Farm, due to the difference in our social rank, especially in view of Mr. Martin's vulgar drooling. Now my friendship is secure with you for ever."

This consequence struck Harriet forcibly. "You could not have visited me!" she cried, looking aghast. "That would have been too dreadful! Dear Miss Woodhouse, I would not give up the pleasure and honour of being friends with you for anything in the world."

"Indeed, Harriet, it would have been a severe pang to lose you. You would have thrown yourself out of all good society."

"Dear me! How should I ever have borne it! It would have killed me never to come to Hartfield any more!"

"Dear affectionate creature, banished to Abbey Mill Farm, confined to the society of the illiterate and vulgar all your life! I wonder how the young man could have the boldness to ask it. He must have a pretty good opinion of himself."

"I do not think he is conceited," said Harriet. "At least, he is very good natured, and I shall always feel much obliged to him and have a great regard for him, though I shall not miss the feeling that he can see my bosom through my gown. And you know, I must confess that I have met other gentlemen so very handsome and agreeable. And as to leaving you, I would not do that upon any consideration."

"Thank you, thank you, my own sweet little friend. We shall not be parted. A woman should never marry a man merely because she is asked, or because he is attracted to her, or can write a tolerable letter, or can see through her gown, or can hoist a cow over his head."

"Oh, no. And it is but a short letter too. I am quite determined to refuse him. But what shall I say?"

Emma assured her that would not be difficult and advised the letter be written directly, which was agreed to. And though Emma protested against giving Harriet any assistance, she in fact gave it in the formation of every sentence.

Looking over Mr. Martin's letter again, Harriet was so concerned at the idea of making Mr. Martin unhappy and what his mother and sisters would think that Emma believed if the young man had come to Hartfield at that moment, Harriet would have accepted him after all.

This letter, however, was written, sealed, and sent. The business was finished, and Harriet was safe. She was rather low all evening, but Emma relieved her feelings by speaking of her own affection for Harriet and bringing forward the idea of Mr. Elton.

"I shall never be invited to Abbey Mill Farm again," Harriet said in rather a sorrowful tone. "On the other hand, I would starve to death there, since they never eat any food, and I would never see the sun, because they keep the shades drawn."

That reminded Emma of Mr. Elton. At the mention of his name, Harriet blushed and wondered why he should like her so much. The idea of Mr. Elton was certainly cheering—his eyes were as black as Mr. Martin's, and to his further credit, he possessed that electrifying touch—but still, after a time, Harriet was tenderhearted again towards the rejected Mr. Martin.

"Now he has my letter," said she softly. "I wonder what they are all doing—whether his sisters know. If he is unhappy, they will be unhappy too. I'm glad he never sleeps—therefore, he will not lose any sleep over me."

Emma offered kind words. "Let us think at this moment, perhaps, that Mr. Elton is showing your picture to his mother and sisters, telling them how much more beautiful is the original, and allowing them to hear your name, your own dear name."

"My picture!"

"It is his companion all this evening. It introduces you to his family. How cheerful, how busy their imaginations all are as they gaze upon the image of your fair white plumpness!"

Harriet smiled again, and her smiles grew stronger.

CHAPTER 8

HARRIET SLEPT AT HARTFIELD that night, still quite shaken by both Mr. Robert Martin's unexpected proposal of marriage and the fear of another vampire attack.

In recent weeks, she had been spending more than half her time at Hartfield and soon a bedroom was set aside for her sole use. Emma judged it best in every respect—safest and kindest—to keep her at Hartfield as much as possible at present.

The next morning, Harriet went to Mrs. Goddard's for her lessons. While she was gone, Mr. Knightley called and sat some time with Mr. Woodhouse and Emma, till Mr. Woodhouse made up his mind to take a walk.

"Well, if you will excuse me, Mr. Knightley, if you will not consider me as doing a very rude thing, I shall go out for a quarter of an hour. I believe I had better take my three turns while I safely can—surely none of those vile creatures are prowling about Hartfield while the sun is out."

"Indeed, sir," said Mr. Knightley with a slight smile, "there is no possibility that a vampire lurks near. Do take your leave while you can."

"Why, thank you, Mr. Knightley," said Mr. Woodhouse. "Emma will be happy to entertain you while I am gone."

Mr. Woodhouse at last was off and Mr. Knightley stayed, seemingly inclined for more chat. He expressed his relief that Emma had survived the vampire attack and praised her bravery in the face of such imminent peril. Then, to Emma's great surprise, he began speaking about Harriet with more voluntary praise than Emma had ever heard before.

"Emma, I cannot rate Harriet's beauty as you do," said Mr. Knightley, "but she is a pretty little creature, and I am inclined to think very well of her disposition. Her character depends upon those she is with; but in good hands she will turn out a valuable woman."

"I am glad you think so," said Emma.

"Come," said he, "you are anxious for a compliment, so I shall tell you that you have improved her. You have cured her of her schoolgirl's giggle—she really does you credit."

"Thank you. I should be mortified if I did not believe I had been of some use; but it is not everybody who will bestow praise. You do not often overpower me with it."

He presently added, with a smile, "I must tell you that I have good reason to believe your little friend will soon hear of something to her advantage."

"Indeed! How so? Of what sort?"

"A very serious sort, I assure you," he said, still smiling.

"Very serious?" asked Emma. "I can think of but one thing—who is in love with her?"

Emma was in hopes of Mr. Elton's having dropped a hint. Mr. Knightley was a sort of general friend and adviser—they would often stay awake all night talking—and Emma knew Mr. Elton looked up to him.

"I have reason to think," he replied, "that Harriet Smith will soon have an offer of marriage, and from a most exceptional quarter—Mr. Robert Martin is the man. He is desperately in love and means to marry her."

"But," said Emma, looking down, "is he sure that Harriet wants to marry him?"

"Well, he means to make her an offer. He came to me two evenings ago to consult me about it. He knows I have a thorough regard for him and all his family and, I believe, considers me not only his landlord but also one of his best friends. He came to ask me whether I thought Harriet was too young and whether I approved of his choice, since he felt that she was higher in society than he.

"Mr. Martin is an excellent young man, Emma. We took a lovely walk in the rain, and I had no hesitation in advising him to marry. He proved to me that he could afford it." And, thought Mr. Knightley, he is desperately thirsty. "I was convinced he could not do better. I praised the fair lady too." Indeed, how vibrantly her blood courses through her plump veins! "I sent him away very happy. This happened the night before last."

"I shall tell you something," said she, "in return for what you have told me. Mr. Martin wrote a letter to Harriet yesterday—and she refused him."

Mr. Knightley's face actually grew paler with surprise and displeasure. He stood up in tall indignation and said, "Then she is a greater simpleton than I ever believed her! What is the foolish girl about?"

"Oh! To be sure!" cried Emma. "It is incomprehensible to a man that a woman should ever refuse an offer of marriage. A man always imagines a woman to be ready for anybody who asks her."

"Nonsense! A man does not imagine any such thing. But what is the meaning of this? Harriet Smith refusing Robert Martin? Madness, if it be so—but I hope you are mistaken."

"I saw her answer! Nothing could be clearer."

"You saw her answer? I am certain you wrote her answer, too! Emma, this is your doing. You persuaded her to refuse him."

"And if I did, I should not feel that I had done wrong. Mr. Martin is a very respectable young man, but I cannot admit him to be Harriet's equal."

"Not Harriet's equal!" exclaimed Mr. Knightley, as the purple circles under his black eyes grew darker. Then, more calmly, he added, "No, he is not her equal—he is much her superior in sense and situation. Emma, your infatuation with that girl blinds you. What are Harriet Smith's claims, of birth, nature, or education, to any social status higher than Robert Martin's? She is the natural daughter of Nobody Knows Whom, with certainly no respectable relations. She is known only as a parlour boarder at a common school. She is not a sensible girl, she has been taught nothing useful, and she is young and simple. She is pretty, good-tempered, and a feast for the eyes, and that is all.

"My only purpose in advising the match was on his account. I felt that, in all probability, he could do much better. But I could read his mind, and he was so in love that I agreed. I even thought of you—I remember saying to myself, 'Even Emma, with all her partiality for Harriet, will think this a good match.'"

Emma replied, "You think a farmer—and with all his merit, Mr. Martin is nothing more—is a good match for my intimate friend! I assure you that my feelings are very different. I must think your statement about Harriet to be unfair. Mr. Martin may be the richer of the two, but he is undoubtedly her inferior as to rank in society. The sphere in which she moves is much above his. It would be a degradation."

"A degradation to illegitimacy and ignorance? To be married to a respectable, intelligent gentleman farmer?" And, he thought, a desperately starving fellow vampire?

Emma returned, "As to the circumstances of her birth, though in a legal sense she may be called Nobody, there can scarcely be a doubt that she is a gentleman's daughter. She is superior to Mr. Robert Martin."

"She desired nothing better for herself," said Mr. Knightley, "till you chose to turn her into a friend. She was as happy as possible with the Martins last summer. She had no sense of superiority then. If she has it now, you have given it to her. You have been no friend to Harriet Smith. Robert Martin would never have proceeded so far unless he felt persuaded of Harriet's feelings for him. I know him well."

Emma returned, "Harriet will certainly be admired and sought after, and will choose from among many. Were you, yourself, ever to marry, she is the very woman for you. Is she, at seventeen and just entering into life, to be wondered at because she does not accept the first offer she receives? No, pray let her have time to look around. And besides, with Mr. Martin's black eyes and her blue ones, their children would certainly have eyes the colour of midnight. Can you imagine anything so hideous?"

Believe me, dear Emma, thought Mr. Knightley, I would not see any children in their future after Miss Smith's painful transformation into Mrs. Martin. Then he spoke: "Though I have kept my thoughts to myself till now, I perceive that Harriet's friendship with you will be a very unfortunate one. You will puff her up with such ideas of her own beauty that nobody within her reach will be good enough for her.

"Miss Harriet Smith may not find offers of marriage flow in so fast. Men of good sense do not want silly wives. Men of good background would be afraid of the disgrace of connecting themselves with a girl of such obscurity. Let her marry Robert Martin, and she is safe, respectable, and happy forever." Her skin will grow pale, he thought, her eyes will turn red, and her youth will endure forever.

"But if you encourage her to expect to marry greatly and teach her to be satisfied with nothing less than a man of large fortune, she may be a parlour boarder at Mrs. Goddard's all the rest of her life." Or at least, he thought, until she grows desperate enough to be the grateful luscious snack of some lecherous old vampire.

"Mr. Knightley, we think so very differently on this point that there can be no use in discussing it. We shall only make each other more angry. But as to my letting her marry Robert Martin, it is impossible. She has refused him. As to the refusal itself, I shall not pretend that I did not influence her a little; but I assure you there was very little for me or anybody to do. His appearance is so much against him and his manner so bad, with those slobbering fangs. She knows now what gentlemen are; and nothing but a gentleman in education and manner has any chance with Harriet."

"Nonsense, errant nonsense, as ever was talked!" cried Mr. Knightley.

Emma made no answer and tried to look cheerfully unconcerned, but she was really feeling uncomfortable and wanting him very much to be gone. She did not regret what she had done—she still thought herself a better judge of female refinement than he. But yet she had a respect for his judgement, and to have him sitting opposite her in an angry state was very disagreeable.

Some minutes passed in this unpleasant silence, with only one attempt on Emma's side to talk of the weather, but he made no answer. He was thinking. The result of his thoughts appeared at last in these words: "As you make no secret of your love of matchmaking, it is fair to suppose that you have certain ideas for Miss Smith. And as a friend, I shall just hint to you that if Mr. Elton is the man, I think it will all be in vain."

Emma laughed, but he continued. "Depend upon it, Elton will not do. Elton is a very good sort of man and a very respectable vicar of Highbury, and he and I spend many cordial visits together in his dark house out of the painful sun. He is not likely to make an imprudent match. He knows many fine ladies with large incomes. He knows that he is a very handsome young man with an electrifying touch and a great favourite wherever he goes."

"I am very much obliged to you," said Emma, laughing again. "But at present, I only want to keep Harriet to myself. I am done with matchmaking, indeed. I could never hope to equal my own success with Miss Taylor. I shall leave off while I am ahead."

"Good morning to you, then," said he, rising and dashing off with a speed that took Emma's breath away.

Emma remained in a state of vexation. She did not always feel satisfied with herself and was not always so convinced that her opinions were right and her adversary's wrong.

The return of Harriet restored Emma's mood. Harriet's staying away so long had made Emma uneasy. The possibility of Mr. Martin's coming to Mrs. Goddard's that morning and meeting with Harriet and pleading his own cause or, even more horrendous to contemplate, the possibility of Harriet's being attacked on her way to Hartfield put alarming ideas in Emma's mind.

Mr. Knightley had frightened Emma a little about Mr. Elton—but Mr. Knightley had not observed Mr. Elton's attention towards Harriet as Emma had.

Harriet's cheerful look and manner answered all questions. She came back, not to think of Mr. Martin but to talk of Mr. Elton. Miss Nash, the head teacher at Mrs. Goddard's school, had told Harriet that Mr. Perry, the doctor, had seen Mr. Elton on the road to London carrying something exceedingly precious. Mr. Perry was very sure there must be a lady involved, and when he mentioned it, Mr. Elton only smiled and rode off in great spirits.

Miss Nash had told Harriet all this and said that she did not pretend to understand what Mr. Elton's business might be, but she only knew that any woman whom Mr. Elton could prefer, she should think the luckiest woman in the world.

CHAPTER 9

M R. KNIGHTLEY WAS SO displeased
it was longer than usual before he c
again; and when they did meet, his grave lo
Emma was not forgiven. She was sorry but
On the contrary, her plans to unite Harrie t
were more and more justified to her by the e
few days.

The *Picture of Harriet*, elegantly framed
Hartfield soon after Mr. Elton's return and
the mantelpiece of the common sitting roo
up to stare at it, careful not to walk too cl
fire, and sighed out his admiration just as he
heartbeat, it would surely be audible now.

As for Harriet's feelings, they were visib ll
strong and steady attachment to Mr. Elton
perfectly satisfied that Mr. Martin was a dist

Emma's plans of improving her little fr
a great deal of reading and conversation,
beyond the first few chapters. It was much e
to study; and the only literary pursuit which r
at present was the collecting of riddles and o
sort into a little book.

In this age of literature, such collection
not uncommon. Miss Nash had written

seen Mr. Elton on the road to London carrying something exceedingly precious. Mr. Perry was very sure there must be a lady involved, and when he mentioned it, Mr. Elton only smiled and rode off in great spirits.

Miss Nash had told Harriet all this and said that she did not pretend to understand what Mr. Elton's business might be, but she only knew that any woman whom Mr. Elton could prefer, she should think the luckiest woman in the world.

CHAPTER 9

M R. KNIGHTLEY WAS SO displeased with Emma that it was longer than usual before he came to Hartfield again; and when they did meet, his grave looks showed that Emma was not forgiven. She was sorry but could not repent. On the contrary, her plans to unite Harriet with Mr. Elton were more and more justified to her by the events of the next few days.

The *Picture of Harriet*, elegantly framed, came safely to Hartfield soon after Mr. Elton's return and was hung over the mantelpiece of the common sitting room. Mr. Elton got up to stare at it, careful not to walk too close to the raging fire, and sighed out his admiration just as he ought. Had he a heartbeat, it would surely be audible now.

As for Harriet's feelings, they were visibly forming into a strong and steady attachment to Mr. Elton. Emma was soon perfectly satisfied that Mr. Martin was a distant memory.

Emma's plans of improving her little friend's mind, by a great deal of reading and conversation, had not gotten beyond the first few chapters. It was much easier to chat than to study; and the only literary pursuit which engaged Harriet at present was the collecting of riddles and charades of every sort into a little book.

In this age of literature, such collections of riddles were not uncommon. Miss Nash had written out at least three hundred; and Harriet hoped, with Miss Woodhouse's help, to get a great many more.

Mr. Woodhouse was almost as interested in the business as the girls and tried very often to recollect something worth putting in. So many clever riddles there used to be when he was young—he wondered why he could not remember them! But he hoped he should in time. And each riddle always ended in "Kitty, a fair but frozen maid."

Mr. Elton was the only other person whose assistance Emma asked. He was invited to contribute any really good riddles that he might recollect; but the one he recalled was already well known, and Emma was quite sorry to acknowledge that they had already written it down some pages ago.

"Why will you not write one yourself for us, Mr. Elton?" she asked. "That is the only guarantee for its originality, and I am sure nothing could be easier for you."

"Oh, no! I have never written anything of the kind in my life. I am the stupidest fellow! I am afraid not even Miss Woodhouse"—he stopped a moment—"or Miss Smith could inspire me. I should be awake all night without a single riddle."

The very next day, however, produced some proof of inspiration. He visited for a few moments just to leave a piece of paper with Emma. He touched her hand with his pale, chilly finger, and a bolt like lightning shot through her body. She picked herself up off the floor and smiled in wonderment at the divine effect Mr. Elton had on her.

Mr. Elton told Emma that the paper contained a riddle which a friend of his had written for a young lady whom he admired. But from his manner, Emma was immediately convinced the riddle must be his own.

"I do not offer it for Miss Smith's collection," said he. "Being my friend's, I have no right to make it public, but perhaps you may enjoy looking at it."

The speech was more to Emma than to Harriet, which Emma could understand. Mr. Elton found it easier to meet Emma's eye than her friend's. He was gone the next moment in a flash.

"Take it," said Emma, smiling and pushing the paper towards Harriet. "It is for you."

But Harriet was in a tremor and could not touch it; so Emma, never shy, examined the riddle herself:

"My first word speaks of the pomp of kings,
Lords of the earth! Their luxury and ease.
A different view of man, my second word brings,
Behold him there, the monarch of the seas!
But the two words united, a new word we have!
With thy clever wit, the word will soon supply,
May its approval beam in thy soft eye!"

Emma read it, pondered it, caught the meaning, and read it through again to be quite certain—the first clue was *court*, the second was *ship*, and united the answer to the riddle was *courtship*. Emma was convinced the riddle foretold a proposal of marriage.

Then she passed it to Harriet, who puzzled over the riddle in all her confusion of dullness while Emma sat happily smiling and saying to herself, "Very well, Mr. Elton, very well indeed. I have read worse riddles. I give you credit for it. This is saying very plainly, 'Pray, Miss Smith, give me permission to pay my respects to you. Approve my riddle and my intentions in the same glance.'"

Emma re-read certain lines to herself. "May its approval beam in thy soft eye!"—Harriet exactly. Soft is the very word

for her eye. "Thy clever wit the word will soon supply."
Humph. Harriet's clever wit? A man must be very much in
love to describe her so.

Ah, Mr. Knightley, she thought, I wish you had the
benefit of reading this—I think it would convince you of
Mr. Elton's intentions towards Harriet. An excellent riddle
indeed! And very much to the purpose. Things are moving
along nicely now.

Emma was obliged to break off from these very pleasant
observations by the eagerness of Harriet's wondering questions about Mr. Elton's riddle.

"What can it mean, Miss Woodhouse? I have not a single
idea—I cannot guess it in the least. I never saw anything so
hard. Who could be the young lady? It must be very clever,
or he would not have brought it."

"There is so particular a meaning in this compliment,"
said Emma, "that I cannot doubt as to Mr. Elton's intentions.
You are the object of his affections, and you will soon receive
the most complete proof of it—a proposal of marriage. Yes,
Harriet, I have been wanting this for so long. I am very happy.
I congratulate you, my dear Harriet, with all my heart. Mr.
Elton is someone who will give you everything you want.
An attachment with him will place you in the centre of all
your real friends, close to Hartfield and me, and confirm our
friendship forever."

"Dear Miss Woodhouse! Dear Miss Woodhouse!" was
all that Harriet, with many tender embraces, could articulate
at first.

"Whatever you say is always right," cried Harriet, "but it
is so much beyond anything I deserve. Mr. Elton, who might
marry anybody! I am sure a month ago I had no more idea
myself! The strangest things do take place!"

Emma smiled. "You and Mr. Elton belong to one another. Your marriage will be equal to the match at Randalls. There does seem to be a *something in the air* at Hartfield which gives love exactly the right direction and sends it into the very channel where it ought to flow."

"That Mr. Elton should really be in love with me—me, of all people! And he, the very handsomest man that ever was, a man that everybody looks up to, quite like Mr. Knightley! Dear me!"

Harriet paused, then said, "This riddle! But how shall I ever be able to return the paper or say I have found out the answer? Oh! Miss Woodhouse, what can we do about that?"

"Leave it to me. You do nothing. He will be here this evening, I daresay, and then I shall return it to him. Your soft eyes will choose their own time for beaming. Trust me."

"Oh! Miss Woodhouse, what a pity that I may not write this beautiful riddle into my book!"

"Leave out the two last lines, and there is no reason why you should not."

"Oh! but those two lines are—"

"The best of all, granted, and for private enjoyment. Give me the book. I shall write it down, and then there can be no possible reflection on you."

Harriet submitted. "I shall never let that book out of my own hands."

"Very well," replied Emma. "A most natural feeling; and the longer it lasts, the better I shall be pleased. But here is my father coming; you will not object to my reading the riddle to him. It will give him so much pleasure!"

Mr. Woodhouse came in and very soon he inquired, "Well, my dears, how does your book go? Have you got anything fresh for it?"

"Yes, Papa, we have something to read to you, something quite fresh. A piece of paper was found on the table this morning—dropped, we suppose, by a fairy—containing a very pretty riddle, and we have just copied it in."

She read it to him, just as he liked to have anything read, slowly and distinctly, and two or three times over, with explanations of every part as she proceeded. He was very pleased and, as Emma had foreseen, especially struck with the complimentary conclusion.

"Aye, that's very properly said. Very true. It is such a pretty riddle, my dear, that I can easily guess what fairy brought it. Nobody could have written so prettily but you, Emma." She only nodded and smiled.

After a little thinking and a very tender sigh, Mr. Woodhouse added, "Ah! It is no difficulty to see who you take after! Your dear mother was so clever at all those things! It makes me think of poor Isabella. I am glad we shall have her here next week. Have you thought, my dear, where you will put her? And what room there will be for the children?"

"Oh yes! She will have her own room, of course, the room she always has. And there is the nursery for the children, just as usual."

"Yes, but the children never sleep—nor does John. They are up all the night long, running everywhere while John paces. And they all keep disappearing into the forest, for what reason I haven't the slightest notion. It worries me exceedingly, with so many wild vampires about. But it will be wonderful to see Isabella—it is so long since she was here! How sorry she will be to not see Miss Taylor here when she comes!"

"We must ask Mr. and Mrs. Weston to dine with us while Isabella is here."

"Yes, my dear, but we must set the table with only half the food. The children will not partake, and neither will their father, nor Mr. Weston, nor Mr. George Knightley. And they will insist on a cold room without a fire. Oh, Emma! I am saddened that Isabella is coming for only one week."

"Harriet must give us as much of her company as she can while my sister and brother-in-law are here. I am sure she will be pleased with the children."

"Poor little dears, having to live in London—how glad they will be to come," he said. "They are very fond of being at Hartfield, Harriet."

"I daresay they are, sir."

"Henry is a fine boy, and John is very like his mamma. They have pale blue eyes, just like their father. And they all stare at me without blinking—makes me quite agitated. I think their father is too rough with them very often."

"He appears rough to you," said Emma, "because you are so very gentle yourself. But if you could compare him with other papas, you would not think him rough. He wishes his boys to be active and hardy, he once told me, so that some day they can hunt for small animals on their own. And if they misbehave, he can give them a sharp word now and then. But he is an affectionate father. The children are all fond of him."

"And then their Uncle George Knightley comes in and tosses them up to the ceiling in a very frightful way!"

"But they like it, Papa. There is nothing they like so much."

"Well, I cannot understand it."

"That is the case with us all, Papa. One half of the world cannot understand the pleasures of the other."

⤝⤞

Later in the morning, Mr. Elton came to call again. Emma opened the door and greeted him. Harriet turned away, but Emma received him with the usual smile, and she returned the paper to him, careful not to touch his hand.

"Here is the riddle which you were so obliging to leave with us; thank you for the sight of it. We admired it so much that I have ventured to write it into Miss Smith's collection. Your friend will not take it amiss, I trust. Of course, I have not copied the last two lines."

Mr. Elton certainly did not know what to say. Seeing the open book on the table, he took it and examined it very attentively.

"I have no hesitation in saying," replied Mr. Elton, "that if my friend feels at all as I do, I am sure that if he could see his little riddle honoured as I see it," looking at the book again and replacing it on the table, "he would consider it the proudest moment of his life."

After this speech he was gone in an instant, leaving tender and sublime feelings of pleasure for Harriet to share.

CHAPTER 10

THE NEXT MORNING, UNDER a dark, overcast sky, Emma and Harriet paid a charitable visit to a poor, sick family who lived a little way out of Highbury.

Their road to this detached cottage was down Vicarage Lane, where the blessed abode of Mr. Elton was located. An old and not very good house, the vicarage had been very much smartened up by Mr. Elton, and there could be no possibility of Emma and Harriet passing by without slowing their pace and observing it.

"Oh, what a sweet house!" said Harriet. "How very beautiful! Made more beautiful by the black curtains that Miss Nash admires so much to keep the sunlight out."

Harriet, of course, had never in her life been inside the vicarage, and her curiosity to see it was so extreme that Emma could only regard it as proof of her love for Mr. Elton.

"I wish we could see inside," said Emma, "but I cannot think of any tolerable pretence for going in."

As they passed the vicarage, Harriet turned to Emma with a look of consternation. "Miss Woodhouse, this road is quite isolated, and we are quite alone. Do you not fear that we shall encounter some of those vicious creatures?"

Emma smiled with sympathy and comfort. "Dear Harriet, we are travelling on Vicarage Road. It is holy and blessed. No vampire would dare tread near such sacred ground."

"True, quite true. Oh, Miss Woodhouse, you are so courageous! And so wise! I am filled with gratitude that you have chosen me to be your friend."

"My befriending you, dear Harriet, is ample evidence of my great wisdom."

They continued walking. After a mutual silence of some minutes, Harriet said, "I do so wonder, Miss Woodhouse, why you are not married, or going to be married, so charming as you are!"

Emma laughed and replied, "My being charming, Harriet, is not quite enough to induce me to marry—I must find at least one other person charming. And not only am I not going to be married at present, but I have very little intention of ever marrying at all."

"Ah! So you say. But I cannot believe it."

"I must see somebody very superior to anyone I have seen yet to be tempted. Mr. Elton, you know, is quite out of the question. Although the touch of his cold hand sends a shock of passion through my body, I would rather not be tempted. I cannot really change for the better. If I were to marry, I would expect to regret it."

"Dear me! It is so odd to hear a woman talk so!"

"I have none of the usual inducements of women to marry. Were I to fall in love, indeed, it would be a different thing, but I have never been in love. It is not my way or my nature, and I do not think I ever shall. And without love, I am sure I would be a fool to change such a situation as mine. Fortune I do not need, employment I do not want, and importance I do not lack. I believe few married women are half as much mistress of their husband's house as I am of Hartfield; and never, never could I expect to be so truly beloved and important, so always first and always right in any man's eyes, as I am in my father's."

"But then, to be an old maid, like Miss Bates?"

"That is as formidable an image as you could present, Harriet. And if I thought I would ever be like Miss Bates—so silly, so satisfied, so smiling, so undistinguishing and unfastidious, and so apt to gossip about everything and everybody around me—I would marry tomorrow."

"But still, you will be an old maid! And that is so dreadful!"

"Never mind, Harriet. I shall not be a poor old maid; and it is only poverty which makes single women contemptible to the public. A single woman with a very narrow income must be a ridiculous, disagreeable old maid! But a single woman of good fortune is always respectable and may be as sensible and pleasant as anybody else. A very narrow income has a tendency to contract the mind and sour the temper. Those who can barely live and who live in a very small and inferior society may well be narrow-minded and cross.

"This does not apply, however, to Miss Bates. She is too silly to suit me, but she is very much to the taste of everybody, though single and poor. Poverty certainly has not contracted her mind. I really believe that if she had only a shilling in the world, she would very likely give away sixpence of it. And nobody is afraid of her—that is a great charm."

"Dear me! But what will you do? How will you employ yourself when you grow old?"

"If I know myself, Harriet, mine is an active, busy mind, with a great many independent resources; and I do not perceive why I should be more in need of employment at forty or fifty than at twenty-one. Women's usual occupations will be as open to me then as they are now. If I draw less, I shall read more; if I give up music, I shall take to gardening. If I retire my wooden stake, I shall take to making a needle-point sheath for it.

"And as for objects of affection, I shall be very well off with my nephews and nieces to care about, with their adorable pale blue eyes. There will be enough of them for every hope and every fear; and though my attachment to them cannot equal that of a parent, it suits me fine. And besides, they will be quite useful, catching the mice and rats at Hartfield for their own pleasure. My nephews and nieces! I shall often have a niece with me."

"Do you know Miss Bates's niece, Jane Fairfax?" asked Harriet. "I know you must have seen her a hundred times, but are you acquainted?"

"Oh yes! We are always forced to be acquainted whenever she comes to Highbury. Heaven forbid that I should ever bore people half so much as Miss Bates does about Jane Fairfax. One is sick of the very name Jane Fairfax. Every letter from her to Miss Bates is read forty times over, her compliments to all her friends go round and round again, and if she sends her aunt a pair of garters, one hears of nothing else for a month. I wish Jane Fairfax very well, but she tires me to death. One could almost wish that Jane Fairfax should take a walk down a lonely road some dark night and satisfy the bloodlust of a vampire."

They were now approaching the cottage of the sick family, and all idle topics were ended. Emma was very compassionate, and the family was as comforted by her personal attention, kindness, counsel, and patience as from her purse. She entered into their troubles with ready sympathy and gave her assistance with as much intelligence as goodwill.

After remaining there as long as she could reasonably give comfort or advice, Emma left the cottage with such an impression of the scene that she said to Harriet, as they walked away, "These are the sights, Harriet, to do one good.

How trifling they make everything else appear! I feel now as if I could think of nothing but these poor creatures all the rest of the day. And yet, who can say how soon it may all vanish from my mind?"

"Very true," said Harriet. "Poor creatures! One can think of nothing else."

Suddenly, from a thicket of shrubbery, the young ladies heard a shriek that would chill a bowl of steaming porridge.

"Dear Miss Woodhouse!" exclaimed Harriet, as they froze in their tracks. "What was that?"

Emma was already reaching down to unfasten her pink ribbon. "Fear not, Harriet. I shall protect you."

With blinding speed, the hideous creature leapt out of the bushes, baring his fangs and uttering yet another ear-splitting shriek.

Emma struggled to locate her wooden stake beneath her skirt.

Meanwhile, the vampire clasped its hands onto Harriet's arms, preventing her from retrieving her own wooden stake. The creature, salivating with lust, drew closer to Harriet's fair neck.

"Miss Woodhouse! Hurry!"

Then suddenly the vampire's black eyes grew wide, and its aspect was filled with horror. It screeched loudly, released Harriet from its vice-like grip, cowered quickly back through the hedge, and was gone from sight just as quickly as it had appeared.

"Dear Miss Woodhouse!" wailed Harriet, shaking with distress, the tears flowing down her round cheeks.

Emma embraced Harriet and comforted her. "Oh, my dear, dear Harriet! The creature is gone. It will not harm you now."

"Dear Miss Woodhouse! I thought my brief, insignificant existence was soon to come to a grisly end!"

"Indeed, Harriet, I feared the same as I watched, help-lessly tangled amongst my silly undergarments. But what could have dissuaded the creature from devouring you?"

"Oh! Miss Woodhouse! I cannot imagine! Perhaps he did not like my perfume! Or perhaps because I neglected to bathe this morning!" she said with mortifying embarrassment.

At that moment, the sun peeked out from behind the grey clouds and illuminated something on Harriet's bosom.

"What is that you are wearing around your neck, my dear Harriet?"

Harriet touched a small silver cross hanging from a fine chain. "Why, it is my Sabbath cross from yesterday's church service."

Emma smiled. "Of course! Silver! I think that perhaps you should continue to display your cross on your bosom whenever you venture out."

"Indeed I shall, Miss Woodhouse! Indeed I shall!"

Harriet felt quite a bit relieved that she wore a modicum of prevention against future attacks.

They walked on. The lane made a slight bend, and when that bend was passed they saw an object before them and realised it was Mr. Elton.

He greeted them warmly, as Emma took caution not to touch his hand, then he joined them on their walk.

The young ladies recounted to Mr. Elton their horrifying experience. But when Harriet displayed her silver cross to the vicar, he quickly moved to the other side of Emma. She thought it peculiar that a man of God should react with fear at the sign of the cross. No, no, rejoined Mr. Elton, he merely wanted to position himself between the ladies and the edge of the road to protect them against any future attacks. How gallant! thought Emma.

The next subject of conversation concerned the wants and sufferings of the poor family they had just visited.

Mr. Elton, meeting Harriet on such a charitable errand as this, thought Emma, will bring a great increase of affection on each side. I should not be surprised if it were to bring about his declaration of love. It certainly would if I were not here. I wish I were anywhere else.

Anxious to separate herself from them as much as she could, Emma stopped under the pretence of having to secure the pink ribbon around her wooden stake and, stooping down, begged them to have the goodness to walk on, and she would follow in half a minute. They did as they were told.

By the time Emma judged it reasonable to have done with her ribbon, she slowly gained on them. Mr. Elton was speaking with animation, Harriet listening with a very pleased attention. But Emma was disappointed when she found that he was only giving Harriet an account of yesterday's party at his friend Mr. Cole's house.

They now walked on together quietly till, within view of the vicarage, Emma's sudden decision to get Harriet into the house made her again find something very much amiss about her pink ribbon and fall behind to secure it once more. She then broke the ribbon off short and, dexterously throwing it into a ditch, was presently obliged to beg them to stop and mentioned her inability to walk home in tolerable comfort.

"Part of my ribbon is gone," said she, "and I do not know what to do. I really am a most troublesome companion to you both. Mr. Elton, I must beg to stop at your house and ask your housekeeper for a bit of ribbon or string or anything just to keep my wooden stake around my leg."

Mr. Elton looked all happiness at this proposition; and nothing could exceed his alertness and attention in escorting them into his house and endeavouring to make everything pleasant.

The room they were taken into was the one he chiefly occupied—the windows darkened by curtains and many candles for illumination.

Emma passed into the next room with the housekeeper to receive her assistance. She left the door ajar between the two rooms. By engaging the housekeeper in conversation, Emma hoped to make it practicable for Mr. Elton to make his declaration of love to Harriet. After ten minutes, Emma was then finished and made her appearance.

The two lovers were standing together at one end of the room, Harriet shivering from lack of warmth, there being no activity in the fireplace. Emma could see Harriet's visible breath but, curiously, no breath coming from Mr. Elton.

Nonetheless, everything looked most promising between them and, for half a minute, Emma felt the glory of having schemed successfully.

But it was not to be; he had not come to the point. He had been most agreeable, most delightful—other little gallantries and allusions had been made—but nothing serious.

Cautious, very cautious is Mr. Elton, thought Emma, as he advances his affections inch by inch, risking nothing till he believes himself secure in Harriet's affection.

Still, however, though everything had not been accomplished by her ingenious device, Emma could not but flatter herself that the occasion had been of much enjoyment to both and must be leading them forward to the great event.

CHAPTER 11

M R. ELTON MUST NOW be left to himself. It was no longer in Emma's power to manage his happiness or quicken his decision to marry Harriet.

The visit of Emma's sister Isabella and her family was so very near at hand that first in anticipation and then in reality, it became henceforth her prime object of interest. And during the ten days of their stay at Hartfield, it was not to be expected that Emma could help Mr. Elton's decision along.

After all, there are people who the more you do for them, the less they will do for themselves.

Mr. and Mrs. John Knightley's visit was exciting more than the usual interest. Till this year, every long vacation since their marriage had been divided between Isabella's home at Hartfield and Donwell Abbey, the home of John's brother Mr. George Knightley.

But all the holidays of this season were to be given to Emma and Mr. Woodhouse, who consequently were now most nervously happy in anticipating this visit.

Mr. Woodhouse was very much concerned about the evils of the journey for Isabella, with so much danger about the countryside, but his alarms were needless. Mr. and Mrs. John Knightley, their five children, and a competent number of nurserymaids all reached Hartfield in safety.

The bustle and joy of such an arrival, the many people to be talked to, welcomed, encouraged, and variously dispersed and disposed of produced a noise and confusion which Mr. Woodhouse's nerves could not have borne under any other circumstance.

But with regard to the five children, Isabella so respected her father that, in spite of all their playing and noisemaking and capturing bunnies in the woods for their strange enjoyment, the little ones were never allowed to be a disturbance to their grandfather.

Mrs. John Knightley was a pretty, elegant little woman of gentle, quiet manners and a disposition remarkably amiable and affectionate. She was wholly wrapped up in her family, a devoted wife, a doting mother, and so tenderly attached to her father and sister that a warmer love might have seemed impossible. She could never see a fault in any of them.

Isabella was not a woman of strong intellect or any quickness. She also inherited much of her father's constitution— delicate in health, over-careful of her children, with many fears and many nerves. She had a general distrust of food, like her father, which was fortunate since John and her five children rarely consumed any that she had prepared.

Mr. John Knightley was a tall gentleman, very handsome and clever, with dark hair, pallid skin, pale blue-coloured eyes, and a very appealing scent. He was a lawyer and, as he never slept, worked all night long, thus excelling in his profession.

He had reserved manners which prevented his being generally pleasing, and he was capable of being sometimes out of humour. He was not an ill-tempered man, but his temper was not his great perfection. He could sometimes be ungracious or say a severe thing. And he had a special power which allowed him, at times, to discern the future.

John was not a great favourite with his fair sister-in-law, Emma. Nothing wrong in him escaped her. She was quick to feel the little injuries to Isabella, which Isabella never felt herself. Perhaps Emma might let more pass over had John's manners been flattering to her, but they were usually without praise.

But John's greatest fault in Emma's eyes was the lack of respect for her father. There had not always been the patience that could have been wished. Mr. Woodhouse's peculiarities and fidgetiness sometimes provoked John to a sharp retort ill bestowed.

They had not been seated long when Mr. Woodhouse, with a melancholy shake of the head and a sigh, mentioned the recent vampire incidents in Highbury.

Emma then related to her family, with a great deal of consternation, the details of the two vicious attacks involving Harriet Smith and herself.

"My dear Emma, how absolutely hideous!" cried Isabella. "We have had a few isolated incidents in London, but the very thought of so much danger within the vicinity of Hartfield simply curls my toes!"

Mr. Woodhouse then added, "Emma's natural modesty prevents her from revealing that she slew one of those horrid creatures herself!"

"Dear me!" exclaimed Isabella. "Do tell!"

Emma then recounted the terrifying event, but gave Mr. George Knightley due credit for advising her to strap a wooden stake to her leg. Mr. John Knightley nodded his approval of his brother's wise counsel.

Mr. Woodhouse, distressed that this unpleasant topic should sour the joy of Isabella's visit, called his daughter's attention to the sad change at Hartfield since she had been there last.

"Poor Miss Taylor," said he. "It is a grievous business."

"Oh yes, sir," cried Isabella with ready sympathy. "How you must miss her! And dear Emma, too! What a dreadful loss to you both! I have been so grieved for you. I could not imagine how you could possibly do without her. But I trust she is doing well, sir."

"Pretty well, my dear, I trust. I suppose marriage agrees with her well enough, though she is perpetually cold in that large house without a fire blazing."

Mr. John Knightley asked Emma quietly whether there were any doubts about Mr. Weston.

"Oh no! None in the least. I never saw Mrs. Weston better in my life—never looking so well."

I should certainly expect so, thought Mr. John Knightley, considering that Mr. Weston, being a vegan like myself, has never feasted upon Mrs. Weston, just as I have never sunk my fangs into my own wife Isabella.

"And do you see Miss Taylor often, Father?" asked Isabella with a note of sadness which pleased him greatly.

Mr. Woodhouse hesitated. "Not nearly so often, my dear, as I could wish."

"But Papa," said Emma, "we have missed seeing them only one day since they were married. Either in the morning or evening of every day, except one, have we seen them. They are very, very kind in their visits. Mr. Weston is really as kind as Miss Taylor."

"Just as it should be," said Mr. John Knightley.

"I believe," said Isabella, "that Mr. Weston is one of the very best-tempered men that ever existed. He has a strange power about him that causes happiness in the people around him. I have been convinced there could not be a more feeling heart nor a better man in existence. If anybody can deserve him, it must be Miss Taylor."

"Where is Mr. Weston's son, Frank Churchill?" asked John Knightley. "Has he been here on this occasion?"

"He has not been here yet," replied Emma. "There was a strong expectation of his coming soon after Miss Taylor's marriage, but it ended in nothing; and I have not heard him mentioned lately."

"But you should tell them of the letter, my dear," said Mr. Woodhouse. "He wrote a letter to Mrs. Weston to congratulate her on the marriage, and a very proper, handsome letter it was. She showed it to me. I thought it very well done of him indeed. Some of the words were difficult to read, with so many dark red stains, but still it was a most handsome letter. Whether it was his own idea, you know, one cannot tell. He is but young, and—"

"Papa, he is three and twenty. You forget how time passes."

"Three and twenty! My, my! Nonetheless, it was an exceedingly good letter and gave Mr. and Mrs. Weston a great deal of pleasure."

"How very pleasing and proper of him!" cried the good-hearted Isabella. "But how sad it is that he should not live at Randalls with his father! There is something so shocking in a child's being taken away from his parents and natural home. I never could comprehend how Mr. Weston could part with him. I really could never think well of anybody who did such a thing. Does he not have a heart that beats inside him?"

"Not likely, I fancy," observed Mr. John Knightley. "I am sure Mr. Weston felt not the pain that you would feel, Isabella, if you had to give up our children. Mr. Weston is an easy, cheerful man, rather than a man of strong feelings; he finds his comfort in the enjoyment of life, rather than upon family affection or anything that home affords."

Emma did not like John Knightley's reflection on Mr. Weston and had half a mind to take it up with him. She struggled but let it pass. She would keep the peace if possible; and there was something honourable and valuable in her brother-in-law's strong family beliefs. It had a high claim to tolerance.

CHAPTER 12

THAT EVENING, MR. GEORGE Knightley was to dine with them—rather against the wishes of Mr. Woodhouse, who did not like to share Isabella with anyone on her first day at Hartfield.

Emma had decided to offer the invitation, due to the recent disagreement between Mr. Knightley and herself. She hoped they might now become friends again. She thought it was time to make up. She certainly had not been in the wrong, and she suspected he had read her mind and knew as much but would never admit it. Still, it was time to appear to forget that they had ever quarreled.

Emma hoped it might assist the restoration of friendship that, when Mr. Knightley came into the room, she had one of the children with her—the youngest niece, a nice little vampiress about eight months old, who was now making her first visit to Hartfield. The girl possessed the same cold, pale skin and appealing scent as her father and Uncle George, which Emma concluded were strong family traits.

The child on her lap did help matters, for though Mr. Knightley began with grave looks and short questions, he soon talked in the usual way and took the child out of Emma's arms.

Emma felt they were friends again. She could not help saying with a little sauciness as he was admiring the baby,

"What a comfort it is, that we think alike about our nephews and nieces. As to men and women, our opinions are sometimes very different; but with regard to these children, I observe we never disagree."

Mr. Knightley answered, "If you were as much guided by nature in your opinion of men and women as you are with these children and less by fancy and whim, we might always think alike."

"To be sure," said Emma, "our disagreements always arise from my being in the wrong."

"Yes," said he, smiling, "and for good reason. I was thirty-seven years old when you were born."

"And you still are!" exclaimed Emma gleefully. "No doubt you were much my superior in judgement then; but does not the passage of my twenty-one years bring our understandings a good deal nearer?"

"Yes—a good deal nearer."

"But still not near enough," said she, "to give me a chance of being right if we think differently."

"I still have the advantage over you of so much experience and of not being a pretty young woman and a spoiled child. Come, my dear Emma, let us be friends and say no more about it."

He then smiled at his niece. "Little Emma, tell your aunt that she ought to set you a better example than to be renewing old grievances and that if she were not wrong before, she is now."

"That's true," said Emma, "very true. Little Emma, grow up a better woman than your aunt. Be infinitely more clever and not half so conceited. Now, Mr. Knightley, a word or two more. Concerning Harriet's refusal of Mr. Robert Martin—as far as good intentions went, we were both right, and nothing on my side of the argument has yet proved wrong. I only want to know that Mr. Martin is not very bitterly disappointed."

"He was very disappointed, indeed," was his answer. "He heaved a cow over the fence in frustration."

"Ah! I am very sorry for the poor cow! Come, shake hands with me."

This had just taken place and with great cordiality when John Knightley made his appearance, and "How do you do, George?" and "John, how are you?" succeeded in the true English style, revealing a vampire bond so strong that it was apparent they would do anything for each other.

The evening was quiet and full of conversation, as Mr. Woodhouse made comfortable talk with his dear Isabella on one side of the room near the fireplace and, on the other side, far away from the raging heat, sat the two Mr. Knightleys, and Emma only occasionally joined one group or the other.

"My poor dear Isabella," said Mr. Woodhouse, fondly taking her hand and interrupting for a few moments her busy duties for some of her five children, "how terribly long it is since you were here! And how tired you must be after your journey! You must go to bed early, my dear, and I recommend a little porridge to you before you go. My dear Emma, suppose we all have a little porridge?"

Emma could not suppose any such thing, and only two bowls were ordered. After a little more discussion in praise of porridge, wondering why it was not taken every evening by everybody, Mr. Woodhouse proceeded to say, with an air of grave reflection, "It was an awkward business, my dear Isabella, your spending the autumn in London instead of coming here. The truth is, my dear, that nobody is healthy in London, and nobody can be. It is a dreadful thing to have you forced to live there! So far off! The air so bad! And did I not hear of a vampire menace in London that had nearly overrun the city?"

"No, indeed—our part of London is very superior to most others. We are so very airy and safe from the threat of attacks!"

"Ah, my dear, I know you make the best of it. But London is not like Hartfield. After you have been a week here, you are a different creature. To be sure, I cannot say I think any of you are looking well at present—all so pale, so very pale, as if you never see the sun."

"I am sorry to hear you say so, Father. But I assure you, excepting those little nervous headaches and palpitations which I am never entirely free from anywhere, I am quite well myself. And the children are naturally pale anyway, like their father. I trust that you do not think Mr. Knightley is looking ill," turning her eyes with affectionate anxiety towards her husband.

"Middling, my dear; I cannot compliment you. I think Mr. John Knightley very far from looking well—in fact, his skin is quite a bit colder and paler than the rest of you, perhaps from lack of food or sleep—I know he works very hard. Look at the dark circles under his eyes."

"What is the matter, sir? Did you speak to me?" cried Mr. John Knightley, hearing his own name from across the large room, his sense of hearing being particularly acute.

"I am sorry to find, my love, that my father does not think you looking well, but I trust it is only from being a little fatigued."

"My dear Isabella," John exclaimed, "pray do not concern yourself about my looks. Be satisfied with coddling yourself and the children, and let me look as I choose."

Isabella then made a kind inquiry after Jane Fairfax and, though no great favourite with Emma in general, she was at that moment very happy to assist in praising.

"That sweet, amiable Jane Fairfax!" said Isabella. "It is so long since I have seen her! I always regret excessively on dear Emma's account that she cannot be more at Highbury. She would be such a delightful companion for Emma."

Mr. Woodhouse agreed to it all but added, "Our little friend Harriet Smith, however, is just such another pretty kind of young person. You will like Harriet. Emma could not have a better companion than Harriet. And Harriet is fortunate to have a vampire slayer such as Emma for a friend."

The mention of vampires once again raised the ire of Mr. George Knightley.

"These wild, vagrant creatures have gotten entirely out of control!" he bellowed. "It is becoming impossible to enjoy our society anymore without constantly looking over our shoulders with the trepidation of someone's blood being sucked dry at any moment!"

"Hear, hear!" said Mr. John Knightley. "I do wish there were some sort of legal censure that could be implemented against them."

"Nonsense, John!" returned his brother. "This is no task for lawyers. This is a task for vigilantes!"

"Dear Mr. Knightley!" said Emma. "I am shocked that you, as a gentleman, would advocate such a coarse and vulgar rejoinder to this menace! We simply do not do such things in Highbury."

"Then what do you propose, my dear Emma? That young ladies tiptoe around flashing their silver crosses as they make their way along each day? I believe staunch action is required, and we, as the natural leaders of this village, are just the ones to do it!"

Emma and her father and Isabella and John remained shocked and silent after Mr. George Knightley's impassioned soliloquy, then quietly let it pass.

This topic was soon forgotten and the porridge came, supplying a great deal to be talked about—much praise of and many comments on its wholesomeness for every constitution. Mr. Woodhouse ended the evening with the soothing attentions of his daughters.

CHAPTER 13

THERE COULD HARDLY BE a happier creature in the world than Mrs. John Knightley in this short visit to Hartfield, calling every morning on her old acquaintances with her five children and talking over what she had done every evening with her father and sister. It was a perfectly delightful visit, though much too short.

Isabella looked forward especially to Christmas Eve dinner with the Westons at their small estate, Randalls. Even Mr. Woodhouse was persuaded to join them, and it did not take Emma long to convince him that they might include Harriet and Mr. Elton also.

The evening before this great event—for it was indeed a very great event that Mr. Woodhouse should dine out on Christmas Eve—had been spent by Harriet at Hartfield, and she had gone home much indisposed with a cold.

❧

Emma called on her little friend the next day at the boarding school and found her very feverish with a bad sore throat. Mrs. Goddard was full of care and affection, but Harriet was too ill to attend the Westons' dinner, causing her many tears.

Emma sat with Harriet as long as she could to attend to her and raise her spirits by saying how much Mr. Elton would be depressed when he learned of her illness; and she left her at least tolerably comfortable.

Emma had just left Mrs. Goddard's when she was met by Mr. Elton himself, evidently coming to visit Harriet. As they walked slowly together in conversation about the invalid, Mr. John Knightley's carriage drew up. John was just returning from his daily visit with his brother George along with his two eldest young boys, whose healthy, glowing faces showed all the benefit of having feasted on the blood of raccoons and rabbits running wild in the countryside of Donwell Abbey.

The carriage slowed and kept pace with Emma and Mr. Elton as they walked. Mr. Elton inhaled the scent of fresh blood on the others and dreamed of having a wife. Emma was just describing the nature of Harriet's complaint: "A throat very much inflamed, with a great deal of heat about her, a quick, low pulse." And she was sorry to find out from Mrs. Goddard that Harriet "was susceptible to very bad sore throats."

Mr. Elton looked all alarmed, his black eyes growing wider, as he exclaimed, "A sore throat! I hope not infectious. I hope not of a putrid infectious sort. Has Mr. Perry seen her? Indeed, Emma, you should take care of yourself as well as your friend. Let me beg you to run no risks. Why does not Perry see her?"

Emma, who was not really at all frightened herself, assured Mr. Elton of Mrs. Goddard's experience and care.

Then, after a moment of contemplation, she added, "The day is so cold, so very cold—and looks and feels so very much like snow, Mr. Elton, that perhaps you should excuse yourself tonight from the Westons."

"I can assure you, dear Miss Woodhouse, that the cold and snow agree with me quite pleasantly."

Emma saw no breath coming from Mr. Elton's nose or mouth and grew very concerned. "You appear to me a little hoarse already, and I think it would be common sense to stay at home and take care of yourself tonight."

Mr. Elton looked as if he did not know what answer to make, for he had not the least inclination to give up the dinner.

But Emma, intending that he miss the dinner so that he might spend time with the ailing Harriet, blurted out, "We shall make your apologies to Mr. and Mrs. Weston."

But hardly had she spoken when Mr. John Knightley offered Emma and Mr. Elton a seat in his carriage, and Mr. Elton promptly accepted the offer, Emma likewise obliging.

Mr. Elton had made up his mind. He was going to the Westons, and never had his pale, handsome face expressed more pleasure than at this moment; never had his smile been wider, his vampire scent stronger or more appealing, nor his eyes darker than when he gazed into Emma's eyes.

Well, Emma thought to herself, this is most strange, that Mr. Elton would choose the dinner party and leave Harriet ill behind! Most strange indeed! But there is, I believe, in many single men such a passion for dining out that anything gives way to it, and this must be the case with Mr. Elton. A most amiable, pleasing young man and very much in love with Harriet, but still he cannot refuse a party invitation, even though he would consume nary a biscuit all evening. What a strange thing love is!

Soon afterwards Mr. Elton departed the carriage, and Emma felt there was a great deal of sentiment in his voice when assuring her that he would call at Mrs. Goddard's for news of Harriet.

After a few minutes of entire silence, John Knightley said to Emma, "I never in my life saw a man more intent on

being agreeable than Mr. Elton where ladies are concerned."
He must need sustenance very badly, he thought.

"Mr. Elton's manners are not perfect," replied Emma,
"but there is such perfect good temper and goodwill in Mr.
Elton as one cannot but value "

"Yes, Emma," said Mr. John Knightley presently, with
some slyness, "he seems to have a great deal of goodwill
towards you." As if he could feast upon you all night,
thought he.

"Me!" she replied with a smile of astonishment. "Are you
imagining *me* to be Mr. Elton's object of affection?"

"Such a thought has crossed my mind, I admit, Emma;
and if it never occurred to you before, you may as well take
it into consideration now."

"Mr. Elton in love with me! What an idea!" exclaimed
Emma. She knew that Mr. John Knightley had a special
power to see the future, but she did not think it included the
foretelling of a match between Mr. Elton and herself.

"I do not say it is so," he said, "but you will do well
to consider it and to regulate your behaviour accordingly.
I think your manners are encouraging to him. I speak as a
friend, Emma."

"I thank you, John, but I am sure you are quite mistaken.
Mr. Elton and I are very good friends and nothing more."

Emma departed the carriage and walked on, not very
pleased with her brother-in-law for imagining her blind and
ignorant and in need of advice.

⚜

That evening, the cold had become severe. Mr. Woodhouse
set out for Randalls with Isabella in his own carriage. By the
time the second carriage was in motion, with Emma and

Mr. John Knightley, a few flakes of snow were finding their way down, and the sky had the appearance of producing a very white world in a very short time.

Emma soon saw that her companion was not in the happiest humour. She could not see Mr. John Knightley's breath, his skin was cold and pale, and his mood anticipated nothing in the visit that could be at all worth the effort; and the whole drive to the vicarage, to fetch Mr. Elton, was spent expressing his discontent.

"A man such as Mr. Weston," said John Knightley, "must have a very good opinion of himself when he asks people to leave the coldness of their own fireside and travel on such a day as this for the sake of coming to see him. It is the greatest absurdity—it is actually snowing at this moment! Here we are, setting forward to spend five dull hours in another man's house, with nothing to say or hear that was not said and heard yesterday and may not be said and heard again tomorrow. Going in dismal weather to return probably in worse."

Emma dreaded being quarrelsome. She allowed him to talk and wrapped herself up without opening her lips.

They arrived at the vicarage, and Mr. Elton, smiling, was with them instantly. As the carriage continued on to the Westons', Mr. Elton was so very cheerful that Emma began to think Harriet must be feeling better.

But when she inquired about her young friend, his face lengthened immediately, and his voice was one of sentiment as he answered, "Oh, no! I am grieved to find that, when I called at Mrs. Goddard's door, I was told that Miss Smith was not better, by no means better—rather worse. Very much grieved and concerned was I."

Emma answered, "It is a most severe cold indeed. Mr. Perry has been with her. I trust tomorrow morning will bring us both a more comfortable report. But it is impossible not to feel uneasiness. Such a sad loss to our party tonight!"

"Dreadful," said Mr. Elton calmly. "Exactly so, indeed— she will be missed every moment."

But Mr. Elton's sigh should have lasted longer. Emma was rather in dismay when only half a minute afterwards he began to speak of other things and in a voice of the greatest enjoyment.

"How excellent," said he, "the use of a sheepskin for carriages. How very comfortable they make it. The contrivances of modern days have indeed rendered a gentleman's carriage perfectly complete. Ha! Snows a little, I see."

"Yes," grumbled John Knightley, "and I think we shall have a good deal more of it."

"Christmas weather," observed Mr. Elton. "Quite seasonable, and what a lovely chill! 'Tis quite the season indeed for friendly meetings. At Christmas everybody invites their friends about them. Nothing could be pleasanter."

At another time, Emma might have been amused. But she was too much astonished now at Mr. Elton's spirits for other feelings. Harriet seemed quite forgotten in the expectation of a pleasant party.

"Charming people, Mr. and Mrs. Weston," continued Mr. Elton, "and everything in the greatest comfort. It will be a small party, but where small parties are select, they are perhaps the most agreeable of any, though Mr. Knightley perhaps is used to the large parties of London."

"I know nothing of the large parties of London, sir—I never dine with anybody. My first enjoyment," replied John Knightley as they passed through the Westons' gate, "will be to find myself safe at Hartfield again."

CHAPTER 14

A CHANGE OF EXPRESSION was needed for each gentleman as he walked into Mrs. Weston's drawing room—Mr. Elton must compose his joyous looks, and Mr. John Knightley disperse his ill humour. Mr. Elton must smile less and Mr. John Knightley more.

Only Emma might act naturally and show herself just as happy as she was. To her it was real enjoyment to be with the Westons. Mr. Weston was a great favourite, and there was no one in the world to whom Emma spoke so freely as the former Miss Taylor—who would listen and understand, and always be interested in the little affairs, arrangements, perplexities, and pleasures of her father and herself.

The very sight of Mrs. Weston—her smile, her touch, her voice—was grateful to Emma, and she determined to think as little as possible of Mr. Elton's oddities, or of anything else unpleasant, and enjoy all that was enjoyable to the utmost.

The misfortune of Harriet's cold had been pretty well gone through before her arrival. Mr. Woodhouse had been safely seated long enough to give the history of it, everyone wholly engrossed in their attention.

Emma's attempt to forget Mr. Elton became difficult when in the drawing room she found herself seated next to him, far away from the fire. The attention he paid Emma was so great as she stared into the black void of his eyes that she could not help thinking, "Can it really be as my brother-in-law imagined? Can it be possible for this man to be beginning to transfer his affections from Harriet to me? Absurd and insufferable!"

Yet he was so concerned that she was warm enough—though he would have preferred to converse outside in the snow—and he was so interested about her father, and so delighted with Mrs. Weston, and admired Emma's drawings with so much zeal, and behaved so much like a would-be lover as he stared at her neck that it took some effort to preserve her good manners.

For her own sake, she could not be rude; and for Harriet's, in the hope that all would yet turn out right, she was even positively polite. But it was truly an effort, especially as another conversation was going on which she particularly wished to eavesdrop on.

Emma heard enough to learn that Mr. Weston was giving some information about his son, Frank Churchill. From a few half-syllables, she suspected he was announcing an impending visit from his son; but before she could quiet Mr. Elton, the subject was so completely past that any reviving question from her would have been awkward.

Now, it so happened that in spite of Emma's resolution of never marrying, there was something about Mr. Frank Churchill that always interested her. She had been told he was strikingly handsome, with perfect white skin and large black eyes like Mr. Elton's and Mr. Knightley's—in fact, quite like so many other gentlemen in Highbury. How curious!

Emma had frequently thought—especially since Frank's father, Mr. Weston, had married Miss Taylor—that if Emma were to marry, Frank Churchill was the very person to suit her in age, character, and condition. He seemed, by this connection between the families, quite to belong to her.

Emma had to suppose it was a match which had been thought of by everybody who knew them. She convinced herself that Mr. and Mrs. Weston thought of it; and she had a great curiosity to see Frank Churchill, a decided intention of finding him pleasant and of being liked by him, and a sort of pleasure in the idea of their being matched in their friends' imaginations.

At the dinner table, Emma was seated next to Mr. Weston, who talked the whole time but never ate a thing. He recoiled in the most curious way, thought Emma, from the garlic-seasoned minced chicken, which she found herself consuming with delight, admittedly in a most unladylike fashion.

Mr. Weston then said, "We wish two more people were here tonight—your pretty little friend Miss Smith and my son—and then I should say we were quite complete. I believe you did not hear me telling the others in the drawing room that we are expecting Frank. I had a letter from him this morning, and he will be with us in a fortnight."

Emma spoke with a very proper degree of pleasure and fully agreed that Mr. Frank Churchill and Miss Smith would make their party quite complete.

"He has been wanting to visit," continued Mr. Weston, "ever since September. Every letter has been full of it, but he could not get away; but now I have no doubt of seeing him here about the second week in January."

"What a very great pleasure it will be to you!" said Emma. "And I know Mrs. Weston is so anxious to be acquainted with him that she must be almost as happy as yourself."

"Yes, but she thinks there will be another delay. The case, you see—this is between ourselves, there are secrets in all families, you know—the case is, that it all depends on his aunt, Mrs. Churchill. She is an odd woman!

"But I never allow myself to speak ill of her, on Frank's account. I used to think she was not capable of being fond of anybody except herself, but she has always been kind to Frank. I would not say this to anybody else, dear Emma, but Mrs. Churchill has no more heart than a stone to people in general and the devil of a temper."

Emma liked the subject of Frank Churchill's visit so well that she mentioned it to Mrs. Weston very soon after their moving into the drawing room after dinner. Mrs. Weston agreed but added, "I am very much afraid that it will all end in nothing. Mr. Weston, I daresay, has been telling you exactly how the matter stands?"

"Yes—it seems to depend upon the ill humour of Mrs. Churchill."

Mrs. Weston smiled and nodded at Emma, then turning to Emma's sister said, "You must know, my dear Isabella, that we are by no means sure of seeing Mr. Frank Churchill. It depends entirely upon his aunt. Mrs. Churchill rules at Enscombe, and his coming now depends upon her being willing to spare him."

"Oh yes—Mrs. Churchill. Everybody knows Mrs. Churchill," replied Isabella, "and I am sure I never think of that poor young man without the greatest compassion—a life of misery. What a blessing that she never had any children!"

"He ought to come," said Emma. "If he could stay only a couple of days, he ought to come; and one can hardly conceive a young man's not being able to spend a week with his father if he desires it."

"My dearest Emma," said Mrs. Weston, "do not pretend with your sweet temper to understand a bad one or to lay down rules for it. You must let it go its own way."

Emma listened and then coolly said, "I shall not be satisfied unless he comes."

CHAPTER 15

AFTER DINNER, MR. WOODHOUSE was soon ready for his tea, and when he had drunk it was entirely ready to go home. It was as much as his three companions could do to convince him to stay.

Mr. Elton, in very good spirits, entered the drawing room. Mrs. Weston and Emma were sitting together on a sofa. He joined them immediately and, with scarcely an invitation, seated himself between them. His hand touched Emma's and an electric shock nearly sent her flying off the sofa.

Emma quickly recovered and, still in good spirits from pondering the visit of Mr. Frank Churchill, was willing to forget Mr. Elton's impropriety; and when he spoke of Harriet, Emma was ready to listen with most friendly smiles.

Mr. Elton declared himself extremely anxious about Emma's fair, lovely, amiable friend. He confessed that the nature of Harriet's illness alarmed him considerably. But then it seemed all at once that he was more anxious that Emma should escape the infection. He begged her with great earnestness to refrain from visiting the sick chamber again; and though Emma tried to laugh it off, there was no putting an end to Mr. Elton's extreme concern about her.

Emma was vexed. It did appear—there was no concealing it now—that Mr. Elton was in love with her instead of

Harriet, which, if true, was most contemptible and abominable! She had difficulty in minding her temper.

Mr. Elton turned to Mrs. Weston, and his large ebony eyes implored her assistance. "Would you not give me your support? Would you not add your persuasions to mine to induce Miss Woodhouse not to go to Mrs. Goddard's till it was certain that Miss Smith's disorder had no infection?"

Emma saw Mrs. Weston's surprise. Emma was too provoked and offended to say anything directly. She could only give Mr. Elton such a look as she thought must restore him to his senses, and then Emma left the sofa, moving to a seat by Isabella and giving her sister all her attention.

Mr. John Knightley now came into the room from examining the weather, with the information that the ground was covered with snow and it was still snowing fast, with a strong, drifting wind, and predicted an imminent blizzard.

Poor Mr. Woodhouse was silent from consternation; but everybody else had something to say or some comfort to offer. Mrs. Weston and Emma tried earnestly to cheer him and turn his attention from his son-in-law John, who was pursuing his triumph rather unfeelingly.

"I admired your resolution very much, sir," said Mr. John Knightley, "in venturing out in such weather. If one carriage is blown over, rest assured the other one will be at hand. I daresay we shall all be safe at Hartfield again before midnight."

"What is to be done, my dear Emma?" was Mr. Woodhouse's first exclamation. He looked to her for comfort, and her assurances of safety revived him a little.

Isabella's alarm was equal to her father's. The horror of being snowed in at Randalls while her children were at Hartfield was full in her imagination; she was eager for John and herself to set forward instantly through the drifted snow that might impede them.

"You had better order the carriage directly, my love," said Isabella to her husband. "I daresay we shall be able to get along if we set off directly."

They were still discussing the point when Mr. George Knightley, who had left the room immediately after his brother's first report of the snow, came back again and told everyone that the snow was nowhere above half an inch deep, very few flakes were falling, the clouds were parting, and the full moon was bright in the evening sky.

But for Mr. Woodhouse the alarm could not be appeased, and all decided to leave. The bell was rung, the carriages came, and all stepped outside into the light snow.

Suddenly, and to everyone's surprise and horror, four despicable creatures lunged from behind the tall privet near the house. The vampires—rags hanging from their bones, limbs thrashing, and fangs drooling—raced towards the assembled gentry.

The next sequence of events unfolded with blinding speed. Mr. Elton shielded Isabella and Mrs. Weston, who screamed in terror. Mr. Woodhouse fainted and collapsed on the ground. Mr. George Knightley dashed into the house and returned with two sabres, one of which he tossed to Mr. Weston, who expertly caught it. John Knightley dashed to his carriage and produced his hunting rifle. Emma deftly retrieved her wooden stake from beneath her bombazines, having practiced the exercise repeatedly at home.

Thus armed, the gentlemen and lady advanced towards the unwelcome intruders and the battle began.

Mr. Weston and George Knightley each raised their sabres and quickly dispatched two of the fiends, decapitating them.

The third vampire shrieked and raged towards John Knightley, who aimed his rifle and fired two shots. Both hit their mark in the torso of the monster. It staggered and fell. The fourth creature bared its claws, snatching at Emma but was repelled by the aura of garlic which permeated her body. As it stood paralysed, Emma drove her wooden stake into its heart and it fell to the ground.

The vampire who had been shot was still alive, for John Knightley had forgotten that mere bullets cannot vanquish the supernatural. It suddenly regained its stance and lurched towards John, whose back was turned. George Knightley hastened to rescue his brother and, with a gallant swipe of his sabre, relieved the vampire of its head.

The cream of Highbury society stood silent and stunned, and surveyed the carnage. Mrs. Weston helped Mr. Woodhouse to his feet. A mixture of relief and revulsion filled their hearts and minds.

Mr. George Knightley was the first to speak: "Is everyone quite all right?"

No one in the party could find a single word to utter. Isabella and Mrs. Weston wiped away their tears. Mr. Woodhouse gasped at the now-familiar sight of headless vampires splayed on the ground. Mr. Weston laid down his sword, and John Knightley placed his hunting rifle in the carriage. Emma withdrew her wooden stake from the dead creature and re-tied it to her leg.

Mr. Elton spoke a few words of prayer and thanksgiving for having been delivered from the valley of death.

Quietly, the guests took to their carriages. Isabella stepped in after her father, and John Knightley joined them.

Emma found herself being escorted into the second carriage by Mr. Elton. She would rather it had not happened.

For scarcely had they passed the gate when Mr. Elton seized Emma's hand!

To her utter astonishment, Mr. Elton then professed his ardent love to Emma—availing himself of the precious opportunity, declaring sentiments, hoping, fearing, adoring, ready to die if she refused him!

Mr. Elton was flattering himself that his love and passion would be seriously accepted by Emma. It was really happening. Mr. Elton, the lover of Harriet, was professing himself Emma's lover!

His fang-like teeth glistened in the night as his black, unblinking eyes stared hungrily at her lovely neck. His cold white hand touched hers and sent another shock through her body.

Still reeling from the vampire attack, Emma now had to cope with Mr. Elton's unwelcome and unexpected advances. She reached for her wooden stake to fend him off.

"No, not that!" screamed Mr. Elton. "Anything but the wooden stake! You needn't take such harsh measures. I shall compose myself."

"Why, Mr. Elton! You recoil as if you were a vampire. But I shall take your word as a gentleman that you will keep your passion under control. I am very much astonished, indeed, Mr. Elton! This? To me? You forget yourself—you mistake me for my friend. Any message to Harriet I shall be happy to deliver; but no more of this to me, if you please."

"Miss Smith? Message to Miss Smith? What could Harriet possibly mean to me?"

"Mr. Elton, this is the most extraordinary conduct! Command yourself to say no more, and I shall endeavour to forget it."

But Mr. Elton resumed the subject of his own passion and pressed Emma for a favourable answer. He pressed his chest against hers, and though she felt no heartbeat, the scent of his venom was overwhelming. Moreover, it appeared that her scent of garlic had faded. Oh! That she had only partaken of a second helping of minced chicken, which perhaps could have dissuaded him from his passion.

"Mr. Elton, my astonishment is much beyond anything I can express. After such attention to Miss Smith as I have witnessed during the past month, to be addressing me in this manner—believe me, sir, I am very far from happy in being the object of your professions of love."

"Good Heavens!" cried Mr. Elton. "What can be the meaning of this? I never thought of Miss Smith or paid her any attentions but as your friend! I never cared whether she were dead or alive but as your friend. If she has fancied otherwise, her own wishes have misled her, and I am very sorry—extremely sorry. But Miss Woodhouse! Who can think of Miss Smith, when Miss Woodhouse is near! No, upon my honour, I have thought only of you. Everything I have said or done for many weeks past has been with the sole view of marking my adoration of you. I am sure you have seen and understood that."

"No, sir," cried Emma. "I have been in a most complete error with respect to your views till this moment. Am I to believe that you have never thought seriously of Harriet?"

"Never, madam," cried he, affronted. "Never, I assure you. Miss Smith is a very good sort of girl; and I should be happy to see her respectably married. I wish her extremely well and, no doubt, there are men who would relish her plumpness. But as for myself, I am not so despairing of a socially equal marriage as to be addressing myself to Miss Smith! No, madam, my visits to Hartfield have been for yourself only; and the encouragement I received—"

"Encouragement! I gave you encouragement? Sir, you have been entirely mistaken in supposing it. I have seen you only as the admirer of my friend. In no other light could you have been more to me than a common acquaintance. I am exceedingly sorry, but I have no thoughts of matrimony at present."

He was too angry to say another word, and Emma's manner was too decided; and in this state of swelling resentment and mutually deep mortification, they had to continue together a few minutes longer.

When the carriage turned into Vicarage Lane, they found themselves all at once at the door of his house; and he was out of the carriage in a blur of light.

Emma wished him a good night. The compliment was returned coldly and proudly, and under indescribable irritation of spirits, she was then conveyed to Hartfield.

There she was welcomed with utmost delight by her father. Mr. John Knightley, ashamed of his ill humour and grateful for his life having been spared, was now all kindness and attention; and the day was concluding in peace and comfort to all their little party, except for Emma. Her mind had never been so disturbed, and she needed a very strong effort to appear cheerful till the evening was over and she could engage in quiet reflection of all that had transpired.

CHAPTER 16

EMMA SAT DOWN IN her room to think and be miserable about Mr. Elton. It was a wretched business indeed! Such an overthrow of everything she had been wishing for! Such a blow for Harriet—that was the worst of all. Every part of it brought pain and humiliation, but compared with the evil to Harriet, all was light.

"If I had not persuaded Harriet into liking Mr. Elton, I could have borne anything. He might have doubled his presumption to me—but poor Harriet!"

How could Emma have been so deceived? Mr. Elton had claimed that he had never thought seriously of Harriet—never! She looked back as well as she could, but it was all confusion. His manners must have been dubious or she could not have been so misled.

The picture! How eager he had been about the picture! And the riddle! And a hundred other circumstances—how clearly they had seemed to point to Harriet. Certainly she had often, especially of late, thought his manners towards her to be unnecessarily gallant—the electrifying touch of his pale hand, the gaze of his coal-coloured eyes—but till this very day she had never for an instant suspected it to mean anything but grateful respect to her as Harriet's friend.

She was indebted to Mr. John Knightley for first suggesting the possibility—indeed, he quite accurately predicted it. She remembered what Mr. George Knightley had once said to her about Mr. Elton, the caution he had given. It was dreadfully mortifying; but Mr. Elton was proving himself, in many respects, the very reverse of what she had believed him—proud, assuming, conceited, very full of his own claims, and little concerned about the feelings of others.

She thought nothing of his proposal and was insulted by his hopes. He wanted to marry well and had the arrogance to pretend to be in love. There had been no real affection either in his language or manners. She need not pity him. He only wanted to enrich himself—and, unbeknownst to Emma, sink his drooling fangs into her fair white neck. If Miss Emma Woodhouse of Hartfield, the heiress of thirty thousand pounds, was not quite so easily won as he had fancied, she was certain he would not sleep until he found Miss Somebody Else with twenty thousand or with ten.

Mr. Elton must know that in fortune and consequence, Emma was greatly his superior. He must know that the Woodhouses had been settled for several generations at Hartfield, the younger branch of a very ancient family—and that the Eltons were nobody. And the Woodhouses had long held a high place in the reputation of the neighbourhood, which Mr. Elton had first entered just two years ago to make his way as best he could without anything to recommend him but his occupation and his politeness.

But he had fancied Emma in love with him. She was willing to admit that her own behaviour to him had been full of courtesy and attention and that an ordinary man like Mr. Elton might fancy himself a decided favourite. If she had so misinterpreted his feelings, it was no wonder that he should have mistaken hers.

The first and worst error was hers. It was foolish, it was wrong, to take so active a part in bringing any two such people together as Harriet and Mr. Elton. She was quite concerned and ashamed and resolved to do matchmaking no more.

Here have I, thought she, actually talked poor Harriet into being very much attached to this man. She might never have thought about him but for me, and certainly never would have thought of him with any hope if I had not assured her of his attachment. For she is as modest and humble as I used to think him.

Oh! That I persuaded her not to accept young Mr. Martin. But there I was quite right. That was well done of me; but there I should have stopped and left the rest to time and chance. I was introducing her into good company and giving her the opportunity of pleasing a gentleman worth having—I ought not to have attempted more. But now, poor girl, her peace is disturbed for some time. I have been but half a friend to her.

I am sure I have no idea of anybody else who would be at all desirable for her. Perhaps William Cox—Oh no! I could not endure William Cox, that rude young lawyer.

She stopped to blush and laugh at her own thoughts about another match for Harriet.

She then became more serious, realising the distressing explanation she had to make to Harriet; and all that poor Harriet would be suffering, with the awkwardness of future meetings, the difficulties of continuing or discontinuing the acquaintance, and concealing resentment, were enough to make Emma unhappy for some time longer. She went to bed that night with nothing settled but the conviction of her having blundered most dreadfully.

Emma got up the next morning, on Christmas Day, with her natural cheerfulness returned, ready to see answers for the evil before her and to depend on getting tolerably out of her situation. It was a great consolation that Mr. Elton should not be really in love with her, that Harriet's nature was not of the sort that would stay unhappy forever, or that no one except the three of them would need to know what had transpired.

These were very cheering thoughts; and the sight of a great deal of snow on the ground further cheered her, for she was therefore safe from either giving or receiving unpleasant news for many days, being a most happy prisoner of Hartfield. No contact with Harriet was possible but by note and, with no church for her on Sunday, no chance of encountering Mr. Elton.

These days of confinement would have been remarkably comfortable; but amidst all the cheerfulness of the holiday and all the present comfort of delay, there was still such a worry hanging over her, anticipating her explanation to Harriet, as made it impossible for Emma to be perfectly at ease.

CHAPTER 17

THE WEATHER SOON IMPROVED enough for Mr. and Mrs. John Knightley to end their visit at Hartfield. Mr. Woodhouse, as usual, tried to persuade his daughter to stay behind with all her children. But he was obliged to see the whole party off and return to his dismay over the destiny of poor Miss Taylor.

That evening brought a note from Mr. Elton to Mr. Woodhouse, a long, polite, ceremonious note to say "that he was proposing to leave Highbury the following morning on his way to Bath, where he had engaged to spend a few weeks with friends."

Emma was most agreeably surprised. Mr. Elton's absence just at this time was the very thing she desired. Her name was pointedly excluded from the note, which, she thought, could not possibly escape her father's suspicion. It did, however. Her father was quite surprised at so sudden a journey and saw nothing unusual in the language of Mr. Elton's note.

Emma resolved to keep Harriet in the dark no longer.

❧

Harriet now being reasonably recovered from her cold, Emma went to Mrs. Goddard's the very next day to undergo the necessary communication, and a severe one it was.

Emma had to destroy all Harriet's hopes for marriage which she had been so industriously feeding and acknowledge herself grossly mistaken and misjudging in all of her ideas, all her observations, all her convictions, and all her prophesies for the past six weeks.

The confession and the sight of Harriet's tears caused Emma great shame. But Harriet bore the news very well—blaming nobody—and betrayed a lowly opinion of herself. Harriet did not consider herself deserving of a man such as Mr. Elton, and nobody but so kind a friend as Miss Woodhouse would have thought such a match possible.

Harriet's tears fell abundantly, and Emma tried to console her with all her heart and understanding. Her duty now was to make Harriet comfortable, so she took her friend to Hartfield and showed her every kindness, striving to occupy and amuse her and, by books and conversation, to drive Mr. Elton from her thoughts.

Time, Emma knew, must be allowed for this healing to be thoroughly done; and it seemed to Emma that by the time of Mr. Elton's return, they could all meet again as friends.

But still did Harriet think Mr. Elton all perfection, and she maintained that no one was equal to him in goodness. Harriet did, in truth, prove herself more in love than Emma had foreseen. Yet Emma felt the feelings would not last.

If Mr. Elton, on his return, showed the indifference towards Harriet that Emma believed he would, she could not imagine Harriet's persisting to place her happiness in the sight of him. All three would certainly encounter each other at some point, so they would have to make the best of it.

It was unfortunate for Harriet that, at Mrs. Goddard's, Mr. Elton was adored by all the teachers and girls in the school. It was only at Hartfield that Harriet could have any chance of hearing him spoken of with cold, hard truth.

There must be a cure somewhere for the wound Harriet had been given; and Emma felt there could be no peace for herself until there was peace for her friend.

CHAPTER 18

M R. FRANK CHURCHILL DID not come after all. When the proposed time drew near, Mrs. Weston's fears were justified in the arrival of a letter of excuse. For the present, he could not be spared, to his "very great mortification and regret; but still he looked forward with the hope of coming to Randalls in the near future."

Mrs. Weston, who was now exceedingly happy to have just learned that she was going to have a baby, was exceedingly disappointed by the news about Frank—much more disappointed, in fact, than her husband.

For half an hour, Mr. Weston was surprised and sorry; but then he began to perceive that Frank's coming two or three months later would be a much better plan, a better time of year, better weather, and that he would be able to stay considerably longer with them. These feelings rapidly restored his comfort, while Mrs. Weston, of a more apprehensive disposition, foresaw nothing but a repetition of excuses and delays.

Emma was not at this time in a state of spirits to really care about Mr. Frank Churchill's not coming. She wanted, rather, to be quiet and out of temptation. But for the sake of friendship with the Westons, she expressed appropriate disappointment.

She was the first to announce it to Mr. George Knightley; and after he complimented Emma again on her valour during the vampire attack at Randalls, he remarked upon the conduct of the Churchills in keeping Frank away. Emma found herself involved in a disagreement with Mr. Knightley again.

"The Churchills are very likely at fault," said Mr. Knightley coolly, "but I daresay he would come if he wanted to."

"I do not know why you should say so," replied Emma. "He wishes exceedingly to come, but his uncle and aunt will not spare him."

"I cannot believe that he has not the power of coming, if he made a point of it."

"How odd you are! What has Mr. Frank Churchill done to make you suppose him such an unnatural creature?"

Unnatural creature? Of all people, he thought, I am not supposing him to be an unnatural creature. No one with pale skin and black eyes, who never sleeps nor ages nor prefers human blood to that of small animals could be considered unnatural.

"It is natural for Mr. Frank Churchill to care only for his own pleasure, after living with those who have set the example. It is natural that a young man, brought up by those who are proud, luxurious, and selfish, should be proud, luxurious, and selfish too. If Frank Churchill had wanted to see his father, he would have arranged it between September and January. A man of twenty-three certainly has the ability to arrange such a visit."

"That's easily said," replied Emma, "and easily felt by you, who have always been your own master. You do not know what it is to have other tempers to manage."

"It is inconceivable that a man of twenty-three should not have liberty of mind or body. We know that he has much money and leisure. We hear of him forever at some party or resort—up all night, dark circles under his eyes—this proves that he can leave the Churchills whenever he chooses."

"Yes, sometimes he can."

"And those times are whenever he thinks it worth his while, whenever there is any temptation of pleasure."

"It is very unfair to judge anybody's conduct without an intimate knowledge of their situation. We need to be acquainted with Mrs. Churchill's temper before we pretend to decide what her nephew can do."

"There is one thing, Emma, which a man can always do if he chooses, and that is his duty. It is Frank Churchill's duty to pay this visit to his father. He knows it is true, by his promises and letters. If he wished to do it, it would be done. He should say at once, simply and resolutely, to Mrs. Churchill, 'I must go and see my father immediately. I know he would be hurt by such a mark of disrespect to him if I did not.'"

"Such language for a young man entirely dependent on his aunt and uncle!" said Emma, laughing. "Nobody but you, Mr. Knightley, would imagine Mr. Frank Churchill to be making such a speech to the uncle and aunt who have brought him up and still provide for him! How can you imagine such conduct practicable? Does not your heart beat with human compassion?"

"Not in the least, Emma. Depend upon it, a sensible man would find no difficulty in it. He would feel himself in the right; and doing so would do him more good, raise him higher, and fix his interest stronger with the people he depended on. They would feel that the nephew who had done right by his father would do right by them."

"We shall never agree about him," cried Emma, "but that is nothing extraordinary. I have not the least idea of his being a weak young man—I feel sure that he is not."

"Yes, he had all the advantages of sitting still when he ought to move, and of leading a life of mere idle pleasure, and fancying himself extremely expert in finding excuses for it. I should even imagine that, in the heat of a confrontation with the wild creatures of the night, he would blanch and faint along with the ladies present, rather than take up his sword to defend them."

"You seem determined to think ill of him."

"Me! Not at all," replied Mr. Knightley, rather displeased. "I do not want to think ill of him. I should be as ready to acknowledge his merits as any other man; but I hear of none, except what are merely personal—that he is well-grown and good-looking, with smooth, pleasing manners."

"Well, if he has nothing else to recommend him, he will be a treasure at Highbury. We do not often look upon fine young men, well-bred and agreeable. Can you not imagine, Mr. Knightley, what a sensation his coming will produce? There will be but one subject throughout the parishes of Highbury, but one interest, one object of curiosity—it will all be Mr. Frank Churchill. We shall think and speak of nobody else."

"You will excuse my not being so overpowered. If I find him conversable, I shall be glad of his acquaintance; but if he is only a chattering dandy, he will not occupy much of my time or thoughts."

"My idea of him," replied Emma, "is that he can adapt his conversation to the taste of everybody and has the power and wish of being universally agreeable. To you, he will talk of farming; to me, of drawing or music; and so on to everybody, having enough general information to speak extremely well on all subjects; that is my idea of him."

"And my idea of him," said Mr. Knightley warmly, "is that if he turns out anything like that, he will be the most insufferable fellow who never took a breath! What! At twenty-three to be such a great man, a practiced politician who reads everybody's character and dispenses his flatteries round? My dear Emma, your own good sense could not endure such a person. And I might even be put to sleep by him, impossible as that may seem."

"I shall say no more about him," cried Emma. "You turn everything to evil. We are both prejudiced; you against, I for him; and we have no chance of agreeing till he is really here."

"Prejudiced! I am not prejudiced."

"But I am, very much, and without being at all ashamed of it. My love for Mr. and Mrs. Weston gives me a decided prejudice in his favour."

"He is a person I never think of at all," said Mr. Knightley, with a degree of vexation which made Emma immediately talk of something else, though she could not comprehend why he should be angry.

To take a dislike to a young man just because he was of a different disposition was unworthy of the open mind which she always used to acknowledge in Mr. George Knightley; for all the high opinion Mr. Knightley had of himself, Emma had never before supposed it could make him unjust to the merits of another man.

CHAPTER 19

EMMA AND HARRIET HAD been walking together one morning and, in Emma's opinion, had been talking enough of Mr. Elton for that day. But after conversing about what the poor must suffer in winter, Harriet burst out, "Mr. Elton is so good to the poor! He brings them food and keeps none for himself!"

They were just approaching the house where Mrs. Bates and Miss Bates lived. Emma decided to call upon them to rid herself of the subject of Mr. Elton. Mrs. and Miss Bates loved to be called on, and Emma knew she was rather negligent in that respect.

Emma had received many a hint from Mr. Knightley, and some from her own heart, as to her deficiency in not visiting them. But she felt it was a disagreeable waste of time—tiresome women—and brought all the horror of associating with the lower classes of Highbury, who were forever calling on them, and therefore she seldom went near them.

But now she made the sudden resolution of not passing their door without going in—observing, as she proposed it to Harriet—that as best as she could calculate, they were safe from any letter from Jane Fairfax.

The house belonged to some business people, and Mrs. and Miss Bates rented the drawing room floor. There, in the

very moderate-sized apartment, visitors were most cordially
and even gratefully welcomed.

As they entered, the quiet, neat old lady Mrs. Bates, who
with her knitting was seated in the warmest corner, wanted
to give up her chair to Emma; her more active, talky old-
maid daughter Miss Bates was almost ready to overpower
them with care and kindness, thanks for their visit, anxious
inquiries after Mr. Woodhouse's health, horror at the recent
vampire attacks, and sweet cake from the buffet.

"Oh! Miss Woodhouse! So many incidents of violence
have I heard of since witnessing your courage that night at
Hartfield! That poor postboy at Mrs. Goddard's! Dearest me!
To die with a letter in his bloody hands addressed to you, Miss
Smith! Oh, dear me! And then the attack on you both in the
presence of our beloved vicar Mr. Elton! I thank the holy Lord
that he was crucified on the cross so that you, Miss Smith, would
have a silver symbol with which to repel the vicious fiend! And,
oh! Miss Woodhouse! The horrifying events of Christmas Eve,
and all the vampire beheadings and stabbing with wooden
stakes! Oh, Miss Woodhouse! It terrifies me to leave the house
even for one moment! Am I not right, dear Mother?"

Old Mrs. Bates looked up absently from her knitting.
"Eh? What was that, my dear?"

"Oh, Miss Woodhouse! My mother does not hear; she
is a little deaf you know. Ma'am!" she screamed, addressing
her, then repeating the tiresome soliloquy twice more.

The Coles were then mentioned, and Emma knew it was
sure to be followed by another mention of Mr. Elton. There
was a friendship between them, and Mr. Cole had received a
letter from Mr. Elton since his going away.

Emma knew what was coming—they must read the
vicar's letter over and over again and discuss how long he had

been gone, how electrifying was his personality, and what a favourite he was wherever he went.

Emma had been prepared for this when she entered the house. She had not been prepared to have Miss Bates's niece Jane Fairfax discussed.

Emma showed her politeness and asked, "Have you heard from Miss Fairfax lately? I trust she is well."

"Thank you. You are so kind!" replied the happy aunt while eagerly hunting for Jane's recent letter. "Oh! Here it is. I was reading it to my mother, for it is such a pleasure to her—a letter from Jane—that she can never hear it often enough. I really must apologise for Jane writing so short a letter—only two pages, you see."

All this, spoken extremely fast, obliged Miss Bates to stop for breath; and Emma said something very civil about the excellence of Miss Fairfax's handwriting.

"You are extremely kind," replied Miss Bates, highly gratified. "You, Miss Woodhouse, who are such a good judge and write so beautifully yourself. I am sure there is nobody's praise that could give us so much pleasure as Miss Woodhouse's." Then she screamed again to her mother. "Ma'am! Do you hear what Miss Woodhouse is so obliging to say about Jane's handwriting?"

And Emma had the advantage of hearing her own silly compliment repeated twice before the good old lady could comprehend it.

Emma was pondering, in the meanwhile, upon the possibility of making her escape from Jane Fairfax's letter, when Miss Bates turned to her again and seized her attention.

"My mother's deafness is very trifling, you see—just nothing at all. Jane will not find her grandmamma at all deafer than she was two years ago—and it really is full two years, you know, since she was here."

"Are you expecting Miss Fairfax here soon?" asked Emma.

"Oh yes, next week."

"Indeed! That must be a very great pleasure."

"Thank you. You are very kind. Yes, next week. Everybody is so surprised, and everybody says the same kind things. I am sure she will be as happy to see her friends in Highbury as they will be to see her. Yes, she will arrive Friday or Saturday next. Jane has not been quite so well as usual lately. She caught a bad cold, poor thing, as long ago as the seventh of November and has never been well since. A long time, is it not, for a cold to hang upon her? Well, three or four months at Highbury will entirely cure her. Nobody could nurse her as we would do."

"It appears to me the most desirable arrangement in the world."

"And so, she is to come to us next Friday or Saturday. So sudden! You may guess, dear Miss Woodhouse, what a flurry it has thrown me in! If it was not for the drawback of her illness—but I am afraid we must expect to see her grown thin. If Jane does not get well soon, we shall call in Mr. Perry."

"I am afraid we must be running away," said Emma, glancing at Harriet and beginning to rise. "My father will be expecting us. I had no intention of staying more than five minutes. I merely called because I would not pass the door without inquiring after Mrs. Bates; but I have been so pleasantly detained! Now, however, we must wish you and Mrs. Bates good morning."

CHAPTER 20

JANE FAIRFAX WAS AN orphan. The marriage of Lt. Fairfax of the Infantry and Miss Jane Bates, the younger daughter of Mrs. Bates, had its day of fame and pleasure, hope and interest. But nothing now remained of it, save the melancholy remembrance of him dying in action abroad and his widow sinking under consumption and grief soon afterwards, leaving only this girl, Miss Jane Fairfax.

At three years old, upon losing her mother, Jane became the charge of her grandmother Mrs. Bates and aunt Miss Bates. There had seemed every probability of her growing up with no advantages of social position or improvement, relying only on what nature had given her—a pleasing personality, good understanding, and warm-hearted, well-meaning relatives.

But the compassionate feelings of a friend of her father changed her destiny. This was Colonel Campbell, who was a married man with only one living child, Miss Campbell, a girl about Jane's age.

Jane became their guest in London, paying them long visits and becoming a favourite with all; and before she was nine years old, Colonel Campbell offered to take charge of Jane's education. The Bateses accepted his offer, and from that period Jane had belonged to Colonel Campbell's family and lived with them in London, only visiting her grandmother and aunt in Highbury from time to time.

The plan was that Jane should be educated as a governess, the few hundred pounds she inherited from her father not making independence possible. By giving Jane an education, the colonel hoped to supply her the means for respectable employment.

Such was Jane Fairfax's history. She had fallen into good hands, known nothing but kindness from the Campbells, and been given an excellent education. She received every advantage of discipline and culture in London.

At the age of eighteen, she was qualified as a governess for the care of children; but she was much too beloved by the Campbells to be parted with. The evil day of her leaving was put off. Jane remained with them, sharing in all the pleasures of elegant society, knowing that some day all this might be over.

The arrangement continued until the colonel's daughter, Miss Campbell, became engaged to Mr. Dixon, a rich and agreeable young man, almost as soon as they were acquainted; and soon they were married, while Jane Fairfax had yet her bread to earn.

This event had very recently taken place. Jane had long ago decided that at age twenty-one she would gain employment and retire from all the pleasures of life and society. Colonel and Mrs. Campbell did not oppose Jane's decision and, as long as they lived, their home would be hers forever.

But Jane had not been quite well since the marriage of the colonel's daughter; and till she should have completely recovered her usual strength, they must forbid her engaging in governess work.

When Mrs. Dixon and her new husband Mr. Dixon invited Jane to accompany them on a trip to Ireland, Jane decided instead, because of her ill health, to visit her grandmother Mrs. Bates and her aunt Miss Bates.

❧

And so, Miss Jane Fairfax came to Highbury. Emma was sorry to have to show kindness to a person she did not like— for three long months! Why did she not like Jane Fairfax? That might be a difficult question to answer. Mr. Knightley had once told Emma it was because she saw in Jane the really accomplished young woman whom she wanted to be thought herself.

Emma felt that Jane Fairfax had such coldness and reserve. This quality, of course, would make her attractive to the male vampires of Highbury. Everybody made such a fuss over Jane Fairfax, and everybody imagined that, because their ages were the same, Emma and Jane must be so fond of each other. These were her reasons—she had no better.

Jane Fairfax was very elegant—remarkably elegant. Her height was pretty, her figure particularly graceful, her size a most becoming medium between fat and thin, though a slight appearance of ill health seemed to point more towards the thin side.

And then her face—there was more beauty than Emma had remembered; it was not regular, but it was a very pleasing beauty. Her eyes were a deep grey, with dark eyelashes and eyebrows, and the skin had a clearness and delicacy which really needed no fuller bloom. It was a style of beauty of which elegance was the reigning character, a perfect match for a gentleman with black eyes and white skin.

In short, Emma sat during the first visit looking at Jane Fairfax from two sides—a sense of pleasure and a sense of judgement—and decided that she would dislike her no longer.

When Emma took in Jane's history, her situation, and her beauty, it seemed impossible to feel anything but compassion and respect; especially when Emma imagined the possibility that Jane may have seduced her best friend's husband, Mr. Dixon, a circumstance which would have denied her the trip to Ireland and brought her to Highbury instead, resolving to end her relationship with him before beginning her career of laborious duty as a governess.

Upon the whole, Emma ended her first visit with Jane with such softened, charitable feelings that made her lament, while walking home, that no young man in Highbury was worthy of marrying her—nobody that Emma could wish to match her with, at any rate. These were charming feelings, but not lasting.

A few days later, Jane spent an evening at Hartfield with her grandmother and aunt. Jane's offences rose again. They played music—Emma was obliged to play the pianoforte, and the praise which followed appeared to be affected, meant only to show off Jane's own superior performance after Emma's.

Jane was, besides, so cold, so cautious! There was no getting at her real opinion. Wrapped up in a cloak of politeness, she was disgustingly, suspiciously reserved. Most of all, she was reserved on the subject of the Dixons. She seemed bent on giving no real insight into Mr. Dixon's character or her own opinion of him. It was all general approval and smoothness, nothing specific or distinguished.

Jane was concealing something. Emma imagined that perhaps Mr. Dixon had favoured Jane but remained with Miss Campbell for the sake of her future twelve thousand pound inheritance.

Jane's reserve prevailed on other topics. It was known that she and Mr. Frank Churchill were at the same resort in Weymouth at the same time and a little acquainted; but not a syllable of real information could Emma procure as to what he truly was like.

"Was he handsome?"

"I believe he was reckoned a very fine young man."

"Was he agreeable?"

"He was generally thought so."

"Did his black eyes appear to lust after you?"

"I think that is a matter of opinion."

"Did he appear a sensible young man?"

"At a resort, it was difficult to decide on such points. Manners were all that could be safely judged. Everybody found his manners pleasing."

Emma could not forgive her.

CHAPTER 21

M R. GEORGE KNIGHTLEY, WHO had also been at Hartfield the night before, saw only pleasing behaviour between Emma and Jane.

The next morning Mr. Knightley was at Hartfield again, on business with Mr. Woodhouse. After complimenting Emma once more on her bravery on Christmas Eve at the Westons and once more lamenting that Highbury should soon be overrun by the dastardly creatures and that the leaders of Highbury society should truly band together to rid the village of this despicable menace, Mr. Knightley turned his comments to more gentile matters.

He remarked that he had always thought Emma unjust to Jane Fairfax but now had great pleasure in marking an improvement.

"A very pleasant evening," began Mr. Knightley, "particularly pleasant. You and Miss Fairfax gave us some very good music. I am sure Miss Fairfax must have found the evening pleasant, Emma. You left nothing undone."

"I am happy you approved," said Emma, smiling, "but I trust I am not often lacking in what is due our guests at Hartfield."

"No, my dear," said Mr. Woodhouse, "that I am sure you are not. There is nobody half so attentive and polite as you are."

"Miss Fairfax is, however, reserved," said Emma.

"I always told you she was—a little," replied Mr. Knightley, "but you will soon overcome that part of her reserve which is based in shyness."

"You think her shy. I do not see it."

"My dear Emma," said he, moving from his chair into one close by her, "you are not going to tell me, I trust, that you had not a pleasant evening."

"Oh, no! I was pleased with my own persistence in asking questions and amused to think how little information I obtained in return."

"I am disappointed," was his only answer.

"I trust everybody had a pleasant evening," said Mr. Woodhouse, in his quiet way. "I had. Once, I felt the fire rather too much; but then I moved my chair back a little, and it did not disturb me."

"I found the fire rather too hot myself," said Mr. Knightley, "and rather scary, if truth be told."

Mr. Woodhouse nodded in acknowledgement, as if he understood Mr. Knightley's hidden meaning, which he certainly did not. Then he remarked, "Miss Bates was very chatty and good humoured, as she always is, though she speaks rather too quick. However, she is very agreeable, and Mrs. Bates too, in a different way. I like old friends; and Miss Jane Fairfax is a very pretty and well-behaved young lady indeed. She must have found the evening agreeable, Mr. Knightley, because she had Emma with her."

"True, sir; and Emma, because she had Miss Fairfax."

Emma saw Mr. Knightley's anxiety and, wishing to appease him at least for the present, said, with a sincerity which no one could question, "She is an elegant creature that one cannot keep one's eyes from. I am always watching her to admire; and I do pity her from my heart."

Mr. Knightley looked as if he were more gratified than he cared to express. Then he said, "Emma, I have a piece of news for you. You like news—and I heard something on my way here that I think will interest you."

"News! Oh, yes! I always like news. What is it? Why do you smile so? Where did you hear it?"

He was about to speak, when the door was thrown open, and Miss Bates and her niece Jane Fairfax walked into the room. Full of thanks and full of news, Miss Bates knew not which to give quickest. Mr. Knightley soon saw that he had lost his moment.

"Oh! My dear sir, how are you this morning? My dear Miss Woodhouse—I come quite overpowered. Have you heard the news? Mr. Elton is going to be married."

Emma had not had time even to think of Mr. Elton, and she was so completely surprised that she could not avoid a little start, and a little blush, at the news.

"There is my news—I thought it would interest you," said Mr. Knightley, with a smile that accented the dark circles under his black eyes. It seems, thought he, that Mr. Elton will finally get the marital sustenance he needs. I should expect to see his eyes soon turn from black to red.

"But where did *you* hear it?" cried Miss Bates. "Where could you possibly hear it, Mr. Knightley? For it is not five minutes since I received Mrs. Cole's note. A Miss Hawkins— that's all I know. A Miss Hawkins of Bath. But Mr. Knightley, how could you possibly have heard it? For the very moment Mr. Cole told Mrs. Cole of it, she sat down and wrote to me. A Miss Hawkins—"

"I was with Mr. Cole on business an hour and a half ago. He had just read Elton's letter as I was shown in and handed it to me directly."

"Well! That is quite—I suppose there never was a piece of news more generally interesting. Well, Mr. Knightley, and so you actually saw the letter. Well—"

"It was short—merely to announce—but cheerful and exulting, of course," said Mr. Knightley. Here was a sly glance at Emma. "The information was, as you state, that he was going to be married to a Miss Hawkins. By his style, I should imagine it just happened."

"Mr. Elton going to be married!" said Emma, as soon as she could speak. "He will have everybody's wishes for his happiness."

"He is very young to settle down," was Mr. Woodhouse's observation.

Not as young as he appears to be, thought Mr. Knightley wryly.

Mr. Woodhouse continued, "He should not be in a hurry to marry. He seemed to me very well off as he was. We were always glad to see him at Hartfield."

"A new neighbour for us all, Miss Woodhouse!" said Miss Bates, joyfully. "My mother is so pleased! She says she cannot bear to have the poor old vicarage without a mistress. This is great news, indeed. Jane, you have never seen Mr. Elton! No wonder that you have such a curiosity to see him. And to touch his hand at communion is, well, such a shock, like a miracle, like the finger of God!"

Jane's curiosity did not appear too absorbing. "No—I have never seen Mr. Elton," she replied.

"When you have been here a little longer, Miss Fairfax," said Emma, "you will understand that Mr. Elton is the standard of perfection in Highbury, both in person and mind."

"Very true, Miss Woodhouse, so she will," said Miss Bates. "He is the very best young man. His kind attention to my mother—wanting her to sit in the vicarage pew, that she might hear better. Now, here will be Mr. Elton and Miss Hawkins. I think there are few places with such society as Highbury. I always say, we are quite blessed in our neighbours."

"As to who or what Miss Hawkins is," said Emma, "or how long Mr. Elton has been acquainted with her, nothing I suppose can be known. One feels that it cannot be a very long acquaintance. He has been gone only four weeks."

"A Miss Hawkins! Well," said Miss Bates, "I had always rather fancied it would be some young lady hereabouts. Miss Woodhouse lets me chatter on, so good-humouredly. She knows I would not offend for the world. And how does Miss Smith do? She seems quite recovered now. Have you heard from Mrs. John Knightley lately? Oh! Those dear little children."

Miss Bates then turned to her niece. "Jane, do you know I always fancy Mr. Dixon to be like Mr. John Knightley. I mean in person—tall and with that sort of ageless look, a study in black and white with pale blue eyes."

"Quite wrong, my dear aunt," said Jane, appearing uncomfortable. "There is no likeness at all."

"Very odd! Mr. Dixon, you say, is not, strictly speaking, handsome?"

"Handsome! Oh, no! Far from it—certainly plain. I told you he was plain."

"My dear, you said that Miss Campbell would not allow him to be plain and that you yourself—"

"Oh! As for me, my judgement is worth nothing," interrupted Jane Fairfax. "But I gave what I believed was the general opinion when I called him plain. His eyes are green, his hair is brown, and his skin is tan. Extraordinarily plain."

"Well, my dear Jane, I believe we must be running away. The weather does not look well, and grandmamma will be uneasy. Good morning to you all."

Emma was alone with her father, while he lamented that young people were in such a hurry to marry—and to marry strangers, too. For Emma, it was a very welcome piece of news, proving that Mr. Elton could not have suffered long from her refusal of his affections.

But she was sorry for Harriet. Harriet needed to know—and all Emma could hope was that by giving the information herself she would save Harriet from hearing it abruptly from others. It was now about the time that Harriet was likely to call. But what if she were to meet Miss Bates along the way and learn the news from her!

The rain shower was heavy, but short; and it had not been over five minutes when in came Harriet with a heated, agitated look, bursting forth with, "Oh! Miss Woodhouse, what do you think has happened!" which had all the evidence that Harriet knew of Mr. Elton. Emma felt that she could not show greater kindness than in listening; and Harriet ran eagerly through what she had to tell.

She had set out from Mrs. Goddard's half an hour ago—she had been afraid it would rain—but she thought she might get to Hartfield first. But it did begin to rain, so she ran as fast as she could and took shelter at Ford's, the fashionable dress shop in town, when all of a sudden, who should come in but Mr. Robert Martin and his sister Elizabeth!

"Dear Miss Woodhouse! I thought I should have fainted. I did not know what to do. I was sitting near the door. Elizabeth saw me directly, but Mr. Martin did not—he was busy with the umbrella. I am sure she saw me, but she looked away. They both went to the far end of the shop, and I kept sitting near the door! Oh dear, I was so miserable! I am sure I must have been as white as Mr. Martin's skin.

"I could not leave because of the rain; but I did so wish myself anywhere in the world but there. Well, at last, he looked round and saw me. They began whispering to one another. I am sure they were talking about me. Then Elizabeth came up to me and asked me how I did. She tried to be friendly and we shook hands and stood talking for some time. She was sorry we never meet now, which I thought almost too kind!

"Dear, Miss Woodhouse, I was absolutely miserable! By that time, Mr. Martin was coming up towards me too. He came and spoke, and I answered—and I stood for a minute, feeling dreadfully, and said I must go. And so off I went, and I had not gotten three yards from the door when he came after me, only to say that if I was going to Hartfield, he thought I had much better go round by Mr. Cole's stables, for I should find the usual way quite flooded by this rain.

"So I very much thanked him—you know I could not do less—and went on my way. A few minutes later as I walked near Mr. Cole's stables, by the tall hedge, suddenly and without warning, one of those horrid creatures sprang out at me! Oh dear! I thought it would have been the death of me! His eyes were black and sunken, his claws were bared, and his fangs were so large and pointy and dripping with venom!

"I touched my neck to show him my silver cross and ward him off, but oh! Miss Woodhouse! It was not there. I had just bathed, you see, and had forgotten to put my necklace back on. So there I stood, frozen with fear, ready to be sacrificed to the wild vampire who would suck my blood dry!

"And then out of nowhere in a flash of light appeared Mr. Robert Martin! With his great strength, he picked up the creature and flung him over his head into the air and impaled him on the wooden picket fence, killing him instantly. Dear me! I was overcome and still am! I asked Mr. Martin how he came to my rescue, and he said he had followed me to make certain I would be safe!

"I thanked him of course, as any lady would, and he went back to meet Elizabeth. Oh! Miss Woodhouse, I would have rather done anything than have it happen. And yet, you know, there was a sort of satisfaction in seeing him behave so gallantly towards me—his black eyes so kind. Oh! Miss Woodhouse, do talk to me and make me comfortable again."

Very sincerely did Emma wish to do so, but she needed to stop and think. She was not thoroughly comfortable herself. The young man's conduct and his sister's seemed to be the result of real feeling. As Harriet described it, their behaviour showed not only wounded affection but genuine tenderness as well. Of course, Mr. Martin must be sorry to lose her— they must be all sorry.

Emma did try to make Harriet comfortable by considering all that had passed as a mere trifle and quite unworthy of being dwelt on.

"It might be distressing for the moment," said Emma, "but you seem to have behaved extremely well; and it is over and may never—can never—occur again, and therefore you need not think about it."

Harriet said "very true" and she "would not think about it." But she could talk of nothing else; and Emma, at last, in order to put the Martins out of her head, was obliged to hurry on with the news about Mr. Elton, which she had meant to give with so much tender caution.

Emma was rather glad that Harriet had seen the Martins, for it deadened the shock of Mr. Elton's marriage. And Emma knew that a year might pass before Harriet ever saw the Martins again.

CHAPTER 22

HUMAN NATURE IS SUCH that a young person who either marries or dies is sure to be kindly spoken of. A week had not passed since Miss Hawkins's name was first mentioned in Highbury before she was thought by everyone to be handsome, elegant, highly accomplished, and perfectly amiable. So when Mr. Elton himself arrived, there was very little more for him to do than mention her name.

Mr. Elton returned a very happy man. He had gone away rejected and mortified—disappointed in not only losing the right lady but also finding himself matched to a very wrong one. He had gone away deeply offended and came back engaged to another—happy and self-satisfied, eager and busy, caring nothing for Miss Woodhouse, defying Miss Smith, and eagerly awaiting his nuptial night when he would sink his teeth into Miss Hawkins's neck and turn both his and his wife's eyes to red.

The charming Augusta Hawkins, in addition to all the assumed advantages of perfect beauty and merit, was in possession of an independent fortune. Mr. Elton had caught both fortune and affection and was just the happy man he ought to be—talking only of himself and his own concerns and expecting to be congratulated. He now addressed all the young ladies of Highbury with fearless smiles—ladies to whom, a few weeks ago, he would have been more cautiously gallant.

The wedding was to occur soon and, as the event was to be small and there were few preparations to wait for, there was a general expectation that when Mr. Elton left for Bath again, he would return to Highbury with his new bride.

During his present short stay Emma barely saw him, but just enough to feel that pride and pretension had taken him over. She was, in fact, beginning very much to wonder why she had ever thought him pleasing at all; and she would have been thankful never to see him again.

She wished him very well, but he gave her pain. The pain of his continued residence in Highbury, however, must certainly be lessened by his marriage. A Mrs. Elton would almost certainly lead him to begin a life of politeness again.

Emma spent very little time thinking about the lady Miss Hawkins. No doubt she was good enough for Mr. Elton, was accomplished enough for Highbury, and would look plain next to Harriet.

As to social connection, it did not appear that she was at all Harriet's superior. She brought no name, no blood, and no alliance. Miss Hawkins was the younger of the two daughters of a successful Bristol merchant from the lower classes. Her father and mother had died some years ago, and only the elder sister added any status to the family, being very well married to a wealthy gentleman.

But dear Harriet! Emma had talked her into love, and alas, she was not so easily to be talked out of it. Mr. Elton must indeed be replaced by another—nothing could be clearer. Even a Robert Martin would have been sufficient.

But nothing else, Emma feared, would cure her. Harriet was one of those girls who, having once fallen in love, would always be in love. And now, poor girl! She was considerably worse from this reappearance of Mr. Elton.

Harriet was always having a glimpse of him somewhere or other. Emma saw him only once. But two or three times every day Harriet was sure to see him or hear his voice. She was, moreover, perpetually hearing about him, for she was always around those who praised Mr. Elton.

Harriet's regrets were being kept alive and her feelings irritated by constant reports of Miss Hawkins's happiness and by continual observation of how much Mr. Elton was in love!

A few days later, Elizabeth Martin paid a visit to Mrs. Goddard's school. Harriet had not been at home; but a note had been left for her written in a touching style, inviting Harriet to visit the Martins.

Harriet continually pondered over what should be done. On the very morning of Mr. Elton's leaving for Bath again, Emma, to lessen some of Harriet's distress, judged it best for her friend to return Elizabeth Martin's visit.

After much thinking, Emma determined it should be only a formal visit. Emma would take Harriet in the carriage, leave her at Abbey Mill Farm, drive a little farther, then call for her again soon, so as to allow no time for the past to be revisited and to prove to Mr. Martin that the future held no intimacy.

Emma could think of nothing better and, though there was something in the plan which her heart felt was ungracious, it must be done, or what would become of Harriet?

CHAPTER 23

HARRIET HAD SMALL HEART for visiting the Martins. Only half an hour before Emma came to pick her up at Mrs. Goddard's, she had seen Mr. Elton's trunk being lifted into the cart to be conveyed to Bath for his wedding.

Harriet went with Emma, however, her protective silver cross gleaming on her neck and her wooden stake tied to her thigh. When they reached the Martins' farm, the sight of everything which had given her so much pleasure the summer before, including the cow that Mr. Martin had hoisted above his head, revived a bit of anxiety.

When they parted, Emma observed Harriet to be looking round with a sort of fearful curiosity, which made Emma decide not to allow the visit to exceed the proposed quarter of an hour.

Emma returned punctually to the white gate again after the allotted time, and Harriet walked alone down the gravel path—Elizabeth Martin just appearing at the door. It seemed to Emma that she parted with ceremonial politeness.

Harriet could not immediately talk about the visit—she was feeling too much emotion. But at last Emma collected from her enough to understand the pain it caused. Mr. Robert Martin was absent—Harriet had seen only Mrs. Martin and the two girls.

They had received her doubtingly, if not coolly; and nothing beyond the merest courtesies had been talked almost all the time—till just at the end, when Mrs. Martin said, all of a sudden, that she thought Miss Smith was more mature and had a warmer manner, and that she was grateful that her son had saved Harriet from the wild vampire.

They all seemed to be ready to return to the same good understanding, just growing again to like each other, when Emma's carriage reappeared, and it all was over.

The style of the visit and the shortness of it were then felt to be insulting. Fourteen minutes to be given to those with whom she had spent two months! Emma pictured it all and felt how resentful they must have been and how naturally Harriet must have suffered. It was a bad business.

Emma would have given a great deal for the Martins to have had a higher rank in society. They were so deserving that a little higher would have been enough. But as it was, how could she have done otherwise? Impossible! Harriet and Mr. Robert Martin must be separated—there would be no more midnight walks in the moonlight, Harriet holding Robert's cold, pale hand—but there was a great deal of pain in the process.

Emma and Harriet returned to Hartfield, and when they arrived, Mr. and Mrs. Weston were standing outside to speak to Emma. There was instant pleasure in the sight of them.

Mr. Weston immediately accosted her with, "How d'ye do? We have been sitting with your father—glad to see him so well. We have wonderful news! Frank Churchill comes tomorrow. I had a letter this morning. He comes for a fortnight—I knew it would be so! We shall enjoy him completely; everything has turned out exactly as we could wish."

There was no resisting such a happy face as Mr. Weston's, confirmed by the face of Mrs. Weston. The worn-out past was replaced by the freshness of what was coming; and Emma hoped that Mr. Elton would now be talked of no more.

"I shall bring him over to Hartfield," said Mr. Weston. "But you must not expect such a very fine young man; I daresay he is really nothing extraordinary." But his own sparkling pale blue eyes at the moment were speaking a very different conviction.

Emma's spirits were mounted quite up to happiness; everything wore a different air. When she turned round to Harriet, she saw something like a look of spring, a tender smile even there.

The morning of the interesting day arrived, and while walking downstairs from her room Emma told herself, "My dear, dear anxious friend, always over-careful for everybody's comfort but your own; I see you now in all your little fidgets, thinking of the possibility of Mr. Frank Churchill calling here. I am sure they will bring him soon."

She opened the parlour door and saw two gentlemen sitting with her father—Mr. Weston and his son Frank. They had arrived only a few minutes before.

Mr. Woodhouse was yet in the midst of his very civil welcome and congratulations when Emma appeared to have her share of surprise, introduction, and pleasure.

The Frank Churchill so long talked of, so high in interest, was actually presented to her. He was a very good-looking young vampire, with black hair and eyes, and pale white skin;

height, air, address, and enchanting scent all were exceptional, and his countenance had a great deal of the spirit and liveliness of his father's.

Emma felt immediately that she would like him; and there was a well-bred ease of manner and a readiness to talk, which convinced her that he came intending to be acquainted with her and that acquainted they soon must be.

"It is a great pleasure to be here," said the young man, with an easy smile that revealed near-fanglike teeth.

Emma was sure that Frank Churchill knew how to make himself agreeable. He was very much pleased with Randalls, thought it a most admirably arranged house, admired Highbury, admired Hartfield still more, and professed to have always felt an interest in the country and the greatest curiosity to visit it. His manner had no air of study or exaggeration. He did really look and speak as if in a state of uncommon enjoyment.

Their subjects in general were appropriate for an opening acquaintance. On his side were the inquiries: "Was Emma a horsewoman? Pleasant walks? Had they a large neighbourhood? A boarding school for young maidens? Balls—had they balls? Was it a musical society? Was the weather sufficiently cool and cloudy?"

When satisfied on all these points, while their two fathers were engaged with each other, Frank mentioned his mother-in-law, Mrs. Weston, and speaking of her with so much handsome praise, so much warm admiration, so much gratitude for the happiness she secured to his father and her very kind reception of himself was an additional proof of his knowing how to please—and of his certainly thinking it worthwhile to try to please Emma.

Then Frank spoke of Mrs. Weston's youth and beauty.

"Elegant, agreeable manners, I was prepared for," said he, "but I confess that I did not know I was to find a pretty young woman in Mrs. Weston."

"You cannot see too much perfection in Mrs. Weston for my feelings," said Emma.

Emma wondered whether Frank's compliments were designed to please her. She must see more of him to understand his ways; at present she felt they were entirely agreeable.

She had no doubt what Mr. Weston was thinking about. She detected his quick eye again and again, glancing towards herself and Frank with a happy expression—and even when he was not looking, she was confident that he was often listening, for his hearing was as acute as Mr. Knightley's.

A reasonable visit paid, Mr. Weston said, "Frank must be going. He has a great many errands for Mrs. Weston."

His son, too well bred not to hear the hint, rose immediately, saying, "Miss Woodhouse, I shall also take the opportunity of paying a visit to a neighbour of yours, a lady residing in Highbury—a family of the name of Fairfax. I shall have no difficulty, I suppose, in finding the house; though Fairfax, I believe, is not the proper name—I should rather say Bates. Do you know any family of that name?"

"To be sure, we do," cried Mr. Weston. "Mrs. Bates—we passed her house—I saw Miss Bates at the window, looking this way and that for vagrant vampires. True, I remember you are acquainted with Miss Fairfax from the Weymouth resort, and a fine girl she is. Call upon her, by all means."

"There is no necessity for my calling this morning," said the young man. "Another day would do as well; but there was that degree of acquaintance at Weymouth which—"

"Oh! Go today. Do not defer it. What is right to be done cannot be done too soon. And, besides, I must give you a hint, Frank; any lack of attention to Miss Fairfax should be carefully avoided. In London, she was the equal of everybody she mixed with, but here she is with a poor old grandmother. If you do not call early, it will be a slight."

The son looked convinced.

"I have heard Miss Fairfax speak of her acquaintance with you," said Emma. "She is a very elegant young woman."

Frank agreed to it, but with so quiet a *yes* as made Emma almost doubt his real eagerness.

"If you were never particularly struck by her manners before," said Emma, "I think you will be today. You will see her and hear her—no, I am afraid you will not hear her at all, for she has an aunt who never holds her tongue."

"You are acquainted with Miss Jane Fairfax, sir, are you?" said Mr. Woodhouse, always the last to make his way in conversation. "Then let me assure you that you will find her a very agreeable young lady. She is staying here on a visit to her grandmamma and aunt, very worthy people; I have known them all my life."

With a cordial nod from one and a graceful bow from the other, the two gentlemen took leave. Emma remained very well pleased with this beginning of the acquaintance and could now engage to think of them all at Randalls any hour of the day with full confidence in their comfort.

CHAPTER 24

T HE NEXT MORNING BROUGHT Mr. Frank Churchill again to Hartfield, accompanied by Mrs. Weston. He had been sitting with his stepmother most companionably at home after a full breakfast of which he declined to partake, till her usual hour of exercise; and desiring to choose their walk, he immediately fixed on Hartfield.

"He did not doubt there being very pleasant walks in every direction, but if left to him, he should always choose the same—Hartfield, that airy, cheerful, happy-looking Hartfield, would be his constant attraction." They walked there directly.

It was an agreeable surprise to Emma to see them strolling up to the house together, arm in arm. She was eager to see Frank again and especially to see him in company with Mrs. Weston. Emma's opinion of Frank would depend on his treatment of her. If he were deficient there, nothing could make amends for it.

But on seeing them together, Emma became perfectly satisfied. It was not merely his fine words or compliments to Mrs. Weston but also his unblinking gaze and his clear wish to consider her as a friend and secure her affection. And there was time enough for Emma to form a reasonable judgement, as their visit included all the rest of the morning.

All three walked together for an hour or two—first round the shrubberies of Hartfield and afterwards towards

Highbury. He was delighted with everything and confessed his wish to become acquainted with the whole village.

As they walked, Emma recounted to Frank the long, sordid tale of the recent vampire menace. She saw his nose rise a bit in the air, as if he regarded the wild vagrants as beneath him socially. Then, as they walked along a bosky stretch of road leading to the village, Frank looked around nervously, as if a bit terrified of suddenly being attacked. Emma's thoughts recalled Mr. Knightley's disapproval of Frank Churchill as a spoiled, selfish young man—was he also a coward?

Frank begged to be shown the house which his father had lived in so long and which had been the home of his father's father. Altogether, he showed a goodwill towards Highbury in general. Emma watched and decided that, with such feelings as were shown, he was not acting a part or being insincere.

Their first stop in the village was at the Crown Inn, the main lodging in town. Emma gave him the history of the large room that had been built many years ago for a ballroom. Such brilliant days had long since passed.

Mr. Frank Churchill was immediately interested. Its character as a ballroom caught his attention, and he stopped for several minutes to look in and lament that its original purpose should have ceased.

Frank thought they ought to have balls there at least every fortnight through the winter. Why had not Miss Woodhouse revived the former good old days of the room? She, who could do anything in Highbury!

Emma mentioned the lack of enough proper families in town to attend, but he believed it would not be inconvenient for families of all social classes to mix together for an evening of dancing. She then mentioned the danger of assembling so many tender young maidens in one place, the better to tempt an attack by the wild creatures of the night.

But Mr. Churchill scoffed at her trepidation. He argued like a young man very much bent on dancing, though Emma wondered how a man without a heartbeat and who never breathed could possibly last the evening on the dance floor. Emma was rather surprised to see all the life and spirit, cheerful feelings, and social inclinations of his father and little of the pride or reserve of the Churchills, except as regarding his social opinion of wild vampires.

At last he was persuaded to move on from the front of the Crown Inn and, now almost facing the house where the Bateses lived, Emma remembered his visit the day before and asked him if he had paid it.

"Yes, oh yes," he replied. "A very successful visit. I saw all three ladies. Ten minutes would have been all that was necessary, but with the talking aunt there was no getting away before nearly three-quarters of an hour."

"And how did you think Miss Fairfax looking?"

"Ill, very ill. Miss Fairfax is naturally so pale—almost as pale as I, including the dark circles under her eyes—she almost always gives the appearance of ill health. A most deplorable want of complexion." She already looks like a vampiress, he thought, even without being yet bitten.

Emma would not agree to this and began a warm defence of Miss Fairfax's complexion. "It was certainly never brilliant, but she would not allow it to have a sickly hue in general; and there is a softness and delicacy in her skin which gives peculiar elegance to the character of her face."

Frank listened with all due respect and agreed that he had heard many people say the same. Yet, he must confess that to him nothing could make amends for the lack of the fine glow of health—although he realised privately that sinking his teeth into her neck, while giving him much needed sustenance, would do nothing to improve her complexion.

"Well," said Emma, "there is no disputing about taste. At least you admire her, except for her complexion."

He shook his head and laughed. "I cannot separate Miss Fairfax and her complexion."

"Did you not see her often at Weymouth? Were you not often in the same group?"

"I must pronounce your question unfair. It is always the lady's right to decide on the degree of friendship. Miss Fairfax must already have given her account. I shall not say more than she chose to."

"Upon my word!" said Emma. "You answer as discreetly as she did. She is so very reserved, so very unwilling to give the least information about anybody that I really think you may say whatever you wish about your acquaintance with her."

"May I, indeed? Then I shall speak the truth, and nothing suits me so well. I met her frequently at Weymouth. I had known the Campbells a little in London, and at Weymouth we were very much in the same set. Colonel Campbell is a very agreeable man and Mrs. Campbell a friendly, warmhearted woman. I like them all."

"You know Miss Fairfax's situation in life, I assume—what she is destined to be?"

"Yes," he said, rather hesitatingly, "I believe I do."

"You get upon delicate subjects, Emma," said Mrs. Weston smiling. "Remember that I am here. Mr. Frank Churchill hardly knows what to say when you speak of Miss Fairfax's situation in life. I shall move a little farther off."

"I certainly do forget to think of her," said Emma, "as having been anything but my dearest friend."

Frank Churchill looked as if he fully understood and honoured such a sentiment. Then he asked, "Did you ever hear Miss Fairfax play the piano?"

"Ever hear her!" repeated Emma. "You forget how much she belongs to Highbury. I have heard her every year of our lives since we both began. She plays charmingly."

"You think so, do you? I wanted the opinion of someone who could really judge. She appeared to me to play quite well, also. I am excessively fond of music, but without the smallest skill or right of judging anybody's performance. I have heard Miss Fairfax's playing admired. In fact, I remember a man—a very musical man, engaged to another woman, on the point of marriage—would never ask his fiancée to play if he could hear Miss Fairfax."

Emma was highly amused. "So, Mr. Dixon is very musical, is he? We have learned more about them all in half an hour from you than Miss Fairfax would have revealed in half a year."

"Yes, Mr. Dixon and Miss Campbell were the persons to whom I referred."

"How did Miss Campbell appear to like Miss Fairfax's playing?"

"She is Miss Campbell's very dear friend, you know."

"If Miss Fairfax played whenever she was asked by Mr. Dixon, one may guess which one he preferred."

"Miss Campbell and Miss Fairfax appeared to have a perfectly good understanding between them—" he began rather quickly, but checking himself, added, "however, it is impossible for me to say on what terms they really were— how it might all be behind the scenes. I can only say that there was smoothness outwardly. But you, who have known Miss Fairfax from a child, must be a better judge of her character and of how she is likely to conduct herself in sensitive situations than I can be."

"I have known her from a child—we have been children and women together. And it is natural to suppose that we should be very close, but we never were. It was her reserve—I never could befriend anyone so completely reserved."

"It is a most repulsive quality, indeed," said he. "Oftentimes very convenient, no doubt, but never pleasing. There is safety in reserve, but no attraction. One cannot love a reserved person." But then, he thought, what matters love when a hearty feast presents itself?

"Intimacy between Miss Fairfax and me is quite out of the question," said Emma. "I have no reason to think ill of her—not the least—except that such extreme and perpetual cautiousness of word and manner, such a dread of giving a distinct idea about anybody is apt to suggest suspicions of there being something to conceal."

He perfectly agreed with her, and after walking together so long and thinking so much alike, Emma felt herself so well acquainted with him that she could hardly believe it to be only their second meeting.

Frank Churchill was less of a man of the world, less the spoiled child of fortune, therefore better than she had expected. His ideas seemed more moderate, his feelings warmer. Whether he would retreat like a scared rabbit from a vampire attack remained yet to be seen.

Emma was particularly struck by his manner of considering Mr. Elton's impending marriage. Mr. Churchill felt that if Mr. Elton's vicarage were to be shared with the woman he loved, then he should not be pitied for having such a small house. There must be ample room in it for every real comfort, and the black curtains made it even more attractive. The man must be a blockhead who wanted more, he reasoned.

Mrs. Weston laughed and said Frank did not know what he was talking about. Accustomed to a large house himself, he could not possibly be a judge of the inconvenience of a small one. But Emma, in her own mind, determined that he did know what he was talking about and that he showed a very positive inclination to settle down early in life and to marry from worthy motives. He no doubt felt that Enscombe could not make him happy and that whenever he married, he would willingly give up much wealth to be allowed a small house of his own—and, Frank Churchill would have added if asked, an ample supply of fresh blood.

CHAPTER 25

Emma's very good opinion of Frank Churchill was a little shaken the following day by hearing that he was gone off to London merely to have his hair cut. There was certainly no harm in his travelling sixteen miles twice over on such an errand; but there was an air of foppery and nonsense in it which she could not approve.

It was not in accordance with the rationality, moderation, or unselfish warmth of heart which she had discerned in him yesterday. Rather, it spoke of vanity, extravagance, love of change, and restlessness.

Emma was blithely unaware, however, that as Frank Churchill's vampire hair never grew, he was merely having its style updated to the more modern custom of the present century.

But, with the exception of this little blot, Emma found that Mr. Churchill's visit thus far had given Mrs. Weston only good ideas of him. Mrs. Weston was very ready to say how attentive and pleasant a companion he made himself and how much she liked his disposition. He appeared to have a very open mind, certainly a very cheerful and lively one; she could observe nothing wrong in his ideas, a great deal decidedly right.

Frank spoke of his uncle Mr. Churchill with warm regard, and he acknowledged his aunt Mrs. Churchill's kindness with gratitude, speaking of her with respect. This was all very promising, and Emma felt there was nothing to deem him unworthy of the honour of being very nearly in love with her, save only her own resolution of never marrying.

Mr. Weston told Emma that Frank admired her extremely—thought her very beautiful, especially her long, fair neck, and very charming; and with so much to be said for him, Emma found she must not judge him harshly.

There was one person among Frank's new acquaintances not so favourably inclined—Mr. Knightley. While visiting at Hartfield, he was told of Frank's haircut in London. Mr. Knightley was silent a moment, but Emma heard him almost immediately afterwards say to himself, "Hum! Just the trifling, silly fellow I took him for. A man does not need a haircut more than every hundred years."

Emma had half a mind to object but decided to let it pass, since she had no decent understanding of what he meant.

Mr. and Mrs. Weston's visit at Hartfield that morning gave Emma the opportunity to ask their advice about a dinner invitation of great importance. It seemed that the Coles had been settled some years in Highbury and were a very good sort of people, friendly and unpretentious. But on the other hand, they were of low class, engaged in trade, and only moderately genteel.

On their first coming to Highbury, they had lived quietly, in proportion to their income, keeping much to themselves. But the past year or two had brought the Coles a considerable increase in wealth. They bought a larger house, added servants, and soon were second only to the Woodhouses of Hartfield in grandeur.

The Coles' desire to be accepted into proper society prepared everybody for invitations to their dinner parties. Emma could hardly suppose they would presume to invite the best families—Mr. Knightley, the Woodhouses, or the Westons.

The Coles were very respectable in their way, but they ought to be taught that it was not for them to decide when the superior families would acknowledge them. This lesson Emma would teach them by refusing their invitation when it arrived.

But when invitations came for Mr. Knightley and the Westons, none had come for herself and her father. Emma wanted to have the power of refusal. But the idea that the party would consist of those people whose society was dearest to her caused Emma to think that she might be tempted to accept after all.

Harriet was to be there and the Bateses. And Frank Churchill would most earnestly lament her absence—he might not sleep for many nights from despondency.

Nonetheless, this very invitation for Emma and her father finally arrived while the Westons were visiting Hartfield, which made their presence so helpful.

Though Emma's first remark upon reading it was that "of course it must be declined," she very soon proceeded to ask the Westons what they advised her to do.

She admitted that she was not completely sure of declining. The invitation was so proper and considerate of her father: "We would have invited you earlier, but we had been waiting for the arrival of a folding screen from London, which we hoped might keep Mr. Woodhouse from any draught of air, and therefore encourage him to accept our invitation."

As for his going, Emma did not wish him to think it possible—the hours would be too late and the guests too numerous. He was soon pretty well resigned.

"I am not fond of dinner parties," said he to the Westons. "I never was. No more is Emma. Especially when uninvited guests suddenly leap out of the privet. Late hours do not agree with us. However, as the Coles are so very desirous to have dear Emma dine with them and as you will both be there and Mr. Knightley too, to take care of her, I do not wish to prevent it.

"Emma, we must write an answer to Mrs. Cole. You will make my excuses, my dear, as civilly as possible. You will say that I am quite an invalid and go nowhere and therefore must decline their obliging invitation, beginning with my compliments, of course. Emma dear, you must come home at an early hour. You will not like staying late. You will get very tired when tea is over."

"But my dear sir," cried Mr. Weston, "if Emma leaves early, it will be breaking up the party."

"And no great harm if it does," said Mr. Woodhouse. "The sooner every party breaks up, the better."

"But you do not consider how it may appear to the Coles. Emma's going away directly after tea might be giving offence. They are good-natured people, and Miss Woodhouse's hurrying away would be more hurtful than any other person's in the room. You would not wish to disappoint and mortify the Coles, I am sure, sir."

"No, Mr. Weston," relented Mr. Woodhouse, "I should be extremely sorry to be giving them any pain. I know what worthy people they are. My dear Emma, you will not consider being tired. You will be perfectly safe among your friends."

"Oh yes, Papa. I have no fears at all for myself, and I should have no scruples of staying as late as Mrs. Weston, but on your account. I am only afraid of your sitting up for me instead of going to bed at your usual time. You must promise me not to sit up."

He did, on the condition that if she came home cold, she would be sure to warm herself thoroughly; if hungry, that she would take something to eat; that her own maid should sit up for her; and that the butler should see that everything was safe in the house, as usual, and that an ample supply of sabres and wooden stakes be readily at hand.

CHAPTER 26

FRANK CHURCHILL RETURNED FROM London with his new hairstyle and laughed at himself with a very good grace but without seeming at all ashamed of what he had done. He was quite as undaunted and lively as ever. His black hair was no shorter, but appeared somewhat different nonetheless and complemented his black eyes and the purple circles against his alabaster skin.

After seeing him, Emma thus moralised to herself, "Certainly silly things cease to be silly if they are done by sensible people. It depends upon the character of those who handle it."

With Tuesday came the agreeable prospect of seeing Mr. Frank Churchill again at the Coles' dinner, and for a longer time than before. Emma would be able to judge the meaning of his behaviour towards her and observe the other dinner guests seeing Emma and Frank together for the first time.

Mrs. Bates and Mrs. Goddard arrived at Hartfield to keep Mr. Woodhouse company at home during the party. Emma had prepared a full dinner for them and, before she left the house, paid her respects by helping them to large slices of cake and full glasses of wine.

❧

Arriving at the Coles' door, Emma was received with cordial respect and given all the attention she could wish for. When the Westons arrived with Frank Churchill, the kindest looks of love and admiration were for Emma, from both husband and wife. Frank approached her with a cheerful eagerness which marked her as special, and at dinner she found herself seated next to him.

The party was rather large, as it included one other family, the Coxes, he being the lawyer of Highbury. The less worthy females were to come later in the evening, along with Miss Bates, Miss Fairfax, and Miss Harriet Smith.

At dinner, Emma surrendered all her attention to the pleasantness of Frank Churchill. They were seated away from the fireplace at Frank's insistence. Emma attributed his lack of appetite to his being overcome by her ravishing beauty.

The first time Emma's attention was diverted from Mr. Churchill was upon hearing the name of Jane Fairfax. Mrs. Cole seemed to be relating a story that appeared very interesting.

Emma listened and found it well worth listening to. Mrs. Cole said that she had visited Miss Bates, and as soon as she entered the room had been struck by the sight of a pianoforte—a very elegant-looking instrument—which had arrived the day before, entirely unexpected.

Jane Fairfax herself was quite at a loss, quite bewildered to think who could possibly have ordered it. Mrs. Cole and Miss Bates were perfectly satisfied that it could be from only one person—Colonel Campbell.

But Jane, it seems, recently had a letter from the Campbells, and not a word was mentioned about a pianoforte. Many at the table agreed with Mrs. Cole, that it must have come from Colonel Campbell. But Emma had her own opinion about it.

"I declare," said Mrs. Cole, "it has always quite hurt me that Jane Fairfax, who plays so delightfully, should not have her own pianoforte, and now she does. I really was ashamed to look at our new grand pianoforte in the drawing room, while I do not know one note from another. We are in great hopes that Miss Woodhouse may be prevailed upon to try it this evening."

Emma nodded to Mrs. Cole that she would, then turned back to Frank Churchill.

"Why do you smile?" said she.

"Nay, why do you?"

"Me! I suppose I smile for pleasure at Colonel Campbell's generosity. It is a handsome present."

"Very," said he.

"Your expression says that your thoughts on this subject are very much like mine."

"I probably suspect whatever you suspect—if Colonel Campbell is not the person, then who can it be?"

"What do you say to Miss Campbell?" asked Emma.

"Miss Campbell! Very true. It would be so like her to send it."

"Then you must also suspect her new husband Mr. Dixon."

"Mr. Dixon. Yes, we were speaking the other day, you know, of his being so warm an admirer of her performance."

"Yes, and I cannot help suspecting that he had the misfortune to fall in love with Miss Fairfax."

"And upon my word," returned Frank Churchill, "that has an air of great probability, considering Mr. Dixon's preference of Jane's music to Miss Campbell's."

"And Mr. Dixon saved Jane's life," said Emma. "Did you ever hear of that? A boating party. And by some accident Jane was falling overboard. He caught her."

"Yes, he did. I was there—one of the party."

"Were you really? Then this tells me quite enough. Depend upon it, we shall soon hear that it is a present from Mr. and Mrs. Dixon."

There was no occasion to press the matter further. The rest of the dinner passed, with much of the food uneaten, so many gentlemen vampires being present, then the dessert followed and a few clever things said.

The ladies had not been long in the drawing room before the other ladies arrived. Emma watched the entrée of her own particular little friend Harriet. There she sat—and who would have guessed how many tears she had lately been shedding over Mr. Elton? To be nicely dressed, to sit and smile and look pretty was enough for the happiness of the present hour.

Jane Fairfax did look and move superiorly, but Emma did not approach her. She did not wish to speak of the piano-forte—she felt too involved in the secret. But the subject was immediately mentioned by others, and Emma saw the blush of guilt which accompanied the name of "my excellent friend Colonel Campbell."

They were soon joined by some of the gentlemen. Frank Churchill walked in, the first and the handsomest, and sat down next to Emma. She sensed what everybody else must be thinking—that she was the object of Mr. Churchill's attention.

She introduced him to her friend Miss Smith and, at convenient moments afterwards, heard what each thought of the other.

"I have never seen so lovely and plump a face," said he.

"I think he looks a little like Mr. Elton, with those big dark eyes," said she.

Emma restrained her indignation at Harriet's reference to Mr. Elton and turned away from her in silence.

Frank Churchill then spoke handsomely of Highbury again. Emma questioned him as to the society at Enscombe, and she discerned there was very little going on. The best that could be said was that no vampire menace existed there.

Frank thought to himself that Enscombe was not satisfactory and that Highbury might reasonably please a young vampire such as himself, with its large selection of fine young ladies for sustenance.

"I have made a most wretched discovery," said he, after a short pause. "I have been here a week tomorrow—half my time. I never knew days to fly so fast. A week tomorrow! And I have hardly begun to enjoy myself, having just gotten acquainted with Mrs. Weston and others!"

The rest of the gentlemen being now in the room, Emma noticed how much they resembled one another, with the same black hair and pale skin, the only exception being the eyes, some black and some pale blue. Mr. Knightley appeared especially gallant, for now he wore his sabre at his side whenever he ventured away from Donwell Abbey.

Emma found herself obliged to turn from Frank for a few minutes while Mr. Cole spoke to her. When Mr. Cole had moved away, she saw Frank Churchill looking intently across the room at Miss Fairfax.

"What is the matter?" asked Emma.

He was startled. "I believe I have been very rude to stare at Miss Fairfax," he replied. "But really she has done her hair in so odd a way that I cannot keep my eyes from her. Those curls! I must go and ask her whether it is an Irish fashion. Shall I? Yes, I will, and you will see how she takes it, whether she blushes."

He was gone in a blur, and Emma next saw him standing before Miss Fairfax and talking to her. But since he stood exactly in front of her, Emma could see absolutely nothing. Before he could return to his chair, it was taken by Mrs. Weston.

"My dear Emma," said she, "do you know how Miss Bates and her niece Jane Fairfax came here tonight?"

"They were invited, were they not?"

"Oh, yes! But the way they arrived?"

"They walked, I conclude. How else could they come?"

"Well, a little while ago it occurred to me how very sad it would be to have Jane Fairfax walking home again, late at night, as cold as the nights are now, and with so much danger lurking about. So I approached her, to offer her our carriage before it took us home. She was grateful, you may be sure, but she said Mr. Knightley's carriage had brought them and was to take them home again. I was quite surprised."

"I know of no man more likely than Mr. Knightley to do such a considerate sort of thing."

"Well," said Mrs. Weston, smiling, "you give him credit for more simple benevolence than I, for a suspicion darted into my head. The more I think of it, the more probable it appears. I have made a match between Mr. Knightley and Jane Fairfax. What do you say to it?"

"Mr. Knightley and Jane Fairfax!" exclaimed Emma. "Dear Mrs. Weston, how could you think of such a thing? Mr. Knightley must not marry! You would not have my little nephew Henry cut out as the Donwell Abbey heir! Oh no, no, Henry must have Donwell. I cannot at all consent to Mr. Knightley's marrying, and I am amazed that you should think of such a thing."

"My dear Emma, I have only told you what led me to think of it. I do not want the match—I do not want to injure dear little Henry. But if Mr. Knightley really wished to marry, you would not have him refrain on Henry's account—a boy of six years old who knows nothing of the matter?"

"Yes, I would! I could not bear to have Henry cut out.
Mr. Knightley marry! No, I have never had such an idea, and
I cannot adopt it now. And Jane Fairfax, too, of all women!
The only thing they have in common is their pale white skin!"

"Well, she has always been a favourite with him, as you
very well know."

"But the imprudence of such a match!"

"I am not speaking of its prudence—merely its probability."

"I see no probability in it, unless you have any better
foundation than what you mention. My dear Mrs. Weston,
do not take to matchmaking—you do it very ill."

"But except for inequality of fortune and perhaps a little
disparity of age, I can see nothing unsuitable."

"But Mr. Knightley does not want to marry. Why should
he marry? He is as happy as possible by himself—with his
farm, and his library, all the parish to manage, and taking his
brother's children hunting in the woods."

"My dear Emma, if he really loves Jane Fairfax—"

"Nonsense! He does not care about Jane Fairfax. It would
be a very shameful and degrading marriage. How would
he bear to have Miss Bates belonging to him? To have her
haunting the Abbey and thanking him all day long for his
great kindness in marrying Jane? And then to fly off, through
half a sentence, about her mother's old petticoat. 'Not that
it was such a very old petticoat either—for still it would last
a great while.'"

"For shame, Emma! Do not mimic her. I have heard him
speak so very highly of Jane Fairfax! Such an admirer of her
performance on the pianoforte and of her voice. I have heard
him say that he could listen to her forever, even from miles
away. This pianoforte that has been sent to her—might it not
be from Mr. Knightley? I cannot help suspecting him."

"I see no sign of affection. I believe nothing about the pianoforte—and only proof will convince me that Mr. Knightley has any thought of marrying Jane Fairfax."

At that moment Mr. Cole approached Emma to beg her to try out the new pianoforte. Frank Churchill stood up from his seat next to Jane Fairfax and joined Mr. Cole in his request.

Emma played and sang with credit and, to her agreeable surprise, was accompanied in her song by Frank Churchill. He was praised for having a delightful voice, made more remarkable by the fact that he never took a single breath. They sang together once more, then Emma rose and gave her place at the pianoforte to Miss Fairfax.

Emma listened to Jane's performance, which was infinitely superior to her own. Frank Churchill sang again. They had sung together once or twice, it appeared, at the Weymouth resort.

Presently Mr. Knightley came and sat down by Emma. They talked at first only of the performance. His admiration of Miss Fairfax was certainly warm, but not exceptional.

"This present from the Campbells," said Emma, "this pianoforte, is very kindly given."

"Yes," replied Mr. Knightley, without the least apparent embarrassment, "but they would have done better had they given her notice of it. Surprises are foolish things. I should have expected better judgement in Colonel Campbell."

From that moment, Emma could have taken an oath that Mr. Knightley had no part in giving the instrument to Jane Fairfax.

At the end of Jane's second song, Mr. Knightley said to Emma, thinking aloud, "That will do—she has sung quite enough for one evening. Now we need quiet. My hearing being so acute, my ears are quite ringing."

Frank Churchill was heard to say, "I think you could manage one more effort."

Mr. Knightley grew angry. "That fellow," said he, indignantly, "thinks of nothing but showing off his own voice. This must not be."

Mr. Knightley then caught the attention of Miss Bates, who at that moment walked by, and protested, "Miss Bates, are you mad to let your niece sing herself hoarse in this manner? Go and interfere. They have no mercy on her."

Miss Bates, in her real anxiety for Jane, stepped forward and put an end to all further singing. This ended the concert part of the evening, for Miss Woodhouse and Miss Fairfax were the only performers.

But within five minutes, the proposal of dancing was so well promoted by Mr. and Mrs. Cole that everything was rapidly clearing away to give proper space. Frank Churchill, with gallantry most becoming, came up to Emma, secured her hand with his frigid touch, and led her onto the dance floor.

Emma looked around to see what became of Mr. Knightley. This would be a trial. If he were to engage Jane Fairfax now, it might mean something. But there was no immediate appearance. No, he was talking to Mrs. Cole. Jane was asked to dance by somebody else, and he was still talking to Mrs. Cole.

Emma had no longer any alarm for Henry—his interest was yet safe—and she led off the dance with genuine spirit and enjoyment.

Not more than five couples were dancing, but the rarity and suddenness of it made it very delightful, and she found herself well matched in a partner. Emma Woodhouse and Frank Churchill were certainly a couple worth looking at.

Two dances, unfortunately, were all that could be allowed. It was growing late.

"Perhaps it is just as well," said Frank Churchill. "I would have asked Miss Fairfax next, and her languid dancing would not have agreed with me after yours." *Jane's great value to me,* he thought, *is in her neck, not her feet.*

∽✧∾

The guests stepped outside the house as the carriages were brought round. The Coles waited outside in the cold, still, moonlit night to see their guests off.

Mr. Knightley, with his acute hearing, was the first to hear a rustle in the shrubbery. Instinctively, his hand went to the grip of his sabre.

"What the deuce! Not again!" cried he, as the bushes parted and six vicious, ragged creatures leapt out and charged threateningly towards the assembled group of Highbury's finest.

In unison, several of the ladies screamed with terror.

"Oh, dear me! Oh, dear me!" cried Miss Bates, "Whatever is to become of us! This happening again? It is too much! I shall collapse and die this very moment from absolute fright!"

"Cole!" ordered Mr. Knightley. "We need more weapons!"

Mr. Cole darted into the house and returned instantly with three sabres.

"Weston! Churchill!" exclaimed Mr. Cole, as he hurled a sabre to each.

Mr. Weston adroitly caught his sword by the grip, but Frank Churchill allowed his sabre to fall to the ground.

"I cannot fight!" he sheepishly protested. "I must help the ladies!"

Emma rushed over and picked up the sabre from the ground. "Oh, very well then, I shall make good use of it."

Thus armed, the vampire killers—Emma, Knightley, Weston, and Cole—prepared to defend the ladies, who stood paralysed, shrieking. Frank Churchill stood before the women, his arms spread, in a feigned show of bravado. "Fear not, dear ladies of Highbury! I shall protect you!"

The six wild fiends paused a moment and viciously eyed their four adversaries.

"Mr. Knightley," inquired Mr. Cole, "how shall I best employ my foil?"

"Decapitation, my good man, is the only way. Off with their heads!" bellowed Mr. Knightley.

At that moment, the creatures attacked—clawing and snatching, fangs dripping, eyes black and crazed.

Mr. Knightley quickly beheaded the first vampire; Mr. Weston followed with a second, and Emma decapitated a third—three torsos and three heads rolled upon the ground.

The gruesome sight caused Jane Fairfax to faint. Mr. Frank Churchill caught her in his arms and gently rested her on the ground as Mrs. Cole dashed inside the house to fetch the smelling salts.

Emma dropped her sabre, unfastened her wooden stake, and stabbed the hearts of the three headless vampires.

The three remaining vampires gathered themselves together and bolted past the sabre-wielding gentlemen towards the group of ladies, who screamed in horror.

Harriet Smith boldly stepped in front of Miss Bates and Mrs. Weston. Holding her silver cross in full display, she cried, "Fie, monsters, fie! And away!"

The creatures drew up and halted their advance, terrified of the holy symbol.

Mr. Cole raised his sabre and whacked off the head of one vampire, as Mr. Knightley dispensed with the head of another. Two more ragged torsos splayed onto the ground.

"Harriet!" exclaimed Emma. "We need your wooden stake!"

"At the ready, Miss Woodhouse!" returned Harriet. She leaned down to reach beneath her infinite bombazine folds, but her plumpness made it impossible to reach her thigh. She struggled to grasp the yellow ribbon.

Suddenly, the remaining wild vampire grabbed Harriet's curls and, pulling her head back, prepared to sink its vile fangs into her neck. With mere moments before utter catastrophe, Harriet managed to release the yellow ribbon, retrieve her wooden stake, and drive its full length into the heart of the dastardly creature. It crumpled to the ground.

Harriet stood up, shocked and agape.

"My dear Harriet! You killed a vampire!" exclaimed Emma with great pride.

"Why, indeed I have!" remarked Harriet.

"Brava, Miss Smith. Well done indeed!" complimented Mr. Knightley. "Well done, all!"

Emma then drove her stake into the hearts of the two remaining prostrate torsos, and the terrifying nightmare was over.

Frank Churchill helped Jane Fairfax to her feet, as she had now come to her senses.

"Oh, dear me!" prattled Miss Bates. "Such carnage and devastation on such a beautiful velvety lawn as the Coles! I think I have never seen such horror! Mr. Frank Churchill, you risked your very life to protect us. How can we ever repay your kindness? And Miss Woodhouse, and Mr. Weston, and Mr. Knightley, and Miss Smith—and you, Mr. Cole! Not only did you graciously host one of the loveliest dinners we have ever been blessed with, but rescued our poor souls from a hideous eternity as well!"

"I, for one," said Mr. Cole, "need something to calm my nerves. May I invite all of you inside for a glass of port?"

The guests acceded to his invitation and, after several casks of amontillado had been eagerly consumed, the hosts and guests alike put the alarming incident quite out of their heads.

CHAPTER 27

EMMA DID NOT REGRET going to the Coles. The visit afforded her many pleasant recollections the next day, although there were some unpleasant recollections as well. Certainly she delighted the Coles with her presence—worthy people, who deserved to be made happy!

There were, however, three points on which she was not quite easy. Firstly, she doubted whether she should have revealed her suspicions about Jane Fairfax to Frank Churchill. It was hardly right—but it was so strong an idea, and he did agree with her after all, that perhaps it was right to do so.

The second circumstance of regret related to Frank Churchill as well. Emma was concerned that he demonstrated less than the proper amount of courage that a gentleman should exhibit in the face of danger, especially when ladies were present. Granted, he made a great show of protecting the women from the marauding vampires, but he appeared a bit too interested in Jane Fairfax's fainting spell.

The third, and most important, point of regret also related to Jane Fairfax—and there she had no doubt. Emma absolutely regretted the inferiority of her own playing and singing. She grieved over the idleness of her childhood—and promptly sat down and practised vigorously for an hour and a half.

Emma's playing was interrupted by Harriet's coming in, and if Harriet's praise could have satisfied her, she might have been comforted.

"Oh!" said Harriet. "If I could but play as well as you and Miss Fairfax!"

"Do not class us together, Harriet. My playing is no more like hers than a vampire is like a gentleman."

"Well, besides," returned Harriet, "if Miss Fairfax does play so very well, you know, it will only help her later because she will have to teach it. The Cox girls were wondering last night whether she would become a governess in a great family. How did you think the Coxes looked?"

"Just as they always do—quite vulgar. And cowardly—they hid themselves inside the house during the entire vampire attack."

"They told me something," said Harriet rather hesitatingly, "but it is nothing of any consequence."

Emma was obliged to ask what they had told her, though fearful it would bring up Mr. Elton again.

"They told me that Mr. Martin dined with them last Saturday."

"Oh!"

"Mr. Martin came to their father on some legal business, and he was asked to stay for dinner."

"Oh!"

"The Cox girls talked a great deal about Mr. Martin, especially Anne Cox. I do not know what she meant, but she asked me if I thought I should go and stay with the Martins again next summer."

"Anne Cox was rudely curious, as always."

"She said Mr. Martin was very agreeable. He sat by her at dinner, though he ate nothing. Miss Nash thinks either of the Coxes would be very glad to marry him."

"Very likely. I think they are, without exception, the most vulgar and cowardly girls in Highbury."

Harriet mentioned that she needed to go into town to purchase a new yellow ribbon at Ford's. Emma thought it most prudent to go with her. Another accidental meeting with the Martins or wild vampires was possible, and in her present state it would be dangerous.

At Ford's, Harriet was tempted by every colour of ribbon and always took very long to make a purchase. While she was still dawdling, Emma waited by the door.

Soon she saw Mrs. Weston and Frank Churchill walking into town. They went up to the Bateses' house, across the street from Ford's, when Emma caught their eye.

Immediately they crossed the road and came forward to Emma. Mrs. Weston informed her that they were calling on the Bateses in order to hear the new pianoforte.

"And while Mrs. Weston pays her visit, Emma, I trust I may be allowed," said Frank Churchill, "to join you and wait for Mrs. Weston at Hartfield—if you are going home."

Mrs. Weston was disappointed. "I thought you meant to go with me. The Bateses would be very much pleased. And I am certain they could use some comfort after last night's horrifying scare."

"Me! I should be quite in the way."

"I am not here on business of my own," said Emma. "I am only waiting for Harriet. She will probably be done soon and then we shall go home. Frank, you had better go with Mrs. Weston, hear the pianoforte, and comfort Miss Bates."

"Well, if you advise it."

Emma watched them enter the Bateses' door, then joined Harriet at the counter and convinced her friend that a blue ribbon, be it ever so beautiful, would still never match her yellow bombazine. At last it was all settled, and Harriet purchased an extra long yellow silk ribbon for her wooden stake.

At the door, they were met by Mrs. Weston and Miss Bates.

"My dear Miss Woodhouse," said Miss Bates, "I just ran across to beg you to come and sit down with us a little while and give us your opinion of our new pianoforte—you and Miss Smith. My mother will be so very happy to see you. Would you believe it, Mr. Churchill is back in the house, fastening the rivet of my mother's spectacles, using his remarkable vision to see the tiniest parts."

Emma said, "I should be very happy to visit with Mrs. Bates."

When they were all in the street, Miss Bates said, "Oh, my mother's spectacles! So very obliging of Mr. Frank Churchill! He said, 'I do think I can fasten the rivet. I like a job of this kind excessively.' I do congratulate you, Mrs. Weston, most warmly. He shielded me from harm last evening and now assists my dear mother. He seems everything the fondest parent could dream of. I never shall forget his manner."

CHAPTER 28

THE APPEARANCE OF THE little sitting room as they entered the Bateses' house was tranquillity itself—Mrs. Bates, asleep by the fire; Frank Churchill, at a table as far away from the fire as possible, occupied with her spectacles; and Jane Fairfax, sitting with her back to them, intent on her pianoforte.

Busy as he was, however, Frank was yet able to show a most happy face upon seeing Emma again.

"This is a pleasure," said he. "You find me trying to be useful."

He contrived that Emma should be seated by him. Jane began playing and, though the first bars were feebly given, the power of the instrument was gradually done full justice to.

Mrs. Weston was delighted, Emma joined her in praise, and the pianoforte was pronounced to be of the highest promise.

"Colonel Campbell has chosen his gift well," said Frank Churchill, with a smile and a glance of his onyx eyes at Emma. "Do you not think so, Miss Fairfax?"

Jane did not look round. She was not obliged to hear.

"This is not fair," said Emma to Frank in a whisper. "My guess last night was merely a random one. Do not distress her."

He shook his head with a smile and looked as if he had very little doubt and very little mercy. Soon afterwards he began again.

"Your friends in Ireland must wonder which day the pianoforte will arrive." He paused.

Jane could not avoid answering. "Till I have a letter from Colonel Campbell," said she, in a voice of forced calmness, "I can imagine nothing with any confidence. It must be all conjecture."

"Conjecture—aye, sometimes one conjectures right, and sometimes one conjectures wrong." Then he added, "Mrs. Bates," who was now awake, "I have the pleasure, madam, of restoring your spectacles, healed for the present."

He was very warmly thanked both by mother and daughter; he went to the pianoforte and begged Miss Fairfax, who was still sitting at it, to play something more.

She played.

"What happiness to hear a tune again which has made one happy!" he exclaimed. "If I mistake not, that was danced at Weymouth."

Jane looked up at him for a moment, blushed deeply, and played something else.

Frank took some sheet music from a chair near the pianoforte and, turning to Emma, said, "Here is something quite new. It was sent with the instrument. Very thoughtful of Colonel Campbell, was it not? Only true affection could have prompted it."

Emma wished he would be less pointed, yet she could not help being amused; and when she glanced at Jane Fairfax, she saw that, with all the deep blush, there had been a smile of secret delight.

This upright, perfect Jane Fairfax was apparently cherishing some very naughty feelings!

Frank brought all the music to Jane, then returned to his seat.

Emma whispered to him, "You speak too bluntly. I am sure she must understand your meaning."

"I trust she does. I would have her understand me. I am not in the least ashamed of my meaning."

"But really, I am half-ashamed and wish I had never suggested the idea."

"I am very glad you did," replied Frank, "and that you told me. I now understand all her odd looks and ways. Leave shame to her. If she does wrong, she ought to feel it."

"But I think she is ashamed."

"I do not see much sign of it. She is playing Mr. Dixon's favourite music."

Just then, Miss Bates, passing near the window, spied Mr. Knightley on horseback just outside.

"It is Mr. Knightley, I declare! I must speak to him if possible, just to thank him for last night. I daresay he will come in when he knows who is here."

She opened the window and called Mr. Knightley's name.

"How d'ye do, Mr. Knightley? So obliged to you for the carriage last night and for your gallantry. Such a lovely dinner and such an awful business at the end. Pray come in, do come in. You will find some friends here."

Mr. Knightley replied, "How is your niece, Miss Bates? How is Miss Fairfax? I hope she caught no cold last night after her fainting spell."

As Miss Bates answered, Mrs. Weston gave Emma a look of particular meaning. But Emma still shook her head in steady doubt.

"Do come in, Mr. Knightley. Who do you think is here? Miss Woodhouse and Miss Smith, so kind to call, to hear the new pianoforte. Do put up your horse and come in."

"Well," said he, deliberating, "for five minutes, perhaps."

"And Mrs. Weston and Mr. Frank Churchill are here, too! Quite delightful, so many friends!"

Abruptly, Mr. Knightley changed his mind. "No, not now, I thank you. I could not stay two minutes. I must get on."

"Oh! Do come in. They will be so very happy to see you."

"No, no, your room is full enough. I shall call another day and hear the pianoforte."

"Well, I am so sorry! But do travel with the utmost care. I see you carry your trusty sabre with you. Well done, Mr. Knightley! And a very good morning to you!"

Emma found it really time to leave. The visit had already lasted too long and, upon examining watches, so much of the morning was found to be gone that Mrs. Weston and Frank Churchill took their leave also. They could allow themselves to walk with Emma and Harriet only to the Hartfield gates before they set off for Randalls.

CHAPTER 29

I T MAY BE POSSIBLE to do without blood for a time—
young vampires have been known to pass many months
without it. But once there is a taste for it, it is difficult not to
desire more. The same applies to dancing and attending balls.

Frank Churchill had danced once in Highbury and longed
to dance again. Since he never breathed, he was never out of
breath, and since he never slept, he could go on and on till
the wee hours.

During an evening with the Westons, Frank and Emma
began scheming about a ball. It was Frank's idea, and
Emma was certainly desirous of showing people again how
delightfully Mr. Frank Churchill and Miss Woodhouse
danced—an activity at which she excelled when compared
to Jane Fairfax.

Emma assisted Frank in measuring the rooms at Randalls
in the hope of discovering which room was the largest. He
proposed that the same people in attendance at the Coles'
party should be invited and the same musician engaged.

"You and Miss Smith and Miss Fairfax will be three, and
the two Miss Coxes five, and there will be the two Gilberts,
young Cox, my father, and myself, besides Mr. Knightley.
Yes, that will be quite enough for pleasure. There will be
plenty of room."

"But will there be enough? I really do not think there will."

They thought to include a second young Cox and one family of cousins of Mr. Weston's and another of very old acquaintance who could not be left out. It became a certainty that the five couples would soon become at least ten.

"I believe we have room here for ten couples," said Frank.

Emma demurred. "It would be a crowd—a sad crowd—and what could be worse than dancing without space to turn in?"

"Very true," he gravely replied. "It is very bad."

But still he went on measuring, and still he ended with, "I think there will be very tolerable room for ten couples."

"No, no," said she, "you are quite unreasonable. It would be dreadful to be standing so close! Nothing can be further from pleasure than to be dancing in a crowd in a little room, pressed up against cold-skinned gentlemen!"

Emma perceived that Frank was a little self-willed. Had she ever intended to marry him, it might have been worthwhile to pause and consider this and try to understand the character of his temper.

The next day Frank Churchill visited Hartfield, and he entered the room with an agreeable smile.

"Well, Miss Woodhouse," he almost immediately began, "I trust your inclination for dancing has not been quite frightened away by the terrors of my father's little rooms. I bring a new proposal on the subject—this little ball will be held, not at Randalls but at the Crown Inn."

"The Crown!"

"Yes—you were perfectly right! Ten couples in the Westons' room would have been insufferable! Dreadful! Is it not a good proposal? I hope you consent."

"I think it most admirable. Papa, do you not think it an excellent improvement?"

She was obliged to repeat and explain it to Mr. Woodhouse before it was fully comprehended.

"No," said he, "a very bad plan indeed—much worse than the other. A room at an inn is always damp and dangerous, never properly aired or fit to be inhabited. You would all catch worse colds at the Crown than anywhere."

"I was going to observe, sir," said Frank Churchill, "that although I personally prefer damp and dreary, from the very circumstance of the Crown being larger, sir, we shall have no occasion to open the windows at all. And it is that dreadful habit of opening the windows, letting in cold air upon heated bodies which, as you well know, sir, does the mischief."

"There, Papa! Now you must be satisfied." He reluctantly nodded his consent.

"My father and Mrs. Weston are at the Crown at this moment," said Frank Churchill, "examining the capabilities of the Inn. I left them there and flashed here to Hartfield, Miss Woodhouse, impatient for your opinion and hoping you might be persuaded to join them and give your advice. They can do nothing satisfactorily without you."

Emma was most happy to be called to such a meeting. The two young people set off together without delay for the Crown.

There were Mr. and Mrs. Weston, delighted to see Emma and receive her approval, very busy and very happy in their different ways—Mrs. Weston, in some little distress; and Mr. Weston, finding everything perfect.

"Emma," said Mrs. Weston, "this wallpaper is worse than I expected. Look! In places you can see it is dreadfully dirty."

"My dear, you are too particular," said her husband. "What does all that signify? You will see nothing of it by candlelight."

The ladies exchanged looks which meant "Men never know when things are dirty or not," and the gentlemen thought to themselves, "Women will have their little nonsense and needless cares."

One problem arose, however, regarding a supper room. The small adjoining card room was too small for any comfortable supper. Another room of much better size was at the other end of a long awkward hallway. This made a difficulty.

Mrs. Weston proposed having merely sandwiches set out in the little room; but that was discarded as a wretched suggestion. A private dance, without sitting down to supper, was an infamous fraud upon the rights of men and women.

Mr. Weston and Frank Churchill suggested no supper at all, since they would not themselves eat.

"I wish," said Mrs. Weston, "we could know which arrangement our guests would like best."

"Yes, very true," cried Frank, "very true. You want your neighbours' opinions. Shall I call upon the Coles? They are not far off. Or Miss Bates? She is still nearer."

"Well—if you please," said Mrs. Weston, rather hesitating, "if you think she will be of any use."

"You will get nothing useful from Miss Bates," said Emma. "She will be all delight and gratitude, but she will tell you nothing. She will not even listen to your questions."

"But she is so amusing!" replied Frank Churchill. "I am very fond of hearing Miss Bates talk. And I need not bring the whole family, you know."

Here Mr. Weston joined them. "Aye, Frank. Go and fetch Miss Bates. She will enjoy the plan, I am sure. But fetch them both. Invite them both."

"Both sir! Can the old lady—"

"The old lady? No! The young lady, to be sure. I shall think you a great blockhead, Frank, if you bring the aunt without Miss Jane Fairfax."

And he disappeared like a vampire bat out of hell.

But before he returned, Mrs. Weston had examined the hallway again and found the evils of it much less than she had supposed before—and here ended the difficulties of the decision. The supper would be held in the larger room.

All the rest of the minor arrangements of tables and chairs, lights and music, tea and supper, were mere trifles to be settled at any time. Everybody invited was certain to come.

Frank had already written to his aunt at Enscombe to propose his staying a few days beyond his fortnight. And a delightful dance it was to be.

Most cordially, when Miss Bates arrived, she agreed with everything. Her approval, warm and incessant, was pleasing.

The group did not break up without Emma's being asked for the two first dances by the hero of the evening, Mr. Frank Churchill, nor without Emma overhearing Mr. Weston whisper to his wife, "He has asked her to dance, my dear. That's right. I knew he would!"

CHAPTER 30

ONLY ONE THING WAS needed to make the prospect of the ball completely satisfactory to Emma—that the Churchills allow their nephew to remain a few days beyond his appointed stay.

To Emma's great surprise, Enscombe was gracious. Frank's wish of staying longer evidently did not please, but it was not opposed. All was safe and prosperous.

And now Emma, being certain of her ball, began to adopt as her next worry Mr. Knightley's annoying indifference about it. Perhaps because he did not dance himself or because the plan had been formed without his being consulted or because he feared another vampire attack, he seemed resolved that it should not interest him.

Emma had a sense that, of the three possibilities, Mr. Knightley's indifference towards the ball was guided by his lack of dancing ability. She was pleased that he had no interest in dancing with Jane Fairfax. Emma was therefore more and more convinced that Mrs. Weston was quite mistaken in her surmise about Mr. Knightley and Miss Fairfax.

"If the Westons think it worthwhile to go to all this trouble for a few hours of noisy entertainment," said he, "I have nothing to say against it. Oh yes, I must be there! I could not refuse, and I shall have no trouble staying awake. But I would rather be at home, I confess. Take pleasure in seeing dancing? Not I, indeed. I never look at it. By the by, will Miss Harriet Smith be in attendance at the ball?"

"Most assuredly. She is my dear friend. We are inseparable."

"A pity."

"Upon my word, Mr. Knightley! As of late, I had thought you held Miss Smith in high regard."

"Indeed I do, Emma. However, I have begun to notice that wherever she appears—whether it be Hartfield, the Coles', or walking about Highbury—a band of malicious vampires appears soon thereafter. I have a suspicion that the wild creatures have settled on Harriet's scent and are brazenly following it in hopes that she will lead them to sustenance."

"My dear Mr. Knightley! Surely you cannot presume to think such ill thoughts about our dear, plump, little Harriet! Indeed, if you recall, Harriet was ill on Christmas Eve when they attacked us at the Westons' dinner."

"Then perhaps her scent rubbed off on you, dear Emma. It is not what I wish to think; however, the coincidences are too frequent to suppose otherwise. Therefore, I must forewarn the gentlemen of Highbury who will be in attendance at the ball to arrive fully armed."

"This is a ball, not a pitched battle, sir!"

"Emma, dear, would you rather risk a massacre?"

"Certainly not, Mr. Knightley," she demurred. "I suppose your point is well taken."

But alas! Two days of joyful anticipation were immediately followed by the overthrow of everything. A letter arrived from Frank's uncle, Mr. Churchill, to urge his nephew's instant return.

Mrs. Churchill was unwell—far too unwell to do without Frank. Her husband said that she had been in a very suffering state when writing to her nephew two days before, though from her constant habit of never thinking of herself, she had not mentioned it. But now she was too ill to trifle and must beg Frank to set off for Enscombe without delay.

The substance of this letter was forwarded instantly to Emma in a note from Mrs. Weston. As to his going, it was inevitable. He must be gone within a few hours.

This wretched note was the finale of Emma's breakfast. After she read it, there was nothing to do but lament. The loss of the ball, the loss of Frank Churchill, and all that the young man might be feeling! It was too wretched! Such a delightful evening as it would have been! Everybody so happy! And she and her partner the happiest!

When Frank Churchill arrived at Hartfield to bid farewell, his dejection was most evident. He sat lost in thought for the first few minutes; and when rousing himself, it was only to say, "Of all horrid things, leaving is the worst."

"But you will come again," said Emma. "This will not be your only visit to Highbury."

"Ah!"—shaking his head—"The uncertainty of when I may be able to return! It will be the object of all my thoughts and cares!" Other than, perhaps, the thought of sinking his fangs into a certain lady's fair neck.

"Our poor ball must be quite given up."

"If I can come again, we are still to have our ball. My father depends on it."

Then he continued, "Such a visit it has been! Every day more precious and more delightful than the day before!"

"I shall venture to ask whether you did not come a little doubtfully at first. Did Highbury not rather surpass your expectations? I am sure we did. I am sure you did not much expect to like us so much."

He laughed rather consciously; and though denying the sentiment, Emma was convinced that it had been so.

"And you must be off this very morning?"

"Yes, I must be off immediately."

"Not five minutes to spare even for your friends Miss Fairfax and Miss Bates? How unlucky!"

"Oh, I have already visited them. I went in for three minutes and was detained by Miss Bates being absent. She was out, and I felt I must wait till she came in. It was better to pay my visit—"

He hesitated, got up, and walked to a window.

"In short," said he, "perhaps, Miss Woodhouse, I think you can hardly be without suspicion—"

He looked at her with his large black eyes, as if able to read her thoughts. She hardly knew what to say. It seemed like the beginning of something absolutely serious, which she did not wish. Forcing herself to speak, therefore, in the hope of avoiding it, she calmly said, "You are quite in the right. It was most natural to pay your visit—"

He was silent. Emma believed he was looking at her—probably reflecting on what she had said. She heard him sigh. It was natural for Frank to sigh if he thought Emma was not encouraging him.

A few awkward moments passed. He sat down again, and in a more determined manner said, "It was something wonderful to feel that all the rest of my time might be given to Hartfield. My regard for Hartfield is most warm—"

He stopped again, arose, and seemed quite embarrassed. He was clearly more in love with Emma than she had supposed; and who can say how it might have ended if Mr. Weston had not appeared just then? Mr. Woodhouse soon followed.

Mr. Weston said, "It is time to go."

And the young man, though he sighed, agreed to leave.

"I shall hear about you all," said he. "Mrs. Weston will correspond with me. She will tell me everything. In her letters I shall be at dear Highbury again."

A very friendly shake of the hand sent a lovely chill through Emma's warm body. A very earnest *goodbye* closed the speech, and the door had soon shut out Frank Churchill.

It was a sad change. They had been meeting almost every day since his arrival. Certainly his being at Randalls had given great spirit to the past two weeks—the expectation of seeing him every morning, the assurance of his attentions, his liveliness, his manners, and his enchanting scent! It had been a very happy fortnight.

Furthermore, he had almost told her that he loved her. Emma could not doubt his having a decidedly warm admiration, a conscious preference for her; and this made her think that she must be a little in love with him, in spite of every previous determination against it.

I certainly must be in love, thought she. I would be the oddest creature in the world if I were not. I shall have many fellow mourners for the ball, though Mr. Knightley will be happy.

Mr. Knightley, however, showed no triumphant happiness. He could not say that he was sorry—his very cheerful look would have contradicted him if he had. But he said, and very steadily, that he was sorry for the disappointment of the others, and with considerable kindness added, "You, Emma, who have so few opportunities of dancing, you are really out of luck."

It was some days before she saw Jane Fairfax, but when they did meet, her mood was unpleasant. She had been unwell, suffering from headaches, which made her aunt declare that, had the ball taken place, she did not think Jane could have attended.

CHAPTER 31

A FTER FRANK CHURCHILL LEFT, Emma was quite certain she was in love. She was very often thinking of him and quite impatient for a letter that she might know how he was, how were his spirits, had he eaten anything lately, how was his aunt, and what was the chance of his coming to Randalls again this spring.

But, on the other hand, she was not unhappy without him. Pleasing as he was, he did have his faults, and whenever she imagined him proposing marriage, she always found herself refusing him. She realised that their affection was always to be limited to friendship.

"I suspect that he is not really necessary to my happiness," said she. "So much the better. I certainly will not persuade myself to feel more than I do. He is undoubtedly very much in love indeed! And when he comes again, I must be on my guard not to encourage it. My mind is quite made up.

"I look not upon him to be quite the sort of man who is steady or constant. His feelings are warm, but his skin is cold, his manner is not so gallant in the heat of battle, and I can imagine him rather changeable. I shall do very well again after a little while—for they say everybody is in love once in their lives, and I shall have been let off easily."

When Frank Churchill's letter arrived at the Westons, Emma read it with pleasure and admiration. *Miss Woodhouse* was mentioned several times, always with affection and gratitude. She was certain of it now—it was the language of real feelings towards her—a compliment to her taste, or a remembrance of what she had said. At the end of the letter were these words: "I had not a spare moment on Tuesday for Miss Woodhouse's beautiful little friend. Pray make my excuses to Miss Harriet Smith."

Emma found that the letter had not added any lasting warmth—that she could still do without Mr. Churchill, and that he must learn to do without her. Her intentions were unchanged.

But Frank's remembrance of Harriet, the *beautiful little friend*, suggested to Emma an idea. Could Harriet replace her in his affections? Was it impossible? No. He had been impressed with the loveliness of her face, the plumpness of her bosom, and the warm simplicity of her manner. For Harriet, it would be advantageous and delightful indeed.

"I must not dwell upon it," said she. "I must not think of it. I know the danger of indulging in such matchmaking. But stranger things have happened."

Emma was glad to have an idea in mind for Harriet's future happiness, for Mr. Elton's wedding day was announced. He would soon be back in Highbury again. Soon, *Mr. Elton and his bride* was on everybody's lips. Emma grew sick at the sound.

Poor Harriet was in a flutter of spirits which required all the soothing and attention that Emma could give. Harriet listened submissively and said, "It is very true—it is not worthwhile to think about Mr. Elton and his bride, and I shall not think about them any longer." But she remained as anxious and restless about the Eltons as before.

At last Emma attacked her on another ground.

"Allowing yourself to be so occupied and so unhappy about Mr. Elton's marrying, Harriet, is the strongest criticism of me trying to match you with him. It was all my doing, I know. I have not forgotten it, I assure you. It will be a painful reflection to me forever. But my being saved from pain is a very secondary consideration. I want you to save yourself from greater pain."

This appeal to Harriet's affections did more than all the rest. "You, who have been the best friend I ever had in my life—I care for nobody as I do for you! Oh! Miss Woodhouse, how ungrateful I have been!"

Such expressions made Emma feel that she had never loved Harriet so well, nor valued her affection so highly before.

Afterwards, Emma said to herself, There is no charm equal to tenderness of heart. Warmth and tenderness of heart with an affectionate, open manner will beat all the clearness of head in the world. I do not have it—but I know how to prize and respect it.

Harriet is my superior in all the charm and all the felicity it gives. Dear Harriet! I would not change you for the clearest-headed, longest-sighted, best-judging female breathing. Oh! The coldness of a Jane Fairfax! Harriet is worth a hundred such. And for a wife, a sensible man's wife, she is invaluable. I mention no names, but happy is the man who changes Emma for Harriet!

CHAPTER 32

THE NEW MRS. ELTON finally arrived in Highbury and was first seen at church. But it would be personal visits to her new home that would settle whether she was very pretty, or only rather pretty, or not pretty at all.

Emma was resolved to be among the first to pay her respects to Mrs. Elton. And she made a point of Harriet's going with her to the vicarage, so the unpleasant business might be taken care of as soon as possible.

Emma could not enter Mr. Elton's house again without remembering all the compliments, riddles, and horrible blunders of three months ago. She knew that poor Harriet would be remembering too—but the young girl behaved very well and was only rather pale and silent.

The visit was of course short; and there was so much embarrassment to shorten it that Emma could not form an opinion of the lady beyond the nothing-meaning term of being *elegantly dressed*.

Emma did not really like Mrs. Elton, however. She would not be in a hurry to find fault, but she suspected that there was no elegance—ease, but not elegance. Her face was not unpretty; but neither feature, nor air, nor voice, nor manner were elegant.

Her face was shockingly pale, like Mr. Elton's, and she had the same mysterious, appealing scent as he. Emma was stunned to see that her eyes were bright red with dark circles under them. Mrs. Elton gave the appearance of having just spent the past several days since her nuptials in the most excruciating pain. Was not the wedding night supposed to be pleasurable?

Moreover, Mrs. Elton seemed to constantly fix her red eyes upon Harriet's fair neck, as if the woman could serve up Harriet for lunch. Granted, Harriet had once been Mrs. Elton's rival for the vicar's affections, but could not bygones be bygones?

As for Mr. Elton, it was an awkward visit. When Emma considered how unlucky poor Mr. Elton was to be in the same room at the same time with the woman he had just married, the woman he had wanted to marry, and the woman whom he had been expected to marry, she must allow him the right to look as uneasy as could be.

Mr. Elton's eyes, too, were the colour of fresh blood. He did seem, however, strangely satiated, as if he had recently consumed his first full meal in quite a long while.

After Emma and Harriet left the house, Harriet said, "Well, Miss Woodhouse, what do you think of her? Is not she very charming?"

There was a little hesitation in Emma's answer. "Oh yes, very! A very pleasing young woman."

"I think her beautiful, quite beautiful."

"Very nicely dressed, indeed; a remarkably elegant red dress—matches her eyes," remarked Emma.

"I am not at all surprised that he should have fallen in love with her."

"Oh, no! There is nothing to surprise one at all. A nice fortune, and she wanted to get married."

"I daresay," returned Harriet, sighing again, "I daresay she was very much attached to him."

"Perhaps, but not every man gets to marry the woman who loves him best. Miss Hawkins perhaps wanted a home and thought this was the best offer she was likely to have."

"Yes," said Harriet earnestly, "well, I wish them happy with all my heart. I do not think I shall mind seeing them again. He is just as wonderful as ever—but being married, you know, it is quite a different thing. No, indeed, Miss Woodhouse, you need not be afraid. I can sit and admire him now without any great misery. She does seem a charming young woman, just what he deserves."

As they strolled along Vicarage Lane on their way back to Highbury, Emma suddenly heard the all-too-familiar rustle of leaves from the tall privet on the edge of the road.

"Harriet, quick, at the ready!" cried Emma.

With amazingly quick precision, borne from hours of practise in the comfort of the drawing room at Hartfield, Emma and Harriet both bent down, reached under their bombazine skirts, and untied their wooden stakes. Harriet, having learnt her lesson well at the Coles', had taken to securing her stake round her calf rather than her thigh. This manoeuvre served to make the stake eminently more accessible, as well as saving precious lengths of expensive yellow silk ribbon.

At the moment when the two vulgar, ragged creatures lunged out of the bushes, snapping and growling, Emma and Harriet were poised, with their wooden stakes raised high in the air.

"How dare you affront two ladies in this manner!" exclaimed Emma as she expertly wielded her weapon, driving it into the heart of the first creature.

"Be gone, hideous monster!" cried Harriet, skilfully piercing the chest of the other. The vampires lay vanquished on the ground.

With calm and confident demeanours, as if they had just finished a game of lawn croquet, Emma and Harriet withdrew their wooden stakes, to be employed yet another day.

∽

Several days later, the Eltons visited Emma and her father at Hartfield. Emma made up her mind to see more and better judge Mrs. Elton. Harriet was not present, and Mr. Woodhouse conversed with Mr. Elton.

Thus, Emma had half an hour of the lady's conversation to herself, time enough to quite convince herself that Mrs. Elton was a vain woman, extremely well satisfied with herself, and thinking too much of her own importance; that she meant to shine and be very superior, but with bold and rude manners, and that she would certainly do Mr. Elton no good.

Harriet would have been a better match for Mr. Elton. If not wise or refined herself, she would have connected Mr. Elton with those who were. But Augusta Hawkins's only connection with society was her sister's rich husband near Bristol.

Indeed, the very first subject after being seated was Mrs. Elton's sister and brother-in-law, Mr. Suckling, and his great house, Maple Grove, and how much it resembled Hartfield.

"Your morning room is the very shape and size of the morning room at Maple Grove, and the staircase very similar as well. I assure you, Miss Woodhouse, it is very delightful to be reminded of a place I am so extremely partial to as Maple Grove. Everybody who sees it is struck by its beauty. And the grounds! People who have extensive grounds themselves are always pleased with anything in the same style."

Emma doubted the truth of this sentiment. People who had extensive grounds themselves cared very little for the extensive grounds of anybody else.

"I suppose you have many parties here every summer, Miss Woodhouse? I love parties, and I stay up all night now."

"No, we are a very quiet set of people, I believe—more disposed to stay at home than engage in schemes of pleasure."

"Ah! There is nothing like staying at home for real comfort. And yet, I am no advocate for entire seclusion. I think when people shut themselves up from society, it is a very bad thing. But I perfectly understand your situation, Miss Woodhouse—your father's state of health must be a great drawback and keep you constantly at home. Why does he not try the healing waters at Bath?"

"My father has tried them more than once, but without receiving any benefit."

"Ah! That is a great pity, for it is so cheerful a place and Mr. Woodhouse's spirits are, I understand, much depressed. Bath would be a charming introduction to society for you, who have lived so secluded a life, and I could immediately introduce you to some of the best people there. A letter from me would bring you a host of new acquaintances."

It was as much as Emma could bear, without being impolite. The idea of Mrs. Elton introducing *her* to society!

Emma restrained herself, however, and only thanked Mrs. Elton coolly—"but their going to Bath was quite out of the question."

And then to prevent further outrage and indignation, Emma changed the subject directly. "I did not ask whether you are musical, Mrs. Elton. Highbury has long heard that you are a superior performer."

"Oh! No, indeed. A superior performer—very far from it! I am passionately fond of music, my friends say I am not entirely devoid of taste, and my hearing is so much more acute now. When Mr. E. was speaking of my future home at the vicarage, the small rooms and such, knowing the luxury I had been accustomed to, I honestly said that the world I could give up—parties, balls, plays—I could do very well without those things. Two carriages were not necessary for my happiness, but I simply could not live without a musical society."

"I trust," said Emma, smiling, "that Mr. Elton has not outstepped the truth."

"No, indeed. I trust we shall have many sweet little concerts together. I think, Miss Woodhouse, you and I must establish a musical club and have regular weekly meetings at your house, or ours, as an inducement to keep me in practise. For married women, you know, there is a sad story against them, in general. They are but too apt to give up music."

Emma had nothing more to say, and after a moment's pause Mrs. Elton chose another subject.

"We have been calling at Randalls," said she, "and very pleasant people the Westons seem to be. I like them extremely. Mr. Weston is quite a first-rate favourite with me already," though from the colour of his pale blue eyes, she thought, we have precious little in common, "and Mrs. Weston appears so motherly and kind-hearted. She was your governess, I think?"

Emma was almost too much astonished to reply; but Mrs. Elton hardly waited for the answer before she went on.

"Considering her former employment, I was rather astonished to find her so very ladylike! But she is really quite the gentlewoman."

"Mrs. Weston's manners," said Emma curtly, "were always particularly good. Their propriety, simplicity, and elegance would make them a model for any young woman."

"And who do you think came in while we were there?"

Emma was quite at a loss. The tone implied some old acquaintance—but how could she possibly guess?

"Knightley!" continued Mrs. Elton. "Knightley himself! Was not it lucky? I had never seen him before, and being so particular a friend of Mr. E.'s, I had a great curiosity. *My friend Knightley* had been so often mentioned that I was really impatient to see him; and I must say that Mr. E. need not be ashamed of his friend. Knightley is quite the gentleman. I felt an immediate kinship with him—I think our tastes are quite similar. I like him very much."

Happily, it was now time for the Eltons to leave. They were off, and Emma could finally breathe.

"Insufferable woman!" was her immediate exclamation. "Worse than I had supposed. Absolutely insufferable! Knightley! Never seen him before in her life and calls him Knightley, and *discovers* that he is a gentleman! A little upstart, vulgar being, with her *Mr. E.* and her airs of pretension and underbred finery.

"And to propose that she and I should form a musical club! As if we were bosom friends! And Mrs. Weston—astonished that the person who had brought me up should be a gentle-woman! Worse and worse. I never met with her equal. Much beyond my hopes. Harriet is disgraced by any comparison!"

"Well, my dear," her father deliberately began, "she seems a very pretty sort of young lady; and I daresay she was very much pleased with you. She speaks a little too quick. I do not like strange voices or red eyes. They quite make me nervous. However, she seems a very obliging, well-behaved young lady and no doubt will make Mr. Elton a very good wife."

Emma was done. Her mind returned to Mrs. Elton's offences, and long, very long, did they occupy her.

CHAPTER 33

EMMA FOUND NO REASON to change her ill opinion of Mrs. Elton. Her observation had been correct. The way Mrs. Elton appeared to Emma at Hartfield—self-important, familiar, presuming, ignorant, cold skinned, and ill bred— was the same way she appeared whenever they met again. And the touch of her hand produced the same annoying, jolting shock as her husband's.

Mrs. Elton had a little beauty and a little accomplishment, but she thought herself coming with superior knowledge of the world to enliven and improve a country neighbourhood.

Mr. Elton seemed not merely happy with his new wife but proud. He had the air of congratulating himself on having brought such a woman to Highbury. And most people in town assumed Mrs. Elton must be as clever and as agreeable as she herself claimed. Emma very politely continued talking about her as being "very pleasant and very elegantly dressed."

Mrs. Elton grew even worse than she had appeared at first—her feelings towards Emma changed. Probably offended that Emma did not return her offers of friendship, she drew back and gradually became much more cold and distant. Mrs. Elton—and Mr. Elton too—became sneering and negligent. When they had nothing else to say, it was always easy to begin by abusing Emma.

And their manners towards Harriet were unpleasant. The venom and lack of heart which they dared not show openly towards Emma found a broader vent in contemptuous treatment of Harriet. And their persistent red-eyed stares at Harriet's fair neck and bosom only increased her discomfort.

But the person to whom Mrs. Elton took a great fancy from the first was Jane Fairfax. And without being asked, she wanted to befriend Miss Fairfax and assist her in finding a governess position.

"Jane Fairfax is absolutely charming. I quite rave about Jane Fairfax. A sweet, interesting creature. So mild and ladylike—and with such extraordinary talents! We must bring her talent forward. She is very timid and silent. One can see that she feels the need of encouragement. I like timidity; in those who are inferior, it is extremely pleasing." I must restrain myself, however, she thought, from certain lusty thoughts about her blood.

"I shall certainly have Jane Fairfax very often to my house, shall introduce her wherever I can, shall have musical parties to draw out her talents, and shall be constantly on the watch for an eligible position for her. My acquaintances are so very extensive that I have little doubt of hearing of something to suit her very shortly."

"Poor Jane Fairfax!" said Emma to herself. "She has not deserved this. She may have done wrong with regard to Mr. Dixon, but this is a punishment beyond what she can have merited—the kindness and protection of Mrs. Elton!"

Emma was not long compelled to listen to Mrs. Elton's tiresome speeches or stare into her cold, unblinking red eyes. Mrs. Elton's dislike for Emma soon appeared, and she was left in peace.

She looked at Mrs. Elton's attentions to Jane Fairfax with some amusement. Emma's only surprise was that Jane accepted those attentions and tolerated Mrs. Elton as she seemed to do.

Emma heard of Jane walking with the Eltons, sitting with the Eltons, spending a day with the Eltons! This was astonishing! She could not believe that the good taste or pride of Miss Fairfax could endure such a friendship as the vicarage had to offer.

To Emma, Jane Fairfax was a riddle. She had planned to be in Highbury for three months while the Campbells were in Ireland. But now the Campbells had decided to stay at least till midsummer and had invited Jane to join them abroad.

According to Miss Bates—it all came from her—Jane's dear friend Mrs. Dixon had written most pressingly. Would Jane go? But still she had declined it!

She must have some motive, more powerful than appears, for refusing this invitation, was Emma's conclusion. There is great fear, great caution, and great resolution somewhere. Somebody is forbidding her to be with the Dixons. But why must she be with the Eltons? Here is quite a puzzle.

Emma could not understand Jane's peculiar friendship with Mrs. Elton. When she wondered aloud to Mrs. Weston and Mr. Knightley, both of whom knew Emma's opinion of Mrs. Elton, Mrs. Weston ventured this apology for Jane: "We cannot suppose that Miss Fairfax has any great enjoyment at the vicarage, my dear Emma, but it is better than being always at home. Her aunt is a good creature, but as a constant companion Miss Bates must be very tiresome."

"You are right, Mrs. Weston," said Mr. Knightley warmly. "If Miss Fairfax could have chosen with whom to associate, she would not have chosen Mrs. Elton. But," with a reproachful smile at Emma, "she receives attentions from Mrs. Elton which nobody else pays her."

With a faint blush, Emma presently replied, "Such attentions as Mrs. Elton's, I should imagine, would disgust rather than gratify Miss Fairfax."

"Another thing must be taken into consideration, too," said Mr. Knightley. "You may be sure that Mrs. Elton is awed by Miss Fairfax's superiority both of mind and manner. Such a woman as Jane Fairfax probably never fell into Mrs. Elton's circle before—and no degree of vanity can prevent her from acknowledging her own comparative inferiority." And, thought he, Jane Fairfax would be the closest Mrs. Elton would ever get to tasty aristocratic blood.

"Mr. Knightley, I know how highly you think of Jane Fairfax," said Emma. Her little nephew Henry was in her thoughts, and a mixture of alarm and delicacy made her unsure what else to say.

"Yes," he replied, as his black eyes glowed, "anybody may know how highly I think of Jane Fairfax."

"And yet, perhaps," said Emma, "you may hardly be aware yourself how highly it is. The extent of your admiration may take you by surprise some day or other."

Emma felt her foot pressed by Mrs. Weston.

In a moment Mr. Knightly replied, "That will never be, however, I can assure you. Miss Fairfax, I daresay, would not have me if I were to ask her—and I am very sure I shall never ask her." Mr. Knightley paused, then said, in a manner which showed him not pleased, "So you have been deciding that I should marry Jane Fairfax?"

"No, indeed I have not," said Emma. "You have scolded me too much for matchmaking for me to presume to take such a liberty with you. What I said just now meant nothing.

Oh, no! Upon my word, I have not the smallest wish for your marrying Jane Fairfax or Jane Anybody."

Mr. Knightley was thoughtful again. The result of his reverie was, "No, Emma, I never had a thought of her in that way, I assure you." And soon afterwards, "Jane Fairfax is a very charming young woman—but not even Jane Fairfax is perfect. She has a fault. She has not the open temper which a man would wish for in a wife, despite her fair white neck and delicate manner."

Emma could not but rejoice to hear that Jane Fairfax had a fault.

"Jane Fairfax has feeling," continued Mr. Knightley. "Her sensibilities, I suspect, are strong and her temper excellent in its power of forbearance, patience, and self-control—but it lacks openness. She is more reserved, I think, than she used to be, and I love an open temper. I converse with Jane Fairfax with admiration and pleasure always—but with no thought beyond."

"Well, Mrs. Weston," said Emma triumphantly after he departed, "what do you now say to Mr. Knightley's marrying Jane Fairfax?"

"Why, really, dear Emma, I say that he is so occupied by the idea of not being in love with her, that I should not be surprised if, in the end, he is in love with her after all."

CHAPTER 34

EVERYBODY IN AND ABOUT Highbury paid great attention to Mr. and Mrs. Elton. Invitations for dinner parties
flowed in so fast that Mrs. Elton had soon the pleasure of
worrying that they were never to have a free day. And since
the Eltons—along with Highbury's other vampires—never
ate, their hosts could entertain quite frugally.

"I see how it is now," said Mrs. Elton. "I see what a life I
am to lead here. We really seem quite the fashion."

But Mrs. Elton was quite a little shocked at the lack of
sophistication in Highbury. Mrs. Bates, Mrs. Perry, Mrs.
Goddard, and others were a good deal behind in knowledge
of the world, but she would soon show them how everything ought to be arranged. In the spring she must return
their invitations with one very superior party.

Emma, in the meanwhile, could not be satisfied without
hosting a dinner of her own for the Eltons at Hartfield. After
she had talked about it for ten minutes, Mr. Woodhouse felt
no unwillingness and only made the usual stipulation of not
sitting at the head of the table himself.

The persons to be invited required little thought. Besides
the Eltons, it must be the Westons and Mr. Knightley;
that made seven, and poor little Harriet must be asked to
make the eighth. But Emma was particularly pleased by
Harriet's wish to stay at home. She would "rather not be in

Mr. Elton's company" more than she could help. She was "not yet quite able to see him and his happy wife together without feeling uncomfortable."

Emma was delighted with the fortitude of her little friend—and she could now invite the very person whom she really wanted to make the eighth, Jane Fairfax. Emma's conscience had bothered her since her last conversation with Mr. Knightley—he had said that Jane Fairfax received attention from Mrs. Elton because nobody else paid any.

"This is very true," Emma said to herself, "and it is very shameful. We are the same age and, always knowing her, I ought to have been more her friend. She will never like me now. I have neglected her too long. But I shall show her greater attention than I have done."

Every invitation was successful and all happily accepted. But then a rather unlucky circumstance occurred. Mr. John Knightley proposed visiting Hartfield for a day and bringing his two eldest little children—the very day of this party.

Mr. Woodhouse considered eight persons at dinner as the utmost that his nerves could bear—John Knightley would be the ninth—and Emma feared that it would be a ninth very much out of humour that her brother-in-law would have to attend a dinner party.

Emma comforted her father by pointing out that John Knightley always said little and ate nothing, so his presence would hardly be noticed. In reality, she dreaded his grave looks, reluctant conversation, and dire predictions of the future.

Then Mr. Weston was unexpectedly summoned out of town, so the party was back to eight. Mr. Woodhouse was now quite at ease.

The day came, the party guests were punctually assembled, and Mrs. Elton was as elegant as lace and pearls could offset the pale skin and dark circles under her red eyes.

Mr. John Knightley seemed devoted to being agreeable. Instead of drawing his brother off to a window while they waited for dinner, he was talking to Miss Fairfax. He had seen her that morning before breakfast as he was returning from a walk with his little boys to the forest to search for raccoons when it had just begun to rain.

John now said to Miss Fairfax, "I trust you did not venture far this morning, or I am sure you must have gotten wet. We scarcely got home in time."

"I went only to the post office," said she, "and reached home before the rain was much. It is my daily errand. I always fetch the letters when I am here. It saves trouble and is something to get me out of the house. A walk before breakfast does me good."

Mr. John Knightley replied, "When you have been my age for as long as I have, you will begin to think that letters are never worth going through the rain for."

Jane Fairfax blushed and then answered, "I cannot expect that simply being older should make me indifferent about letters."

"Letters are no matter of indifference; they are generally a very positive curse."

"You are speaking of letters of business; mine are letters of friendship. You have everybody dearest to you at home. I probably never shall again. And therefore, the hope of a letter of friendship draws me out in the rain." Then another blush, a quivering lip, and a tear in her eye showed her deep feelings.

Her attention was now claimed by Mr. Woodhouse, who according to his custom on such occasions paid his compliments to his guests.

"I am very sorry to hear, Miss Fairfax, of your being out this morning in the rain. Young ladies should take care of themselves. Young ladies are delicate plants. They should take care of their health and their complexion. My dear, did you change your stockings?"

"Yes, sir, I did indeed, and I am very much obliged by your kind interest in me."

By this time, the walk in the rain had reached Mrs. Elton, and her protest now opened upon Jane.

"My dear Jane, what is this I hear? Going to the post office in the rain! This must not be, I assure you. You sad girl, how could you do such a thing?"

Jane very patiently assured her that she had not caught any cold.

"Oh! You do not know how to take care of yourself. To the post office indeed! We shall not allow you to do such a thing again. There must be some arrangement made. I shall speak to Mr. E." She thought a moment, then announced, "The man who fetches our letters every morning will inquire for yours, too, and bring them to you." I myself would love to bring them to you, she thought, along with my appetite.

"You are extremely kind," said Jane, "but I cannot give up my early walk. The post office is a fine destination."

"My dear Jane, say no more about it. The thing is settled."

"Excuse me, Mrs. Elton," said Jane earnestly, "I cannot by any means consent to such an arrangement. The errand is a pleasure to me."

Jane then turned to Mr. John Knightley to change the topic. The varieties of handwriting were talked of; Emma and Mr. George Knightley joined in, and the usual observations were made.

"I have heard it asserted," said John Knightley, "that the same sort of handwriting often prevails in a family. But I should imagine the likeness must be chiefly confined to the females, for boys scramble into any hand they can get."

"I never saw any gentleman's handwriting that was—" Emma began, but stopped, then began again, "Mr. Frank Churchill writes one of the best gentleman's hands I ever saw."

"I do not admire it," said Mr. George Knightley. "It is too small—lacks strength. It is like a woman's writing. And he is quite sloppy, with red blotches spotting the fine parchment."

Emma defended him. "No, it is by no means a large hand but very clear and certainly strong."

"Oh! When a gallant young man like Mr. Frank Churchill," said Mr. George Knightley dryly, "writes to a fair lady like Miss Woodhouse, he will, of course, put forth his best. Just do not ask him to defend you against a vampire attack, for then he will cower like a woman!"

Dinner was on the table, and the guests paraded into the dining parlour, though many intended not to partake of the food.

Jane's insistence about fetching her own letters at the post office had not escaped Emma. She suspected that Jane expected to hear from someone very dear, and indeed that had occurred. Emma thought there was an air of greater happiness than usual in Jane—a glow of both complexion and spirits.

CHAPTER 35

WHEN THE LADIES RETURNED to the drawing room after dinner, the ill-behaved Mrs. Elton ignored Emma and sat with Jane Fairfax. Emma was obliged to sit with Mrs. Weston.

It was impossible for Emma not to overhear Mrs. Elton, in a loud half-whisper, discuss the post office, catching cold, fetching letters, friendship, and a subject which must be equally unpleasant to Jane—inquiries into whether she had yet heard of any governess positions.

"I get anxious about you!" said she. "June will soon be here."

"But I have not made any inquiries; I do not wish to make any yet."

"Oh! My dear, you are not aware of the difficulty of procuring exactly the desirable position. You have not seen so much of the world as I have. You do not know how many candidates there always are for the best situations."

"Colonel and Mrs. Campbell are to be in town again by midsummer," said Jane. "I must spend some time with them; afterwards I may probably begin to inquire. But I would not wish you to take the trouble of making any inquiries at present. When I am quite determined as to the time, there are offices in town where inquiry will soon produce something—offices for the sale, not quite of human flesh, but of human intellect."

"Oh! My dear, human flesh! You quite shock me. If you mean a fling with vampires or the slave trade—"

"I was not thinking of the slave trade and certainly not vampires," replied Jane. "The governess trade, I assure you, was all that I had in mind."

"I know what a modest creature you are," repeated Mrs. Elton, "but you must take up with a family that moves in a certain circle, commanding the elegancies of life."

"As to all that, it is no matter to me whether I associate with the rich. A gentleman's family is all that I should care for."

"But with your superior talents, you have a right to move in the first circle. Your musical knowledge alone would entitle you to name your own terms, mix in the family as much as you choose, and have as many rooms as you like, especially if the little darlings never sleep."

"I am exceedingly obliged to you, Mrs. Elton," said Jane. "However, I am very serious in not wishing anything to be attempted at present for me till the summer. For two or three months longer I shall remain where I am, and as I am."

The whole party was just reassembled in the drawing room when Mr. Weston made his appearance among them. He had just returned from London and had walked to Hartfield to join Mrs. Weston at the party.

John Knightley was in quiet astonishment—that a man who might have spent his evening quietly at home after a day of business in London should walk half a mile to another man's house for the sake of being in mixed company.

Mr. Weston, meanwhile, was happy and cheerful as usual and making himself agreeable among the rest. He gave Mrs. Weston a letter, which he was sure would be highly interesting to everybody in the room. It was from Frank Churchill.

"Read it, read it," said he. "It will give you pleasure. Only a few lines—it will not take you long—just ignore the red blotches. Read it to Emma."

The two ladies looked it over together; and Mr. Weston sat smiling and talking to them the whole time in a voice a little subdued but very audible to everybody.

"Well, Frank is coming, you see—good news! I always told you he would be here again soon, did I not? In town next week. As to his aunt's illness, it is all nothing, of course. It is an excellent thing to have Frank among us again."

Mrs. Weston was most comfortably pleased on the occasion. She was happy; her congratulations were warm and open.

But Emma could not speak so fluently. She was a little occupied in weighing her own feelings and trying to understand the degree of her agitation, which she rather thought was considerable.

It was well that Mr. Weston took everybody's joy for granted, or he might not have noticed that neither Mr. Woodhouse nor Mr. Knightley were particularly delighted.

He then proceeded to tell Miss Fairfax, but she was so deep in conversation with John Knightley that it would have been too rude an interruption; and finding himself close to Mrs. Elton, he necessarily began on the subject with her.

CHAPTER 36

M RS. ELTON," SAID MR. Weston, "I trust I shall soon
have the pleasure of introducing you to my son, Frank
Churchill. He will be in London next week, along with his
aunt and uncle Mr. and Mrs. Churchill."

"Oh yes!" said Mrs. Elton, smiling most graciously, as her
cold, pale hand touched his cold, pale hand. "And I shall be
very happy in his acquaintance."

"I received a letter from him, and it tells us that they are
all coming directly on Mrs. Churchill's account. She has not
been well the whole winter and thinks Enscombe too cold
for her. So they are all moving south to London without loss
of time. Mrs. Churchill is not much in my good graces, as
you may suspect—she is not one of *us*, if you get my drift—
but this is quite between ourselves. She is very fond of Frank,
and therefore I would not speak ill of her. Besides, she is of ill
health now—I would not say this to everybody, Mrs. Elton,
but I have not much faith in Mrs. Churchill's illness."

"Frank was here in February for a visit, was he not?"
asked Mrs. Elton.

"Yes, a mere fortnight. Such a short time." He lowered
his voice. "And no sustenance to be found, besides."

"Well, then," said she, "he will find, in myself, an addition to the society of Highbury when he comes again; but
perhaps he may never have heard of me."

This was too loud a call for a compliment to be passed by, and Mr. Weston with very good grace immediately exclaimed, "My dear madam! Not heard of you! I believe Mrs. Weston's letters lately have been full of very little else than Mrs. Elton."

He had done his duty and could return to discussing his son. "When Frank left us," continued he, "it was quite uncertain when we might see him again, which makes this day's news doubly welcome."

Mrs. Elton began to speak but was stopped by a slight fit of warmth and moved farther away from the fireplace. Mr. Weston instantly seized upon the opportunity to continue.

"I trust you will be pleased with my son; he is generally thought a fine young man, but do not expect a prodigy. Mrs. Weston's partiality for him is very great and, as you may suppose, most gratifying to me. She thinks nobody equal to him. He has black eyes, like Mr. Elton had—before you, of course."

"I assure you, Mr. Weston, I have very little doubt that my opinion will be favourable. I have heard so much in praise of Mr. Frank Churchill. At the same time, it is fair to observe, that I always judge for myself. I am no flatterer."

Mr. Weston was musing. "I trust," said he presently, "that I have not been too severe upon poor Mrs. Churchill. If she is truly ill, I should be sorry to do her injustice; but there are some traits in her character which make it difficult for me to speak of her with the kindness I could wish. She has no pretence of family or blood. She was nobody when Mr. Churchill married her, barely the daughter of a gentlemen, and certainly not the daughter of a vampire; but ever since her being turned into a Churchill she has out-Churchill'd them all in high and mighty claims—but, I assure you, she is an upstart."

"Well, that must be infinitely provoking! I have quite a horror of upstarts. Maple Grove has given me a thorough disgust of people of that sort."

They were interrupted. Tea was carrying round and Mr. Weston, having said all that he wanted, soon took the opportunity of walking away.

After tea, the Westons and Mr. Elton sat down with Mr. Woodhouse to cards. The remaining five were left to their own powers. Mr. George Knightley seemed little disposed for conversation, and Mrs. Elton wanted attention which nobody had inclination to pay.

Mr. John Knightley proved more talkative than his brother. He was leaving early the next day. He said to Emma, "Well, my boys will be visiting Hartfield soon, and all that I can recommend to you is—do not spoil them. Just let them hunt raccoons in the woods and they will be content."

"I rather hope to satisfy both you and Isabella," said Emma, "for I shall do all in my power to make my nephews happy."

"And if you find them troublesome—they hardly sleep a wink—you must send them home again."

"You think that is likely, do you not?"

"I am aware that they may be too noisy for your father. They may even be some encumbrance to you, if your social calendar continues to increase as much as it has done lately."

"Increase!"

"Certainly, you must be aware that the last half-year has made a great difference in your way of life."

"Difference! No, indeed."

"There can be no doubt that you are more engaged with company than you used to be. Witness tonight. Here I visit for only one day, and you are hosting a dinner party! A little while ago, every letter to Isabella brought an account of fresh

gaieties—dinners at Mr. Cole's, or balls at the Crown. It
strikes me, Emma, that Henry and John may be sometimes in
the way. And if they are, I only beg you to send them home."

"No," cried Mr. George Knightley, "that need not be the
answer. Let them be sent to Donwell Abbey. I shall certainly
be free to mind them. For I am occasionally pressed to hunt
raccoon myself, and neither do I sleep."

"Upon my word, Mr. George Knightley," exclaimed
Emma, "you amuse me! You have attended every one of
my *numerous engagements*—and what have they been? Dining
once with the Coles and having a ball talked of which never
took place. And as to my dear little boys, I must say that,
if Aunt Emma has not time for them, I do not think they
would fare much better with Uncle George, who is absent
from home about five hours where she is absent one."

Mr. George Knightley seemed to be trying not to smile
and succeeded without difficulty upon Mrs. Elton's winking
her red eye at him and beginning to talk to him.

The evening ended on a pleasant note, there being no
vampire attack after port was passed round.

"You see?" said Mr. George Knightley to Emma. "I need
not have worn my sabre tonight. My suspicion, I believe,
has been proven. The absence of Miss Harriet Smith, while
depriving us of pleasant company, has assured our dinner
party of a peaceful conclusion."

CHAPTER 37

U PON HEARING THE NEWS of Frank Churchill's arrival
from London, Emma quietly reflected on her emotions
and realised that her feelings for him had faded into nothing.

But if he were returning with the same feelings as when he
left, it would be very distressing. She did not want to have her
own affections entangled again, and it would be incumbent
upon her to avoid any encouragement of his. Yet she could
not escape the feeling that spring would not pass without a
crisis, an event, something to alter her peaceful state.

When at last he arrived at Hartfield for a visit, they met
with the utmost friendliness, but it was clear that Frank was
less in love than he had been. He was in high spirits, as ready
to talk and laugh as ever. But what convinced Emma was his
staying only a quarter of an hour, then in a flash, disappearing
to make other calls in Highbury.

This was the only visit from Frank Churchill in the course
of ten days. He kept intending to come but was always
prevented. His aunt could not bear to have him leave her.
It soon appeared that London was not the place for Mrs.
Churchill. She could not endure its noise. Her nerves were
under continual irritation and suffering.

The Churchills then decided to move immediately
to a furnished house in Richmond, only nine miles from
Highbury, for the months of May and June.

Frank Churchill wrote of the news to the Westons, and Mr. Weston was quite delighted. Now it would be really like having Frank in their neighbourhood. What were nine miles to a young man? An hour's ride—or a couple of minutes' run by a swift vampire such as Frank. He would always be coming over.

One good thing was immediately made certain by the Churchills' move—the ball at the Crown Inn. Every preparation was resumed, and very soon after the Churchills had moved to Richmond, a date for the ball was fixed. A very few tomorrows stood between the young people of Highbury and happiness.

Mr. Woodhouse was resigned. The month of May was better for everything than February. Mrs. Bates was engaged to spend the evening at Hartfield with Mr. Woodhouse during the ball, and he hoped that neither dear little Henry nor dear little John, his grandsons who would be visiting, would have anything the matter with them while dear Emma was gone for the evening.

CHAPTER 38

T HE DAY OF THE ball arrived, and no misfortune occurred to prevent it. Mr. George Knightley, however, had forewarned the gentlemen of Highbury to bring their sabres and wooden stakes to the ball, for Miss Harriet Smith, the vampire magnet, would be in attendance.

Mr. Weston had asked Emma to arrive early to be sure the arrangements were satisfactory. She was to bring Harriet with her, and they arrived just after the Randalls party—the Westons and Frank Churchill.

Frank did not say much, but his black eyes were full of mirth and declared that he meant to have a delightful evening.

They all walked about together to see that everything was as it should be. Within a few minutes, a family of old friends arrived, then a carriage of cousins of the Westons, all of whom had been requested to come early on the same errand of preparatory inspection.

The whole party walked about, and looked, and praised again. Frank was standing by Emma, but there was a restlessness. He was looking about, he was going to the door, he was watching for the sound of other carriages—impatient to begin, or afraid of always being near Emma.

A carriage was heard. Mr. and Mrs. Elton appeared, and all the smiles and politeness disappeared. Emma longed to know what Frank's first opinion of Mrs. Elton might be—how he was affected by the studied elegance of her dress and her smiles of graciousness.

After Frank Churchill was properly introduced to Mrs. Elton and politenesses were exchanged, Mrs. Elton took Mr. Weston aside to gratify him by her opinion of his son, such that Frank could not help but overhear.

"A very fine young man indeed, Mr. Weston. You know I candidly told you I should form my own opinion; and I am happy to say that I am extremely pleased with him. I think him a very handsome young vampire, his complexion pale, his hairstyle modern, his scent appealing, and his manners precisely what I like and approve—so truly the gentleman, without the least conceit or puppyism. You must know I have a vast dislike of puppies—quite a horror of them, as pets or as food. He will certainly turn some young maiden's eyes bright red."

Miss Bates and Miss Fairfax walked into the room, Miss Bates coming in talking with her incessant flow.

"This is brilliant indeed! Excellently contrived, upon my word—so well lighted up! Jane, Jane, look! Did you ever see anything like it? Oh! Mr. Weston, you must really have had Aladdin's lamp. Oh! Mr. Frank Churchill, I must tell you my mother's spectacles have never been in fault since; the rivet never came out again. My mother often talks of your good nature. Does she not, Jane? Do we not often talk of Mr. Frank Churchill? Ah! Here is Miss Woodhouse. Dear Miss Woodhouse, how do you do? This is meeting quite in fairyland! How do you like Jane's hair? She did it all herself. Quite wonderful how she does her hair!"

Frank Churchill returned to his station by Emma; and as soon as Miss Bates was quiet, Emma found herself over-hearing the conversation of Mrs. Elton and Jane Fairfax, who were standing a little way behind her.

After complimenting Jane's dress, Mrs. Elton touched her hand and gave her a shock that nearly sent poor Miss Fairfax reeling.

Mrs. Elton was evidently wanting to be complimented herself, and it was, "How do you like my gown? How do you like my trimming? How is my hair? When everybody's eyes are so much upon me, and since this ball is chiefly to honour me, I would not wish to be inferior. And I see very few pearls in the room except mine."

Then she added, "So Frank Churchill is a wonderful dancer, I understand. We shall see if our dancing styles suit each other. He is a fine young vam—that is to say, a fine young man. I like him very well."

At this moment, Frank began talking so vigorously that Emma could not but imagine he had overheard his own praises and did not want to hear more.

"How do you like Mrs. Elton?" asked Emma in a whisper.

"Not at all," replied Frank. "Where is my father? When are we to begin dancing?"

Frank walked off to find his father but was quickly back again with both Mr. and Mrs. Weston. They were perplexed. It had just occurred to Mrs. Weston that Mrs. Elton must be permitted to dance first, to begin the ball— that she would expect it—which interfered with all their wishes of giving Emma that honour. Emma accepted the sad truth with courage.

"And who will be a proper dancing partner for Mrs. Elton?" asked Mr. Weston. "She will think Frank ought to ask her."

Frank turned instantly to Emma to remind her that she promised him the first two dances. Mr. Weston smiled his approval, until Mrs. Weston decided that her husband should dance with Mrs. Elton. The group finally persuaded him to oblige.

Mr. Weston and Mrs. Elton led the way, and Mr. Frank Churchill and Miss Woodhouse followed. Emma submitted to stand second to Mrs. Elton, though she had always considered the ball as uniquely for her. It was almost enough to make her think of marrying.

In spite of this little insult, however, Emma was smiling with enjoyment, delighted to see a respectable number of couples advance onto the dance floor and to feel that she had so many hours of unusual festivity before her.

Emma was more disturbed by Mr. Knightley's not dancing than by anything else. There he was among the standers-by, when he ought to be dancing. His tall, firm, upright figure— there was not one among the whole row of young male vampires who could be compared with him. Whenever she caught his eye, he smiled. He seemed often to be observing her. She must not flatter herself.

The ball proceeded pleasantly, but Emma noticed that the two last dances before supper had begun, and Harriet had no partner—the only young lady sitting down. She observed Mr. Elton sauntering about. She was sure he would avoid asking Harriet to dance if possible.

As if to show his liberty, Mr. Elton stood directly before Miss Smith and spoke to those near her. Emma could not bear to watch—but then she danced near to Mr. Elton and overheard Mrs. Weston say, "Do not you dance, Mr. Elton?" to which his prompt reply was, "Most readily, Mrs. Weston, if you will dance with me."

"Me! Oh, no! I would get you a better partner than myself. There is a young lady whom I should be very glad to see dancing—Miss Smith."

"Miss Smith! Oh, I had not observed. You are extremely kind, but my dancing days are over, Mrs. Weston. You will excuse me."

Emma thought, could this really be Mr. Elton speaking? The amiable, obliging, gentle Mr. Elton!

She could not look again. Her heart was raging, and she feared her face might be as hot. But another moment later, a happier sight caught her eye—Mr. Knightley leading Harriet to the floor! Never had she been more surprised, seldom more delighted, than at that instant. She was all pleasure and gratitude, both for Harriet and herself.

Mr. Knightley's dancing proved to be just what she had believed it—extremely good; and Harriet was in complete enjoyment and a very high sense of the distinction, which her happy features revealed.

Supper was announced. Frank Churchill escorted Miss Bates and Miss Fairfax down the hallway into the dining room, though he himself had no plans to eat. Miss Bates might be heard from that moment, without interruption, until she was seated at a table and taking up her spoon.

Emma had no opportunity of speaking to Mr. Knightley till after supper; but when they were all in the ballroom again, her eyes invited him irresistibly to come to her and be thanked. He was warm in his disapproval of Mr. Elton's conduct—it had been unpardonable rudeness.

"The Eltons did not offend just Harriet but you as well," said he. "Emma, why is it that they are your enemies?" He looked at her with a knowing smile. "Confess, Emma, that you wanted Mr. Elton to marry Harriet."

"I did," replied Emma, "and they cannot forgive me."

He shook his head; but there was a smile of sympathy with it, and he said only, "I shall not scold you. I leave you to your own reflections."

"I admit to having been completely mistaken in Mr. Elton. There is a littleness about him which you discovered and which I did not—and I was fully convinced of his being in love with Harriet. It was through a series of strange blunders!"

"And, in return for your acknowledging so much, I shall do you the justice to say that Harriet Smith would have been the better wife. She has some first-rate qualities which Mrs. Elton, despite her recent transformation, is totally without."

Emma was extremely gratified. They were interrupted by the bustle of Mr. Weston calling on everybody to begin dancing again.

"Come Miss Woodhouse, Miss Otway, Miss Fairfax, what are you all doing? Come Emma, set your companions the example."

"I am ready to dance," said Emma, "whenever I am asked."

"Whom are you going to dance with?" asked Mr. Knightley.

She hesitated a moment and then replied, "With you, if you will ask me."

"May I?" said he, warmly offering his cold, pale hand.

"Indeed I shall. You have shown that you can dance, and you know that we are not really so much brother and sister as to make it at all improper."

"Brother and sister! No, indeed."

At the conclusion of what was generally deemed one of the highlights of Highbury's social season, the doors of the Crown Inn burst open and the partygoers, numbering in excess of fifty, flooded the street.

The assembled multitude waited patiently as carriages were summoned and began to be brought up.

Mr. George Knightley stood with Emma and Harriet Smith, exchanging final pleasantries, when Mr. Knightley abruptly ceased speaking. His acute hearing had detected a worrisome sound.

"Emma, Miss Smith, I fear danger approaches. Best be at battle ready! I shall gather the other swordsmen!"

Instantly, and without the slightest embarrassment, Emma and Harriet pawed through their petticoats to retrieve their wooden stakes—each young lady carried two weapons this night, one on each leg.

"Weston! Cole! Churchill! Elton! Cox!" exclaimed Mr. Knightley. "Arm yourselves!"

The unexpected, terrifying announcement produced screams of fright from the ladies. They instinctively huddled together for protection.

"I shall protect the ladies!" announced Mr. Elton. "I shall shield them with my holy body!"

"Very well," returned Mr. Knightley, "I should not expect a man of God to take up the sword."

"I shall help Mr. Elton!" squealed Frank Churchill, cowering among the ladies.

"Churchill!" thundered Mr. Knightley. "We need your sabre! No room for cowardice tonight!"

"I am no coward, sir, and if you persist in challenging my honour, I shall have no choice but to meet you on the morrow with duelling pistols!"

"Nonsense, you snivelling little mamma's boy. Go stand with the ladies, then!"

With no further warning or opportunity for preparation, a horde of more than twenty vulgar, ragged vampires surged forth from the bushes behind the Crown Inn. Their drooling fangs bared, their claws outstretched, they converged upon the horrified crowd of tasty aristocrats.

Mr. Knightley and his sabre-armed band of gentlemen, in what had become almost instinctive behaviour, began lopping off the heads of the creatures as they hurtled towards the crowd full of ladies and unarmed male guests.

Heads fell left and right, torsos collapsed on the ground, and blood spilled and gushed everywhere.

The ladies screamed at the horrific massacre, with Miss Bates and Mrs. Elton screaming the loudest, as Frank Churchill and Mr. Elton spread their arms out and formed a buffer between the night monsters and their intended victims.

Emma and Harriet Smith, both wielding wooden stakes in each hand, valiantly plunged their weapons into the hearts of one vampire after another.

Within minutes, it was over. The street was a river of blood, severed heads, and stabbed torsos.

The crowd became subdued, with only whimpers and soft cries emanating from the ladies.

Exhausted and covered with blood, the gentlemen swordsmen and Emma and Harriet surveyed the carnage to ensure that all the vampires were indeed dead.

Miss Bates was the first to speak, and speak she did. "Oh! Mr. Knightley, what a brave and gallant soldier you are! Is he not, Jane? Oh! Such devastation! Did you ever see anything like it? I must tell my mother about this. Oh! Mr. Frank Churchill and Vicar Elton, risking your very lives to protect us fair ladies! Jane, were not Mr. Weston and Cole and Cox the most courageous warriors in Highbury history! And Miss Woodhouse and Miss Smith! To have rescued our fairyland ball from this menace! Oh! So much blood! Jane, what has happened to your hair?"

CHAPTER 39

THE NEXT MORNING, WHILE walking about the lawn at Hartfield, one of Emma's most agreeable recollections of the ball, besides her part in the victorious battle with the hideous vampires, was her conversation with Mr. Knightley. She was extremely glad that his opinion of the Eltons was so much in concert with hers; and his praise of Harriet was gratifying.

She hoped that Mr. Elton's rudeness would cure Harriet of her infatuation with him. It seemed as if Harriet's eyes were suddenly opened, and she was able to see that Mr. Elton was not the superior creature she had believed him.

Harriet was thinking rationally, Frank Churchill was not too much in love with Emma, and Mr. Knightley did not want to argue with her—how very happy a summer lay ahead!

Suddenly, the great iron gate of Hartfield opened, and through it passed two people whom Emma had never expected to see together—Frank Churchill with Harriet leaning on his arm!

A moment later, as Emma watched them approach the house, she realised that something extraordinary had happened. Harriet's skin was as pale as Frank's—certainly they had not eloped! But no, she looked frightened, and he was trying to cheer her.

Soon, all three were in the hall, and Harriet immediately sat down in a chair and fainted. A young lady who faints must be recovered—questions must be answered and surprises explained. Soon Emma learned the whole story.

Miss Smith and Miss Bickerton, another boarder at Mrs. Goddard's, who had been also at the ball, had taken a walk together that morning on the Richmond road. About half a mile beyond Highbury, it became deeply shaded and isolated, when the young ladies suddenly came upon a band of wild vampires.

Miss Bickerton, excessively frightened, gave a great scream and, calling on Harriet to follow her, ran up a steep bank and took a shortcut back to Highbury. But poor Harriet could not follow. She had suffered a cramp after dancing and could not make it up the bank to escape. And her cramp prevented her from bending down to retrieve her trusty wooden stake!

Harriet was attacked by half a dozen vampires, who would have devoured Harriet had it not been for the silver cross about her neck which kept them momentarily at bay.

By a most fortunate chance, Frank Churchill had decided to walk from Richmond to Highbury on the same road. He came upon the scene and found Harriet, trembling, and the vampires hovering around her.

He came to her assistance at this critical moment. He had that very morning most fortunately decided to begin carrying his sabre, after having been accused by Mr. Knightley of being a coward at the Crown Inn.

Frank Churchill's superior fencing skills left several assailants headless, and the rest of the vampires retreated hastily to the dense woods.

Harriet, eagerly clinging to him and hardly able to speak, had just strength enough to reach Hartfield before her spirits were quite overcome.

Frank could not stay any longer than to see Harriet well. Emma gave him assurance that she would see Harriet safely back to Mrs. Goddard's. And so, he was gone in a flash of light, with all the grateful blessings that Emma could utter for her friend and herself.

At that moment, Emma's opinion of Mr. Frank Churchill turned to utmost admiration. He was no coward indeed! She must inform Mr. Knightley forthwith!

Such an adventure as this—a fine young man and a lovely young woman thrown together in such a way, Emma thought—could hardly fail to suggest certain ideas. Such a match would help Frank forget about his infatuation with Emma, and Harriet to forget about Mr. Elton!

Everything was to take its natural course, however. Emma would not stir a step, nor drop a hint. No, she had had enough of interference. There could be no harm in a scheme, a mere passive scheme. It was no more than a wish. Beyond it she would on no account proceed.

Emma's first resolution was to keep her father from knowledge of what had happened to Harriet, aware of the anxiety and alarm it would cause—but she soon realised that secrecy would be impossible. Within half an hour it was known all over Highbury.

It was the very event to engage those who talked most, and all the youth and servants in Highbury were soon chatting about the frightful news. Last night's ball became lost in the new vampire attack on Harriet Smith and her gallant rescue by Mr. Frank Churchill.

Poor Mr. Woodhouse trembled as he sat and, as Emma had foreseen, would scarcely be satisfied without her promising never to go beyond the shrubbery again. It was some comfort to him that many inquiries after himself and

Miss Woodhouse, as well as Miss Smith, were coming in during the rest of the day.

The story soon faded out, except to Emma and her nephews. In her imagination it maintained its ground, and Henry and John were still asking every day for the story of Harriet and the vampires and still correcting Emma if she varied in the slightest detail from the original story.

The great benefit, of course, that accrued from the vicious attack was this: The secret hiding place of the wild, vagrant vampires was now revealed. Mr. Knightley immediately began formulating a plan to organise the Vampire Killers of Highbury to wipe out the nest of creatures forever.

CHAPTER 40

A FEW DAYS AFTER this adventure, Harriet came one morning to Emma with a small parcel in her hand and, after sitting down and hesitating, thus began: "Miss Woodhouse, I have something that I should like to tell you—a sort of confession to make—and then it will be over."

Emma was a good deal surprised but begged her to speak. There was a seriousness in Harriet's manner which prepared Emma, quite as much as Harriet's words, for something more than ordinary.

"It is my duty and my wish," continued Harriet, "to tell you that I am happily a changed person, and you should have the satisfaction of knowing it. I am so much ashamed. I can see nothing at all extraordinary in Mr. Elton now. I do not envy his wife in the least—I neither admire her nor envy her. She is very charming, I daresay, but I think she is a shock to one's system and very ill-tempered and disagreeable.

"However, I assure you, Miss Woodhouse, I wish her no evil. No, let them be ever so happy together, to gaze into each other's red eyes in the darkened rooms of the vicarage. And to convince you that I have been speaking the truth, I am now going to destroy what I ought never to have kept. And it is my particular wish to do it in your presence, that you may see how rational I have become. Can you not guess what this parcel holds?"

"Not the least in the world. Did Mr. Elton ever give you anything?"

"No, I cannot call them gifts, but they are things that I have valued very much."

Harriet held the parcel towards her, and Emma read the words *Most Precious Treasures* on the top. Her curiosity was greatly excited.

Harriet unfolded the parcel and Emma looked on with impatience. Within an abundance of pale pink paper was a pretty little inlaid wooden box, which Harriet opened. It was well lined with the softest cotton, but besides the cotton, Emma saw only a small piece of bandage.

"Now," said Harriet, "surely you must remember."

"No, indeed I do not."

"Dear me! I should not have thought it possible you could forget what happened in this very room! It was a few days before I had my sore throat. Do you not remember Mr. Elton's cutting his finger with your new penknife and your recommending a bandage? But, as you had none, I took mine out and cut him a piece; but it was too large, and he cut it smaller, and gave the rest back to me. And then, in my nonsense, I could not help making a treasure of it and looked at it now and then as a great treat."

"My dearest Harriet!" cried Emma, putting her hand before her face and jumping up. "You make me more ashamed of myself than I can bear. I remember it all now—all except your saving this relic. Well," she said, sitting down again, "go on—what else?"

"Here," resumed Harriet, turning to her box again. "Here is something still more valuable, because this is what really did once belong to him."

Emma was quite eager to see this superior treasure. But— it was the end of an old pencil, the part without any lead.

"This was really his," said Harriet. "Do you not remember? One morning, Mr. Elton wanted to make a memorandum in his pocket-book; but when he took out his pencil, there was so little lead that he soon cut it all away, so you lent him another, and this was left upon the table. But I kept my eye on it; and as soon as I dared, took it and never parted with it again from that moment."

"I do remember it," cried Emma. "I perfectly remember it. Well, go on."

"Oh! That's all. I have nothing more to show you or to say except that I am now going to throw them both in the fire, and I wish you to see me do it."

"My poor dear Harriet! And have you actually found happiness in treasuring these things?"

"Yes, simpleton that I was! But I am quite ashamed of it now and wish I could forget as easily as I can burn them. It was very wrong of me, you know, to keep any remembrances after he was married."

As she tossed them in the fire, she said, "There it goes, and there is an end, thank heaven, of Mr. Elton."

And when, thought Emma, will there be a beginning of Mr. Churchill?

About two weeks later, in the course of some trivial chat, Emma advised Harriet that "whenever you marry I would advise you to do so and so" and thought no more of it.

After a minute's silence Harriet said in a very serious tone, "I shall never marry."

Emma then looked up and replied, "Never marry! This is a new resolution."

"It is one that I shall never change, however. I shall devote my life to killing vampires with my wooden stake."

"My dear Harriet, I applaud your noble resolution. And thanks to you, the secret hiding place of the wild, vagrant vampires is now known to us. Mr. Knightley has informed me that he is devising a scheme to invade their nest and vanquish them forever! You will certainly be called upon to assist in this valiant quest."

"Oh, indeed, Miss Woodhouse! I should be honoured to contribute both my wooden stakes to the effort!"

After short hesitation, Emma said, "I trust this decision of yours never to marry is not a result of Mr. Elton?"

"Mr. Elton indeed!" cried Harriet indignantly. "Oh no! So superior to Mr. Elton!"

Emma then took a longer time for consideration. Should she proceed no further? Should she let it pass and seem to suspect nothing? She believed it would be wiser for her to say it. She was decided and thus spoke: "Harriet, does your resolution of never marrying result from an idea that the person whom you might prefer would be too greatly your superior in society to consider you?"

"Oh, yes! Miss Woodhouse, believe me, I would never expect him even to look at me a second time! But it is a pleasure for me to admire him at a distance—and to think of his infinite superiority to all the rest of the world, with the gratitude, wonder, and veneration that I have towards him. His skin is pale and his eyes are ebony like Mr. Elton, but he is so far superior!"

Emma was sure that Harriet was speaking of Frank Churchill. "I am not at all surprised at you, Harriet. The service he rendered you was enough to warm your heart."

"Service! Oh, the very recollection of it and all that I felt at the time—when I saw him coming, his noble look, and my wretchedness before. Such a change! In one moment such a change! From perfect misery to perfect happiness!"

"It is very natural. It is natural, and it is honourable, to fall in love with such a gentleman. But perhaps it will be wise to check your feelings while you can—do not let them carry you far, unless you are persuaded of his liking you. Be observant of him. Let his behaviour be your guide. Remember, we were very wrong before; we shall be cautious now. He is your superior, no doubt, and there do seem serious obstacles. However, such a match is not without hope."

Harriet kissed her hand in silent gratitude. Emma was very decided in thinking that such a romance would be a good thing. It would improve and refine her little friend.

CHAPTER 41

M R. KNIGHTLEY, WHO HAD taken an early dislike to Frank Churchill, was only growing to dislike him more, despite his heroic effort in saving Harriet Smith's life. He began to suspect Frank of a double-cross in his pursuit of Emma. It certainly appeared that Frank was courting Emma. Everything pointed to it—Frank's own attentions, Mr. Weston's hints, and Mrs. Weston's guarded silence.

But, while so many were matching Frank Churchill with Emma, and Emma herself matching Frank with Harriet, Mr. Knightley began to suspect Frank's affections leaning towards Jane Fairfax. There were knowing glances between them which, having once observed, he could not persuade himself were wrong. And then, of course, there was Jane's fair white neck—and Frank's black eyes revealed he was in dire need of fresh blood.

The suspicion first arose when Mr. Knightley was dining with the Westons, and he had seen more than a single look from Frank Churchill at Miss Fairfax which seemed somewhat out of place. When he was again in their company, he could not help observing something of a private understanding between Frank and the young lady.

Mr. Knightley's strongest proof of his suspicion came one day at the end of a walk, which included a large group— Emma and Harriet, Mr. and Mrs. Weston and their son

Frank Churchill, and Miss Bates and her niece Jane Fairfax. Upon reaching the gates of Hartfield, Emma pressed them all to come in and drink tea with Mr. Woodhouse. They all agreed to it immediately.

As they were turning onto the grounds of Hartfield, Mr. Perry passed by on horseback and greeted the group as he rode on.

Frank Churchill said to Mrs. Weston, "What became of Mr. Perry's plan to buy a carriage?"

Mrs. Weston looked surprised, and said, "I did not know that he ever had any such plan."

"But I heard it from you. You wrote me word of it three months ago."

"Me? Impossible!"

"Indeed you did. I remember it perfectly. You mentioned that Mrs. Perry was extremely happy about it because Mr. Perry being out in bad weather did him a great deal of harm. You must remember it now."

"Upon my word, I never heard of it till this moment."

"Really, never? Bless me! Then I must have dreamed it—but I was completely persuaded."

Emma was out of hearing distance. She had hurried on to the house ahead of her guests to prepare her father for their arrival.

"Why, to tell the truth," cried Miss Bates, "I remember that Mrs. Perry herself mentioned it to my mother—but it was quite a secret, known to nobody else. Jane, do you not remember Grandmamma's telling us of it?"

They were entering the hall. Mr. Knightley noticed that Frank Churchill glanced towards Jane's face with a suppressed laugh. But she was behind Mr. Weston and could not see Frank. Mr. Knightley continued to watch the young vampire as he tried to catch Jane's eye, but she looked away. It occurred to Mr. Knightley that perhaps Frank Churchill learned of the new carriage through a secret letter from Jane Fairfax.

There was no time for further remark or explanation. Mr. Knightley took his seat with the rest of the group round the large modern circular table which Emma had introduced at Hartfield. Tea passed pleasantly, and nobody seemed in a hurry to leave.

"Miss Woodhouse," said Frank Churchill, after examining a table behind him, "have your nephews taken away their box of alphabet letters? It used to sit here. We had great amusement with those letters one morning. I want to puzzle you again."

Emma was pleased with the thought and, producing the box, the table was quickly scattered over with alphabets. Emma and Frank were rapidly forming words for each other or for anybody else who wanted to be puzzled.

Frank Churchill placed a word, with the letters scrambled, before Miss Fairfax. She gave a slight glance round the table and applied herself to unscrambling it. Jane figured out the word created by Frank and, with a faint smile, pushed it away.

Harriet, eager to play, took the word aside and tried to solve it. She was sitting by Mr. Knightley and turned to him for help. The word was *blunder*, and as Harriet excitedly announced it, there was a blush on Jane's cheek which gave it a meaning not clear to the others.

Mr. Knightley connected it to the carriage story. He feared there must be some decided involvement between Frank Churchill and Miss Fairfax. These letters were chosen to conceal a deeper game on Frank Churchill's part.

With great indignation, Mr. Knightley continued to observe Frank Churchill. He saw Frank prepare a short word for Emma, given to her with a sly look. He saw that Emma soon made it out and found it highly entertaining, though it was something which she judged improper, for she said, "Nonsense! For shame!"

Mr. Knightley heard Frank Churchill say, with a glance towards Jane, "Shall I give it to her?" and heard Emma objecting with laughing warmth. "No, no, you must not; you will not, indeed."

It was done, however. This gallant young vampire, who seemed to love without feeling, directly handed over the word to Miss Fairfax and asked her to look at it.

Mr. Knightley, excessively curious to know what this word might be, darted his eye towards it, and he saw it was *Dixon*. Jane Fairfax was evidently displeased. She looked up and seeing herself watched blushed more deeply than he had ever perceived her, and saying only, "I did not know that proper names were allowed" angrily pushed away the letters and turned towards her aunt.

"Yes, very true, my dear," cried Miss Bates, having seen the word herself. "I was just going to say the same thing. It is time for us to be going indeed. We really must wish you good night."

Jane immediately stood up to leave, and the group dispersed, ending the evening.

Mr. Knightley remained at Hartfield after all the rest, his thoughts full of what he had seen. He felt that he must, as a friend, give Emma a hint of this. He could not see her in a situation of such danger without trying to help her. It was his duty.

"Pray, Emma," said he, "may I ask what was the great amusement of the last word given to you and Miss Fairfax? I saw the word, and I am curious to know how it could be so very entertaining to you and so very distressing to Miss Fairfax."

Emma was extremely confused. She could not give him the true explanation. "Oh!" she cried in evident embarrassment. "It all meant nothing—a mere joke among ourselves."

"The joke," he replied gravely, "seemed confined to you and Mr. Churchill."

He had hoped she would speak again, but she did not. She would rather busy herself about anything than speak.

Mr. Knightley sat a little while in doubt. At last he said, with earnest kindness, "My dear Emma, do you think you understand the level of friendship between the gentleman and lady we have been speaking of?"

"Between Mr. Frank Churchill and Miss Fairfax? Oh, yes! Perfectly. Why do you ask?"

"Have you ever had reason to think that he admired her, or that she admired him?"

"Never, never!" she cried with a most open eagerness. "Never did such an idea occur to me. And how could it possibly come into your head?"

"I have lately imagined that I saw signs of attachment between them—certain private, expressive looks."

"Oh! You amuse me excessively. I am delighted to find that you let your imagination wander. But there is no admiration between them, I do assure you. They are as far from any attachment from one another as any two beings in the world can be."

She spoke with a confidence which silenced Mr. Knightley. She wanted to hear the particulars of his suspicions, every look described, and all the where's and how's, but his feelings were too much irritated for talking. He soon took a hasty leave and walked home to the coolness and solitude of Donwell Abbey.

CHAPTER 42

Mrs. Elton was quite anxious to take an excursion; she settled on a visit to Box Hill country park. Emma and Mr. Weston had also been planning a trip there—Emma had never been, and she wished to see what everybody found so well worth seeing.

Emma and Mr. Weston had agreed to invite two or three more to join them, and it was to be done in a quiet, unpretending, elegant way, infinitely superior to the bustle, preparation, and picnic parade of the Eltons.

Emma was surprised, then, and felt a little displeasure, on hearing from Mr. Weston that he had invited the Eltons to join their group and that Mrs. Elton had very readily accepted.

Mr. Weston had to be aware of Emma's very great dislike of Mrs. Elton, but since Emma did not want to offend Mrs. Weston, she found herself obliged to consent to the arrangement.

"I am glad you approve of what I have done," said Mr. Weston very comfortably. "But I thought you would. And Mrs. Elton is a good-natured woman after all. One could not leave her out."

Emma denied none of it aloud and agreed to none of it in private.

It was now the middle of June and the weather fine. Mrs. Elton was growing impatient to name the day and settle with

Mr. Weston as to pigeon pies and cold lamb for those mortals in the group who required food.

But then the Eltons' carriage horse became lame and threw everything into sad uncertainty. It might be weeks before the horse was usable, and so preparations could not be continued.

"Is this not most annoying, Knightley?" she cried. "These delays and disappointments are quite odious. What are we to do?"

"You could explore Donwell Abbey," replied Mr. Knightley. "That may be done without horses. The mortals may eat my strawberries. They are ripening fast. And besides, it would present a convenient opportunity to gather all our friends about us and organise a definitive attack to rid Highbury of the secret nest of wild, vagrant vampires.

"Oh! I should like it of all things!" said Mrs. Elton.

Donwell Abbey was famous for its strawberry patches, but for a lady who just wanted to go somewhere—anywhere—cabbage patches would have been enough to tempt Mrs. Elton.

"You may depend upon me," said she. "I certainly will come. Name your day and I shall come. You will allow me to bring Jane Fairfax?"

"I cannot name a day," said he, "till I have spoken to the others whom I would wish to attend."

"Oh! Leave all that to me. Give me a carte blanche. I am Lady Patroness, you know. It is my party. I shall bring friends with me."

"I trust you will bring Mr. Elton," said he, "but I shall give out all the other invitations."

"Oh! Now you are looking very sly. It is my party. Leave it all to me. I shall invite your guests."

"No," he calmly replied, "there is but one woman in the world whom I would ever allow to invite whatever guests she pleases to Donwell, and that one is—"

"Mrs. Weston, I suppose," interrupted Mrs. Elton, rather mortified.

"No, it is Mrs. Knightley. And until she exists, I shall manage such matters myself."

"Ah! You are an odd creature, even for a vampire!" she cried. "You are quite the humourist. Well, I shall bring Jane and her aunt with me—the rest I leave to you."

Mr. Knightley was fortunate in everybody's most ready acceptance, for a universal desire permeated the society of Highbury to consume strawberries and plan the final vampire battle. Mr. Weston promised to get Frank over to join them. Mr. Knightley was disappointed but said he should be glad to see Frank.

Meanwhile, the lame horse recovered so fast that the excursion to Box Hill was now possible. It was agreed that Donwell would be attended one day and Box Hill the next, providing the weather appeared exactly right.

It was so long since Emma had been at Donwell Abbey that she was eager to refresh her memory. The house was larger than Hartfield, rambling and irregular, with many comfortable and handsome rooms. Its ample gardens stretched down to meadows washed by a stream.

Rich pastures, the orchard in bloom—Emma felt an increasing respect for it, as the residence of a family of such true gentility. She had pleasant feelings about the Abbey, and she walked about and indulged them till it was necessary to join the others round the strawberry beds.

The whole party was assembled, except Frank Churchill, who was expected any moment from Richmond. Mrs. Elton, in her large bonnet and basket, was very ready to lead the way in gathering and accepting strawberries.

Afterwards, seats were found in the shade to escape the heat. Mr. Knightley proposed his plan of action for the vampire raid; all were invited to contribute their various thoughts on the matter; and within a short time, a consensus was reached as to the specific date of the attack and the strategy with which to implement it.

Afterwards, as the group engaged in small conversations, Emma was able to overhear what Mrs. Elton and Jane Fairfax were talking of.

Mrs. Elton had received word that morning of a most desirable governess position for Jane and was in raptures. It was with an acquaintance of Mrs. Elton's in Maple Grove.

The situation was delightful, charming, superior, everything—and Mrs. Elton was wild to have Jane accept the offer immediately. Miss Fairfax continued to assure her that she would not at present engage in anything.

Still, Mrs. Elton insisted on being authorised to write an acceptance letter by tomorrow. At last, it was more than Jane could bear. She proposed a walk. "Would Mr. Knightley show them the gardens—all the gardens?"

During this walk, Emma noticed Mr. Knightley and Harriet strolling apart from the rest of the party, quietly leading the way. Mr. Knightley and Harriet! It was an odd sight, but Emma was glad to see it. There had been a time when Mr. Knightley would have scorned Harriet as a companion. Now they seemed in pleasant conversation, perhaps finding a common bond in vampire slaying.

Next they all went into the house to eat, and they were all seated and busy, but still Frank Churchill did not come. Mrs. Weston looked and looked in vain. Frank had assured them he would come.

The meal was over, the food half-eaten, and the party went outside to see the Abbey fishponds. Mr. Woodhouse chose to stay inside, and Emma remained with him.

Emma walked into the hall, when suddenly Jane Fairfax appeared, coming in quickly from the garden with a look of escape about her.

Startled at seeing Emma, Jane said, "Will you be so kind to tell everyone that I am gone home? I am going this moment. I have said nothing about it to anybody. It would only be giving trouble and distress."

"Certainly, if you wish—but you are not going to walk to Highbury alone, are you?"

"Yes—what should hurt me? I walk fast. I shall be at home in twenty minutes."

"But it is too far, indeed it is, to be walking quite alone. And with all the danger lurking about. Let me order the carriage. It can be round in five minutes."

"Thank you, but no, Miss Woodhouse. The greatest kindness you can show me would be to let me have my own way and only mention that I am gone when it becomes necessary."

"Have you any silver on your person, Jane, to ward off an attacker?"

"Why yes, I am wearing my charm bracelet."

Emma had not another word to oppose. She watched Jane safely off with the zeal of a friend. Jane's parting look was grateful, and her parting words were, "Oh! Miss Woodhouse, the comfort of being sometimes alone!" Emma thought they seemed to burst from an overcharged heart.

Jane had not been gone a quarter of an hour when Frank Churchill entered the room. Emma had not been thinking of him—she had forgotten to think of him—but she was very glad to see him.

He had been detained by a nervous seizure in his aunt. The heat was excessive; he almost wished he had stayed at home, and he sat down in a foul mood.

"You will soon be cooler if you sit still," said Emma.

"As soon as I am cooler I shall go back home again. I felt I had to come—it was expected of me! But I should not have come! Madness in such weather, absolute madness!"

Emma listened, looked, and recommended his taking some refreshment to calm his anger.

"No, there is only one thing I should desire to drink right now, but you would not oblige me, I am sure!" and he stalked off.

Emma thought to herself, "I am glad I am done being in love with him. I should not like a man who is so soon discomposed by a hot morning. Harriet's sweet, easy temper will not mind it."

He was gone long enough to have cooled down, coming back with good manners. He was not in his best spirits but seemed trying to improve them.

"As soon as my aunt gets well I shall go to Switzerland and escape this dreadful heat," said he. "I shall never be calm till I have seen some of those places."

"You will never go to Switzerland. Your uncle and aunt will never allow you to leave England."

"I ought to travel. I am tired of doing nothing. I want a change. I am serious, Miss Woodhouse. Whatever your penetrating eyes may fancy, I am sick of England and would leave it tomorrow if I could."

"You are merely sick of prosperity and comfort. Cannot you invent a few hardships for yourself and be contented to stay?"

"You are quite mistaken. I do not look upon myself as either prosperous or comfortable. I do not consider myself at all a fortunate person. Look at these black eyes. If only you knew what I require to satisfy them!"

"We are going to Box Hill tomorrow—join us. It is not Switzerland, but it will be something for a young man so much in want of a change."

"No, certainly not."

The rest of the party was now returning and all were soon collected. With some, there was great joy at the sight of Frank Churchill; others, not so. But there was distress and disturbance upon Miss Fairfax's disappearance being explained.

Then it was time for everybody to go and with a final arrangement for the next day's excursion and satisfaction that they had conceived a viable plan to rid the countryside of vampires, they parted.

Frank Churchill's last words to Emma were "Well, if you wish me to go to Box Hill, I shall."

She smiled her acceptance.

CHAPTER 43

THEY HAD A VERY fine day for Box Hill. Everybody had
a burst of excitement on first arriving, but later there
was a lack of good spirits and they separated too much into
groups. The Eltons walked together, Mr. Knightley took
charge of Miss Bates and Jane Fairfax, and Emma and Harriet
belonged to Frank Churchill.

The two whole hours spent on the hill was downright
dullness to Emma. She had never seen Frank Churchill so
silent and stupid. He said nothing worth hearing and listened
without knowing what she said. While he was so dull, it was
no wonder that Harriet should be dull likewise, and they
were both insufferable.

When they all sat down together, Mr. Knightley attempted
to review details of the anticipated moonlight raid on the wild
vampires' nest. But on this particularly unpleasant outing, he
could elicit no interest whatsoever.

Frank Churchill grew talkative and merry, paying excessive attention to Emma. She, in turn, became merry and
encouraging as well, though her attention to him meant
nothing more than friendship.

Frank Churchill became very excitable. "Our companions are excessively dull and stupid," he said to Emma.
"What shall we do to rouse them? Any nonsense will
serve."

He announced to the group, "Ladies and gentlemen, I am ordered by Miss Woodhouse to say that she desires to know what you are all thinking of."

Some laughed and answered good-humouredly. Mr. Knightley's answer was the most distinct.

"Is Miss Woodhouse sure that she would like to hear what we are all thinking of?"

"Oh! No, no," cried Emma, laughing as carelessly as she could. "It is the very last thing I would want. There are one or two, perhaps," glancing at Mr. Weston and Harriet, "whose thoughts I might not be afraid of knowing."

"It will not do," whispered Frank to Emma. "They are most of them affronted. Ladies and gentlemen, I am ordered by Miss Woodhouse to say that she only requires something very entertaining from each of you—either one thing very clever, or two things moderately clever, or three things very dull indeed."

"Oh! Very well," exclaimed Miss Bates. "Three things very dull indeed. That will be easy for me, you know. I shall be sure to say three dull things as soon as ever I open my mouth."

Emma could not resist. "Ah! Ma'am, but that may be difficult. You are limited to only three at once!"

Miss Bates did not immediately catch her meaning; but then, a slight blush showed that it pained her.

"Yes, I see what she means, and I shall try to hold my tongue. I must be very disagreeable, or she would not have said such a thing to an old friend."

"Allow me to try," cried Mr. Weston. "I shall make a puzzle. What two letters of the alphabet express perfection?"

"I am sure I do not know," said Frank Churchill.

"Ah! And I am sure you will never guess. I shall tell you. M and A. Emma. Do you understand?"

Emma found a great deal to laugh at and enjoy in it, and so did Frank and Harriet. But it did not seem to touch the rest of the party equally.

"Oh! For myself, I must be excused," said Mrs. Elton, offended. "I am not at all fond of this sort of thing. I have nothing clever to say."

"Yes, yes," added her husband, with a sort of sneer. "I have nothing to say that can entertain Miss Woodhouse. Shall we walk, Augusta?" They stormed off.

"Happy couple!" said Frank Churchill, as soon as they were out of hearing. "How well they suit one another! A marriage of blood and money, to be sure! Very lucky, marrying as they did, upon an acquaintance formed only a few weeks. How many a man has committed himself on a short acquaintance and regretted it all the rest of his life!" At least, he thought, Mr. Elton got a night's sustenance from it.

Miss Fairfax, who had seldom spoken before, spoke now. "Such things do occur, undoubtedly. But it can be only weak, indecisive characters who will suffer such an unfortunate acquaintance forever."

"Well," replied Frank Churchill, "I have so little confidence in my own judgement that, whenever I marry, I hope somebody will choose my wife for me. Will you, Emma? I am sure I should like anybody chosen by you."

"Very well," said Emma. "I undertake the commission. You will have a charming wife. She must be very lively and have hazel eyes. She will go abroad for a couple of years for more education then return to be your wife." The very creature she was describing was Harriet.

"Shall we depart now?" said Jane to her aunt.

"With all my heart," said Miss Bates. "I am quite ready."

The group stood up, and Emma relished the prospect of a quiet drive home to close the very questionable enjoyments of this day. Such another excursion, composed of so many ill-assorted people, she hoped never to be talked into again.

While waiting for the carriage, Emma found Mr. Knightley by her side. He looked around, as if to see that no one was near, and then said, "Emma, I must once more speak to you as I used to. How could you be so unfeeling to Miss Bates? How could you be so insolent to a woman of her character, age, and inferior class? Emma, I had not thought it possible."

Emma blushed and was sorry but tried to laugh it off. "Nay, how could I help saying what I did? It was not so very bad. I daresay she did not understand me."

His ebony eyes grew darker. "I assure you, she did. She felt your full meaning."

"Oh!" cried Emma. "I know there is not a better creature in the world than Miss Bates. But you must allow that what is good and what is ridiculous are most unfortunately blended in her."

"They are blended," said he, "I acknowledge. And were she a woman of fortune, I would not quarrel with you for any liberties of manner. But Emma, consider that she is poor; she has sunk from the comforts she was born to. It was badly done, indeed! You, whom she has known from an infant, in thoughtless pride, to laugh at her, humble her in front of many others. This is not pleasant for you, Emma, but I must tell you the truth while I can, proving myself your friend by very faithful counsel."

While they talked, they were advancing towards the carriage. Emma had not been able to speak and, upon entering the carriage, sunk back for a moment, overcome—her face averted from him, full of anger against herself, mortification, and deep concern.

She was vexed beyond what could have been expressed, almost beyond what she could conceal. Never had she felt so agitated or grieved by any circumstance in her life. The truth there was no denying. She felt it in her heart.

How could she have been so brutal, so cruel to Miss Bates! How could she have exposed herself to such ill opinion in Mr. Knightley—a person she so highly valued!

Time did not ease her pain. As she reflected more, she seemed but to feel it more. She never had been so depressed. Happily it was not necessary to speak—there was only Harriet there with her in the carriage, who seemed not in good spirits herself and very willing to be silent.

Emma felt the tears running down her cheeks almost all the way home, without trying to control them, extraordinary as they were.

CHAPTER 44

THE WRETCHEDNESS OF THE trip to Box Hill was in Emma's thoughts all the evening. How it might be considered by the rest of the party, she could not tell. But in her view it was a morning more to be detested than any she had ever spent.

An evening of backgammon with her father was happiness for her. There, indeed, lay real pleasure. As a daughter, she hoped she was not without a heart.

With Miss Bates, she had often been remiss, her conscience told her so—scornful and ungracious. But it should be so no more. In the warmth of true remorse, she would call upon Miss Bates the very next morning, and it should be the beginning of a regular, kindly intercourse.

❧

The next morning Emma went early, that nothing might prevent her. At the Bateses' door, she heard a good deal of moving and talking.

She heard Miss Bates's voice; then the maid, looking frightened and awkward, ushered Emma in, just as Miss Bates and Jane Fairfax rushed into the next room. Emma had a glimpse of Jane, who looked extremely ill.

The poor old grandmother Mrs. Bates, civil and humble as usual, looked as if she did not quite understand what was going on.

"I am afraid Jane is not very well, Miss Woodhouse," said she.

Emma had a moment's fear that Miss Bates might avoid her, but soon she came into the room. Miss Bates had not the usual cheerful look. But after Emma inquired about Jane, Miss Bates's manner changed immediately.

"Ah! Miss Woodhouse, how kind you are to ask! Jane has accepted a governess position. She has a dreadful headache just now, for tears were in her eyes perpetually, she is so distraught. Though she is amazingly fortunate, she is as low as possible. You will please excuse her—she will be sorry to have missed you."

Emma was most sincerely interested. Her heart had been growing kinder towards Jane, whose present suffering left Emma nothing but pity. She spoke as she felt, with earnest regret and concern.

"So very kind!" replied Miss Bates. "But you are always kind."

"Where, may I ask, is Miss Fairfax going?"

"To a Mrs. Smallridge, a charming woman, most superior, to have the charge of her three little girls, delightful children. Jane will be only four miles from Maple Grove."

"Mrs. Elton, I suppose, has been the person to whom Miss Fairfax owes—"

"Yes, our good Mrs. Elton. She would not let Jane say *no*, for when Jane first heard of it, she was quite decided against accepting the offer. Then yesterday evening it was all settled that Jane should go. Quite a surprise to me! I had not the least idea! Jane took Mrs. Elton aside, and after the shock of touching her hand subsided told her that upon thinking over the advantages of Mrs. Smallridge's offer, she had come to the resolution of accepting it."

"And when is Miss Fairfax to leave you?"

"Very soon, very soon, indeed—that's the worst of it. Within a fortnight. Mrs. Smallridge is in a great hurry."

"Her friends will all be sorry to lose her."

"Yes," said Miss Bates, "and she had no time even to tell Frank Churchill, who was called away last night to return to Richmond. It would seem his aunt has taken quite ill again."

"I am so sorry, Miss Bates," said Emma with sincerity. "I do have the pleasure to inform you, however, that Mr. Knightley has organised an effort to rid our lovely village of the hideous vampire menace."

"Oh, Miss Woodhouse! How kind of you to let me know. That will be a blessing indeed."

Emma's thoughts then drifted back to Frank's aunt and her illness, reflecting on the contrast between Mrs. Churchill's importance in the world and Jane Fairfax's—one was everything, the other nothing—and she sat musing on the difference of women's destinies, quite unaware that her eyes were staring at the pianoforte, until Miss Bates spoke again.

"Aye, I see what you are thinking of, the pianoforte— what is to become of that? Poor dear Jane was talking of it just now, how much she would miss it. To this day, I do not believe she knows whether it was Mr. Campbell's present or his daughter's."

Now Emma began to think of the pianoforte, and the remembrance of all her former unfair guessing about Mr. Dixon was so displeasing to her that Emma decided her visit had been long enough; and, repeating all the good wishes which she really felt, took leave.

CHAPTER 45

UPON ENTERING THE PARLOUR at Hartfield, Emma found that Mr. Knightley and Harriet had arrived during her absence and were sitting with her father.

Mr. Knightley immediately got up and, in a manner decidedly graver than usual, said, "I would not go away without seeing you, but I have no time to spare, and therefore must now be gone directly. I am going to London to spend a few days with John and Isabella, to review the plans for our final vampire battle, and to attempt to enlist my brother's assistance in our effort."

Emma was sure he had not forgiven her. He looked unlike himself, as if he had not slept all night. However, she thought, time would tell him that they ought to be friends again. While he stood, as if meaning to go, but not going, her father began his inquiries.

"Well, my dear, and did you get there safely? Mr. Knightley, dear Emma has been to call on Miss Bates and Miss Fairfax."

Emma blushed and looked at Mr. Knightley. There was an instantaneous change in his expression towards her—a smile of regard. She was warmly gratified and, in another moment, Mr. Knightley took her fingers in his pale hand, pressed them, and was about to bring them to his lips, his onyx eyes gazing into hers, when he suddenly let go of her hand.

The intention, however, was unmistakable. Emma thought it so gallant and dignified a gesture of perfect friendship. He left them immediately afterwards—gone in a flash.

Emma wished she had returned ten minutes earlier. It would have been a great pleasure to talk over Jane Fairfax's situation with Mr. Knightley. They parted thorough friends, however; his gallantry assured Emma that she had fully recovered his good opinion.

Emma shared the news about Jane Fairfax with her father. "I am very glad, my dear, to hear she is to be so comfortably settled. I trust that her health will be taken good care of."

The following day brought news from Richmond to throw everything else into the background. News arrived at the Westons to announce the death of Mrs. Churchill! A sudden seizure had carried her off after a short struggle. The great Mrs. Churchill was no more.

Everybody had a degree of gravity and sorrow—tenderness towards the departed, sympathy for the surviving friends, and, in a reasonable time, curiosity to know where she would be buried.

Mrs. Churchill, after being disliked at least twenty-five years, was now spoken of with compassionate allowances. "Poor Mrs. Churchill! No doubt she had been suffering a great deal more than anybody had ever supposed."

Emma considered how it would affect Frank Churchill. He would now be free, she thought. Now, an attachment to Harriet Smith would have nothing to stop it. All that remained was that Frank should form the attachment, which Emma could feel no certainty of happening.

It was a more pressing concern for Emma to show attention to Jane Fairfax. The person whom Emma had spent so many months neglecting was now the very one on whom she wanted to lavish regard and sympathy.

Emma invited Jane to spend a day at Hartfield. A note was written, but the invitation was refused by a verbal message: "Miss Fairfax was not well enough to write."

Mr. Perry called at Hartfield the same morning to report that Miss Fairfax was suffering severe headaches, a nervous fever, appetite gone—and she had not even yet been bitten by a vampire—and he doubted that she could go to Mrs. Smallridge's on the appointed date. He felt that Jane's being confined to one room at Miss Bates's house was harmful.

Emma, eager to be useful, wrote Miss Fairfax again to propose taking her out into the fresh air for an hour or two.

Jane's answer was only in this short note: "Miss Fairfax's compliments and thanks, but is quite unable to have any exercise."

Nonetheless, Emma drove the carriage to Miss Bates's house in the hope that Jane would be induced to join her—but it would not do. Miss Bates came to the carriage door, all gratitude, to say that Jane could not be persuaded.

"Indeed," said Miss Bates, "the truth is that poor dear Jane cannot bear to see anybody at all—except Mrs. Elton, Mrs. Cole, and Mrs. Perry. She has not eaten anything at all."

Emma, on reaching home, speedily dispatched some superior quality herbs to Miss Fairfax with a most friendly note.

In half an hour the gift was returned, with a thousand thanks from Miss Bates, but "dear Jane did not want anything."

When Emma afterwards heard that Jane Fairfax had been seen wandering about the meadows, on the very day which she had refused to go with Emma in the carriage, she concluded that Jane was resolved to receive no kindness from Emma.

Emma was sorry, very sorry. Her heart was grieved that she was valued so little by Jane as a friend. But she had the consolation of knowing that her intentions were good, and if Mr. Knightley had known of Emma's attempts to assist Miss Fairfax, he would not have found anything to criticise.

CHAPTER 46

ONE MORNING, ABOUT TEN days after Mrs. Churchill's decease, Mr. Weston came to Hartfield and wanted particularly to speak with Emma.

He met her at the parlour door, and in a low voice said, "Can you come to Randalls this morning? Mrs. Weston must see you."

"Is she unwell?"

"No, no, not at all, but she must see you alone—can you come?"

"Certainly. It is impossible to refuse what you ask in such a way." To guess what all this meant was impossible even for Emma. Something really important seemed announced by his looks.

They hurried on, and were speedily at Randalls.

"Well, my dear," said Mr. Weston to his wife, as they entered the room, "I have brought Emma. I shall leave you together."

Mrs. Weston was looking so ill that Emma's uneasiness increased.

She eagerly said, "What is it, my dear friend?"

Mrs. Weston said, "Frank Churchill has been here this very morning on a most extraordinary errand. It is impossible to express our surprise. He came to speak to his father on a subject—to announce an attachment—" She stopped to breathe.

Emma thought first of herself and then of Harriet.

"More than an attachment, indeed," resumed Mrs. Weston. "An engagement of marriage. What will you say, Emma, what will anybody say, when it is known that Frank Churchill and Miss Fairfax are engaged—nay, that they have long been engaged!"

Emma jumped with surprise and, horror-struck, exclaimed, "Jane Fairfax! Good God! You are not serious! You do not mean it!"

"It is so," returned Mrs. Weston, still averting her eyes. "There has been a solemn engagement between them ever since October, formed at the Weymouth resort and kept a secret from everybody. Not a creature knowing it but themselves—neither the Campbells, nor her family, nor his."

Emma scarcely heard what was said. Her mind was divided between two ideas—her own former conversations with him about Miss Fairfax and poor Harriet.

"Engaged to her all winter, before either of them came to Highbury?"

"It has hurt me, Emma, very much. It has hurt his father equally. Some part of his conduct we cannot excuse."

Emma pondered a moment and then replied, "Please let me assure you that, in the early part of our acquaintance, I did like him and I was very much disposed to be attached to him. Fortunately, however, it did cease. I have really for some time, for at least three months, cared nothing about him. You may believe me, Mrs. Weston. This is the simple truth."

Mrs. Weston kissed her with tears of joy.

"Mr. Weston will be much relieved," said she. "It was our wish that you might be attached to each other, and we were persuaded that it was so. Imagine what we have been feeling on your account."

"I must say, Mrs. Weston, that I think he bears great blame. What right had he to come among us with such affection and attention while he really belonged to another? It was very wrong, indeed."

"Now, dear Emma, I must defend him. For though he has been wrong in this instance, I have known him long enough to answer for his having many, very many, good qualities, and—"

"Good God!" cried Emma. "Jane has accepted a position as governess. How could he allow her to accept the position?"

"He knew nothing about it, Emma. When he learned of it, he decided to come forward and reveal his secret engagement."

Emma began to listen better.

"I am to hear from him soon," continued Mrs. Weston. "Do not let us be in a hurry to condemn him. Now that I know, I am sincerely anxious for all turning out well. They must both have suffered a great deal under such secrecy."

"His sufferings," replied Emma dryly, "do not appear to have done him much harm. Well, how did his uncle Mr. Churchill take it?"

"Most favourably for his nephew—he gave his consent with hardly any difficulty. Scarcely are Mrs. Churchill's remains at rest in the family vault than her husband acts exactly opposite to what she would have wished. What a blessing it is when influence does not survive the grave!"

"Well," said Emma, "I suppose we shall gradually grow reconciled to the idea, and I wish them very happy. But here have we been the whole winter and spring completely duped."

At this moment, Mr. Weston appeared at a little distance from the window. His wife invited him in and, while he was coming round, she added, "Now, dearest Emma, let me beg you to say you are satisfied with the match. Let us make the best of it. Frank is very fortunate to be engaged to a girl of such steadiness of character and good judgement." And, she might have added, she will turn Frank's eyes from black to red, and Jane Fairfax will be none the paler for it.

Emma met Mr. Weston upon his entrance with a smiling face, exclaiming, "I congratulate you, Mr. Weston, with all my heart, on the prospect of having one of the most lovely and accomplished young women in England for your daughter."

A glance between Mr. Weston and his wife convinced him that all was as right as this speech proclaimed, and its happy effect on his spirits was immediate. He became perfectly reconciled, thinking it the very best thing that Frank could possibly have done.

Mr. Weston then said, "I have met recently with Mr. Knightley, and I believe we are close to finalising our plan to rid Highbury of the wretched creatures in our midst. Dear Emma, we value your friendship and wooden stake immensely!"

CHAPTER 47

HARRIET, POOR HARRIET!" THOUGHT Emma, with the tormenting ideas she could not get rid of. Frank Churchill had behaved very ill towards Emma, but poor Harriet! To be a second time the dupe of Emma's misconceptions and flattery. Mr. Knightley had spoken prophetically when he once said, "Emma, you have been no friend to Harriet Smith."

Emma knew she had been responsible for having encouraged Harriet's feelings towards Frank Churchill. Common sense would have directed her to tell Harriet not to think of him. She was extremely angry with herself. Thank goodness she was angry with Frank Churchill too, or it would all have been too dreadful.

As for Jane Fairfax, Emma need no longer be unhappy about Jane. Her days of insignificance were over. She would soon be well and happy and prosperous and, unbeknownst to her, have red eyes to match Mrs. Elton's and no need to sleep or eat ever again.

Emma now imagined why Jane had slighted her. No doubt it had been from jealousy. In Jane's eyes, Emma had been a rival.

But poor Harriet! Emma was sadly fearful that this second disappointment would be more severe than the first. She must communicate the painful news, however, and as soon as possible. Emma had promised Mr. Weston to keep it secret. But Harriet must be told—it was Emma's superior duty.

Emma's heartbeat quickened on hearing Harriet's footsteps at the front door.

"Well, Miss Woodhouse!" cried Harriet, coming eagerly into the hall. "Is this not the oddest news that ever was?"

"What news do you mean?" replied Emma, unable to guess whether Harriet could indeed have received any hint.

"About Jane Fairfax. Did you ever hear anything so strange? Oh! You need not be afraid of telling me, for Mr. Weston has told me himself. I met him just now. He told me it was to be a great secret and I should not mention it to anybody but you, but he said you already knew it."

Harriet's behaviour was so extremely odd that Emma did not know how to understand it. She seemed to show no concern or disappointment in the discovery of Frank's engagement. Emma looked at her, quite unable to speak.

"Had you any idea," cried Harriet, "of his being in love with Miss Fairfax?"

"Can you seriously ask me, Harriet, whether I imagined him attached to another woman at the very time that I was encouraging *your* feelings towards him?"

"Me!" cried Harriet, blushing and astonished. "I never cared about Mr. Frank Churchill!"

"I am delighted to hear you say that," replied Emma. "But then, who did you give me to understand that you cared about, if it wasn't Frank Churchill?"

Emma could not speak another word. Her voice was lost and she sat down in great terror, waiting till Harriet should answer.

Harriet, who was standing at some distance, with her face turned from Emma, said, "I should not have thought it possible that you could have misunderstood me! But considering how infinitely superior he is to everybody else, I trust I have better taste than to think of Mr. Frank Churchill! If you had not told me that more wonderful things could happen, that there had been matches of greater disparity—those were your very words—I should not have dared to give way to my feelings for—Mr. Knightley!"

"My dear Harriet!" exclaimed Emma. "I perfectly remember what I said! I told you that I did not wonder at your affection, considering the service he had rendered you."

"Oh dear," cried Harriet, "you thought I was referring to Mr. Churchill saving me from the vampires! It was not the vampires—it was not Mr. Frank Churchill that I meant. No! I was thinking of something much more precious—of Mr. Knightley asking me to dance at the ball, which made me feel how superior he was to every other man upon the earth."

"Good God!" cried Emma. "This has been a most unfortunate mistake!"

She paused, and then asked tentatively, "Has Mr. Knightley returned your affection?"

"Yes," replied Harriet modestly but not fearfully, "I must say that he has."

Emma's eyes were instantly withdrawn, and she sat silently meditating for a few minutes, making herself acquainted with her own heart.

She admitted—she acknowledged—the whole truth. It darted through Emma with the speed of an arrow—Mr. Knightley must marry no one but herself!

Harriet had been conscious of a difference in Mr. Knightley's behaviour ever since those two decisive dances. Emma knew that he had found her much superior to his expectation. Harriet had noticed his talking to her much more than he used to and his having a different manner

towards her—a manner of kindness and sweetness, gazing
with his black eyes at her plumpness.

Lately, Harriet had been more aware of it. When they all
had walked together, he had so often come and walked by
her and talked so very delightfully! He seemed to want to be
acquainted with her. Emma knew it was very much the case.
She had often observed the change.

Harriet repeated to Emma how Mr. Knightley had praised
Miss Smith for being without affectation, for having simple,
honest, generous feelings, and for her spectacular valour in
the midst of recent vampire attacks. Emma knew that he saw
such recommendations in Harriet; he had mentioned them
to her more than once.

Emma herself had twice witnessed Mr. Knightley's attentions towards her young friend. First, when he walked with
Harriet apart from the others on the outing at Donwell
Abbey, and he had talked to her in a more particular way
than he had ever done before.

The second instance was the morning Emma returned
from visiting Miss Bates and Miss Fairfax. Mr. Knightley sat
talking with Harriet nearly half an hour before Emma had
returned to Hartfield.

Harriet now appealed to her dear Miss Woodhouse for
reassurance concerning Mr. Knightley.

"I could never have hoped for it if you had not encouraged me. Now I feel that I may deserve him and that if he
does choose me, it will be so very wonderful!"

The many bitter feelings felt by Emma made it necessary for her to reply, "Harriet, I shall only venture to declare
that Mr. Knightley is the last man in the world who would
intentionally give any woman the idea of his feeling for her
more than he really does."

Harriet seemed ready to worship her friend for such an encouraging reply, but the sound of Mr. Woodhouse's footsteps coming through the hall caused Harriet great agitation. She could not compose herself, and so she slipped through another door and was gone from the house.

The moment Harriet was gone, Emma's feelings burst out spontaneously. "Oh God! I wish I had never seen her!"

The rest of the day and the following night, Emma was bewildered by the confusion of all her thoughts. How to understand it all!

To thoroughly understand her own heart was the first effort. How long had Mr. Knightley been so dear to her? When had he replaced Frank Churchill in her affection? She then realised that she had always considered Mr. Knightley superior to every other man in her circle.

How arrogant she was to arrange everybody's romances. She was proven to have been completely mistaken with everyone, and she had brought evil on Harriet, on herself, and, she feared, on Mr. Knightley. He would never have known Harriet at all but for Emma.

Oh! If she had only not prevented Harriet from marrying Mr. Robert Martin, who would have made her happy and respectable in the sort of life to which she truly belonged—all would have been safe and none of these dreadful events would have happened!

CHAPTER 48

EMMA HAD NEVER KNOWN how much of her happiness depended on Mr. Knightley, now that she was threatened with losing him. For a very long time she had felt that, since Mr. Knightley was not married, Emma was first in his eyes.

She knew she had not deserved it—she had often been negligent, slighting his advice, wilfully opposing him, and quarrelling with him because he would not agree with her.

But still, he had loved her and watched over her from a little girl, with an endeavour to improve her and an anxiety for her doing right, which no other person had shared. In spite of all her faults, she knew she was dear to him—might she not say, very dear?

And in the heat of battle against the wild vampires—was she not constantly by his side as his partner, to impale the creatures' torsos as Mr. Knightley beheaded them?

Emma had a slight hope that perhaps Harriet was mistaken about Mr. Knightley's affection. For her own sake, Emma must wish that Mr. Knightley remain single all his life. If he never married at all, Emma believed she could be perfectly satisfied. Let him continue to be the same Mr. Knightley who visited Hartfield regularly.

Emma needed some time away from Harriet. She wrote to her friend and kindly asked that she be absent from Hartfield for a few days to avoid discussing one particular subject. Harriet agreed and left Emma in peace.

Mrs. Weston paid a call to Emma at Hartfield to relate that she had just visited with Jane Fairfax. Due to Jane's recent illness, Mrs. Weston suggested a carriage ride to give her some air. Jane apologised for her ungracious behaviour during her illness.

Jane was very much relieved to be able to talk about her engagement and the misery she suffered while keeping it secret for so many months. She told Mrs. Weston she had not had the blessing of a single peaceful hour during that time.

"Poor girl!" said Emma. "She thinks herself wrong, then, for having consented to a secret engagement?"

"No one could blame her more than she is disposed to blame herself," said Mrs. Weston.

"Poor girl!" said Emma again. "She loves Frank Churchill excessively, then, I suppose."

"Yes, I have no doubt of her being extremely attached to him."

"I am afraid," returned Emma, sighing, "that I often contributed to making her unhappy."

"On your side, my love," said Mrs. Weston, "it was very innocently done. Jane spoke of you, Emma, and of the great kindness you had shown her during her illness and, with a blush, asked me to thank you."

"Oh! Mrs. Weston, you are very kind to bring me these kind words. I trust she will be very happy."

"Are you well, my Emma?" was Mrs. Weston's parting question.

"Oh! Perfectly. I am always well, you know."

Mrs. Weston's visit furnished Emma with more reflection on her past injustice towards Jane Fairfax. She bitterly regretted not having sought a closer acquaintance with her, and she blushed for the envious feelings which had certainly been the cause. Had she followed Mr. Knightley's wishes in paying attention to Miss Fairfax, tried to know her better, she would have been spared the pain which pressed on her now.

The evening of this day was very long and melancholy at Hartfield. A cold stormy rain set in, and nothing of July appeared. Emma would like nothing better than a visit from Mr. Knightley to cheer her, but those sorts of visits might shortly be over.

Emma pondered how lonely Hartfield could soon become. Mrs. Weston would soon give birth to a child, keeping her and Mr. Weston away. Frank Churchill and Jane Fairfax would be married and most likely settle at Enscombe.

Add to these losses the absence of Mr. Knightley, and what would remain of cheerful society within her reach? Mr. Knightley to be no longer coming there for his evening comfort! How was it to be endured?

And if he were to be absent because of his marriage to Harriet, Emma's wretchedness would be all the greater, knowing that she had caused it all.

The only consolation that Emma could draw from all this was to resolve that she would conduct herself better, become more rational and more acquainted with herself. And she sincerely hoped that Mr. Knightley and Harriet Smith would both survive the impending final vampire battle to enjoy their happiness together.

CHAPTER 49

T HE WEATHER CLEARED IN the afternoon and glimpses
of sun would soon appear—it was summer again. Emma
resolved to be out of doors as soon as possible. She longed
for the serenity of nature, so she walked through the gardens,
freshening her spirits and relieving her thoughts a little.

Suddenly she saw someone in the distance—Mr. Knightley
passing through the garden door, coming towards her. He had
just returned from London. She quickly collected her thoughts.

Emma exchanged quiet and constrained greetings with
Mr. Knightley. She thought he neither looked nor spoke
cheerfully. He was perhaps preoccupied with the looming
encounter with the vampires. They walked together; he was
silent. She thought he was often looking at her.

Then Emma thought that perhaps he wanted to speak
to her of his attachment to Harriet. She could not bear this
silence; with him it was most unnatural.

She decided to speak and, trying to smile, began, "Now
that you have returned, I have some news that will rather
surprise you."

"If you mean Miss Fairfax and Frank Churchill, I have
already heard. From Mr. Weston."

"You probably have been less surprised than any of us, for
you had your suspicions. I have not forgotten that you once
tried to give me caution. I wish I had attended to it."

For a moment or two, nothing was said, then Mr. Knightley suddenly took her arm with his cold hand and pressed it against his heart. Emma was so surprised that she did not notice the lack of a heartbeat.

In a tone of great sensitivity, he said, "Time, my dearest Emma, will heal your wound."

And in a louder, steadier tone, he concluded with, "Frank Churchill will soon be gone. I am sorry for Miss Fairfax. She deserves a better fate."

Emma quite understood him and, with a flutter of pleasure, excited by such tender consideration, replied, "You are very kind, but you are mistaken, and I must set you right. I never have been at all in love with Mr. Churchill. I was tempted by his attentions and allowed myself to appear pleased. He never wished to attach me. It was merely a trick to conceal his real attachment to Miss Fairfax."

Mr. Knightley, quite relieved, said, "I have never had a high opinion of Frank Churchill. With such a woman as Miss Fairfax, he has a chance to turn out well. I shall certainly wish him well." He will have sustenance at last, he thought.

"I have no doubt of their being happy together," said Emma. "I believe them to be very sincerely in love."

"He is a most fortunate man!" returned Mr. Knightley, with enthusiasm. "So early in life—to be twenty-three forever—and to have drawn such a prize! Frank Churchill is, indeed, favoured by fortune. Everything turns out for his good. His eyes will grow red with pride!"

"You speak as if you envied him."

"And I do envy him, Emma. In one respect he is the object of my envy."

Emma could say no more. They seemed to be within half a sentence of mentioning Harriet, and her immediate feeling was to avert the subject, if possible.

But Mr. Knightley startled her by saying, "You do not ask me why I am envious, Emma. I must tell you what you will not ask, though I may regret it."

"Oh! Then, don't speak it, don't speak it," she eagerly cried. "Take a little time—consider—do not commit yourself."

"Thank you," said he, with deep mortification. Not another syllable followed.

Emma could not bear to give him pain. She was convinced he wished to confide in her about Harriet.

A moment later, Emma changed her mind. He was her friend and she must help him.

"Mr. Knightley, if you wish to ask my opinion of anything—as a friend—I shall hear whatever you like. I shall tell you exactly what I think."

"As a friend!" repeated Mr. Knightley. "Emma, that is a word which—oh, why should I hesitate? I have gone too far already to turn back. Emma, tell me, have I no chance of ever becoming more than a friend?"

He stopped, and the expression of his onyx eyes overpowered her.

"My dearest Emma," said he, "for dearest you will always be, whatever the event of this hour's conversation, my dearest, most beloved Emma, tell me at once. Say *no* if that is your answer to my profession of love for you."

She was unable to utter a single word in her disbelief of what she was hearing.

"You are silent," he cried with great pain, "absolutely silent! At present I ask no more."

Emma was almost ready to sink under the nervousness of this moment, not wanting to be awakened from the happiest dream of her life.

"I cannot make speeches, Emma," he soon resumed in a tone of such sincere tenderness as was tolerably convincing. "If I loved you less, I might be able to talk about it more. But you know what I am. You hear nothing but the truth from me. I have blamed you and lectured you, and you have borne it as no other woman in England would have borne it. Bear with the truths I would tell you now, dearest Emma, as well as you have borne with them. God knows, I have been a very indifferent lover. But you understand me. You understand my feelings of love towards you and will return them if you can. At present, I ask only to hear your voice say that you feel the same towards me."

While he spoke, Emma's mind was most busy and had been able to comprehend the exact truth of the whole—to see that Harriet's hopes had been entirely a mistake; that Harriet was nothing; that Emma was everything; and to rejoice that she had not revealed Harriet's secret to him.

She spoke then.

What did she say?

Just what she ought, of course. A lady always does. She said enough to show that he need not despair and to invite him to say more.

Within half an hour, Mr. Knightley had passed from a thoroughly distressed state of mind to perfect happiness. This same half hour had given to Emma the precious certainty of being beloved, clearing from both of them all jealousy and distrust.

It was his jealousy of Frank Churchill that had taken him to London. But this very morning, when he learned of the engagement, he felt so much love for Emma that he rushed back to Hartfield.

Mr. Knightley had ridden home through the rain to see how this sweetest and best of all creatures, faultless in spite of all her faults, felt about Frank Churchill's engagement. Then, to learn that she had never loved him at all, Mr. Knightley realised that she was his own Emma, by hand and word.

Mr. Knightley extended his cold, pale hand and took hers.

"United in love, my dear Emma," he said gently, "let us together vanquish the evil vampires!"

❧

That evening, under the full illumination of moonlight, the gentlemen of Highbury, accompanied by Emma and Harriet Smith, assembled at the Crown Inn for a ceremonial glass of sherry before they set out on their quest.

Mr. George Knightley raised a toast to their impending victory, joined by Mr. Weston, Cole, Cox, Churchill, and his brother Mr. John Knightley, who had graciously journeyed from London for the occasion. Mr. Elton was absent, having been forbidden by Mrs. Elton to participate in the noble adventure.

All had sharpened their sabres, including Emma, and all wielded wooden stakes as well. Miss Smith, being inept at swordplay, had tied multiple wooden stakes about both calves.

"Onwards to victory!" exclaimed Mr. George Knightley.

"Hear! Hear!" returned the ebullient band of vampire killers.

They set off on foot along the Richmond road and soon left the village of Highbury behind. The warriors walked silently, full of contemplation about the battle soon to be waged.

About half a mile out of the village, the gentle soldiers slowed their pace; the vampires among them employed their acute hearing, listening carefully for telltale signs of the wild vampire nest.

Mr. George Knightley stopped in his tracks and raised his hand. The others halted as well. They were close now. They could hear activity on the other side of a thick hedge.

George Knightley whispered to Emma, "Their attention is diverted. I can hear them feasting on something—or someone. We shall take them by surprise!"

Mr. Weston pointed to an opening in the hedge and whispered loudly, "Here we may gain access!"

"Indeed!" rejoined George Knightley, also whispering. "Ladies and gentlemen! Tally ho! Charge!"

The warriors surged through the opening in the hedge and came upon a clearing. They stopped and gasped in horror!

The scene they beheld filled them with revulsion, dismay, and anger. Fifty wild, ragged vampires were clustered in groups round six young ladies, feasting viciously on their blood. The creatures had, not long before, attacked Mrs. Goddard's boarding school and carried away the fair maidens to their lair!

Shocked and horrified by the wanton bloodlust, the band of society soldiers felt a surge of vengeance, affording them an energy and ferocity heretofore unseen in ladies and gentlemen.

The warriors of Highbury attacked. Emma and the five gentlemen each lunged towards one of the groups of vampires.

With dazzling speed and expert swordsmanship, the warriors hacked and lopped and sliced and whacked. Heads bounded and rolled like lawn bowling pins. Torsos crumpled and collapsed to the ground. Harriet fairly ran from one fallen body to another, a wooden stake in each hand, finishing the vampires off with plunging stabs to the heart.

Within mere minutes, the vampires were vanquished. The scene of devastation was beyond comprehension. Alas, none of the fair young maidens could be saved. All six had been lost.

Emma, Harriet, and the other soldiers were the only souls standing. All the other creatures lay on the ground, dead.

With a heavy heart but a proud sense of victory, Mr. George Knightley announced, "Ladies and gentlemen, we have rid our dear Highbury of the vampire menace!"

Cheers rose up from among the gentle warriors. Though covered with blood, drenched with aristocratic sweat, and drained of all energy, they were relieved and grateful.

Dragging their blood-stained sabres behind them, the soldiers began a retreat back towards the hedge whence they came.

Suddenly, there rose up a chorus of shrieks that echoed through the forest and chilled the spines of the Highbury warriors.

Then, leaping from the dense trees surrounding the clearing, came at least eighty more feral creatures! Snapping and snatching and baring their fangs and claws, they descended upon the noble fighters.

The weary band of warriors turned to face them and began again, lopping off heads and piercing torsos with wooden stakes.

But soon it became apparent that Emma, George, and the others would be overwhelmed.

"I don't think we can hold them!" cried Emma, as her arms became heavy with the weight of her sabre.

"We must, dear Emma! We cannot fail now!" returned her betrothed, though Mr. Knightley's voice betrayed a hint of doom. A sudden horrible thought flashed through his mind—how could he continue to exist through the centuries to come without dear Emma by his side?

All seemed lost. The vicious unnaturals were closing in fast. It would only be a matter of seconds before the Highbury warriors would be defeated.

"Fear not!" exclaimed a woman's voice coming through the hedge. "We are here!"

Mrs. Goddard and her train of fourteen fair young maidens, all wielding sabres and wooden stakes, charged into the clearing.

"Upon my word!" cried Emma.

"Mrs. Goddard!" exclaimed Harriet. "Thank God you're here!"

"Kill the bastards!" shrieked Mrs. Goddard, and the young ladies, seeking vengeance for the terrible fate of their classmates, with untrained, but ferocious swipes of their sabres beheaded one vampire after another until all the creatures were fallen. Then they drove their wooden stakes into the hearts of the monsters, finishing them off.

In a very short time, all was quiet. The victorious band of heroes and heroines breathed a collective sigh of relief and utter exhaustion and slowly made their way back to Highbury.

CHAPTER 50

THAT NIGHT IN BED, Emma had great difficulty falling asleep. Her nerves were still much frayed from the vicious battle, and, with her engagement to Mr. Knightley set, her thoughts now turned to her father and Harriet.

With respect to her father, she knew she could never marry and leave Mr. Woodhouse alone at Hartfield while he was alive. Mr. Knightley must agree to a prolonged engagement.

How to do her best by Harriet was a more difficult decision—how to spare her from any unnecessary pain. She concluded that it would be desirable to ask Isabella to invite Harriet to London for a few weeks. A separation would avert the evil day when Harriet must learn that Mr. Knightley could not belong to her.

Emma rose early and wrote her letter to Harriet—a duty which left her very sad.

But Mr. Knightley arrived at Hartfield to watch Emma eat breakfast, and soon her happiness was restored. They rejoiced for the peace and tranquillity that had already settled upon Highbury after last night's victory as well as the expectation of the joy of a life together.

After he left, Emma received a packet from the Westons. It contained a letter from Frank Churchill which Mrs. Weston had forwarded to Emma.

Emma read the letter slowly and carefully. Frank Churchill began by explaining his actions concerning Jane Fairfax and begging the forgiveness of those actions by Mr. and Mrs. Weston.

His letter continued with a reference to Emma: "With the greatest respect, the warmest friendship, and the deepest humiliation, do I mention Miss Woodhouse. In order to conceal my engagement to Miss Fairfax, I made Miss Woodhouse my object of affection. But I was convinced that she was not attracted to me, and we seemed to understand each other. I believed she already knew of my attachment to Miss Fairfax because she received my attentions with an easy, friendly, good-humoured playfulness. I beg her forgiveness for leading her astray."

He admitted that he had hurt Jane by showing affection towards Emma, and for that he was truly ashamed.

Frank Churchill then revealed that he sent Jane Fairfax the pianoforte anonymously because she would never have accepted the gift if she knew he gave it.

He explained that he and Jane had had a terrible argument the day of the excursion to Donwell Abbey. He stormed off to Richmond, and she accepted the governess position, sending him a letter ending the engagement.

Fearful of losing her, Frank informed his uncle Mr. Churchill of his attachment to Miss Fairfax, secured the old man's blessing, then returned to Highbury. Though Miss Fairfax was quite ill, he made his true feelings of love known to her, and she agreed once more to marry him.

CHAPTER 51

F RANK CHURCHILL'S LETTER TOUCHED Emma's feelings.
She saw his suffering and sorrow and how much in love he
was with Miss Fairfax. Emma could not judge him severely.

She thought so well of the letter that, when Mr. Knightley
came again, she desired him to read it.

"I shall be very glad to look it over," said he. He began to
read, stopping here and there, furrowing his brow, his black
eyes glowing, and saying, "humph!" several times; and Emma
saw from the expression on his face that Mr. Knightley was
silently critical of Frank Churchill.

When he came to the part about Miss Woodhouse, Mr.
Knightley read it aloud—with a smile, a look, a shake of the
head, and a word or two of assent or disapproval or merely
of love, as the subject required. He concluded, however,
seriously and after steady reflection, "Very bad—though it
might have been worse. Playing a most dangerous game;
respecting no one's wishes but his own. His own mind
full of deceit and suspecting it in others. My dear Emma,
his actions prove more and more the beauty of truth and
sincerity in all our dealings with each other. I do, however,
commend him for his valour last evening. He rose considerably in my estimation."

After this, he made some progress reading the letter
without any pause. Frank Churchill's confession of having

behaved shamefully was the first thing to call for more than a word in passing.

"I perfectly agree with you, sir," was his remark. "You did behave very shamefully. You never wrote a truer line."

Emma knew that he was now getting to the Box Hill party and grew uncomfortable. Her own behaviour had been so very improper! She was deeply ashamed and a little afraid of his next look. It was all read, however, without the smallest remark except one momentary glance at her, instantly withdrawn, in the fear of giving her pain.

Mr. Knightley finished the letter. "Well, there is feeling here. He does seem to have suffered. Certainly, I can have no doubt of his being fond of Miss Fairfax. I trust he may long continue to feel the value of such a marriage."

"You do not appear so well satisfied with his letter as I am, but at least I trust you must think the better of him for it."

"Yes, I certainly do. He has had great faults of inconsideration and thoughtlessness, and I think he is likely to be happier than he deserves. But I am ready to believe his character will improve and acquire from hers the steadiness that it needs." He thought to himself that Jane would make a fitting vampiress for Mr. Churchill. Certainly, her pale skin could not grow any paler. But at least her new red eyes would give her some much-needed colour.

Mr. Knightley handed the letter back to Emma then said, "And now, let me talk to you of something else. Ever since I left you this morning, Emma, my mind has been hard at work on one subject."

The subject was in plain, unaffected, gentlemanlike English, such as Mr. Knightley used even to the woman he was in love with—how to ask her to marry him without attacking the happiness of her father.

Emma's answer was ready at the first word: "While my dear father lives, marriage would be impossible for me. I could never leave him."

Mr. Knightley felt just as strongly as Emma about staying with her father. He had been thinking it over most deeply, most intently. He proposed that he should move to Hartfield. As long as her father's happiness required Emma to remain at Hartfield, Mr. Knightley should do likewise.

Emma felt that, in leaving Donwell Abbey, he would sacrifice a great deal of independence. She promised to consider it; but he was fully convinced, and nothing could change his opinion on the subject. The more she thought about his plan of marrying and living at Hartfield, the more pleasing it became.

Emma reflected on poor Harriet. In time, of course, Mr. Knightley would be replaced in her affections. But it would not be as easy as forgetting Mr. Elton—and those thrilling shocks with his every touch. Mr. Knightley was so kind, so feeling, so truly considerate of everybody.

It really was too much to hope, even for Harriet, that she could be in love with more than three men in one year.

CHAPTER 52

EMMA ARRANGED WITH HER sister Isabella to invite Harriet for two weeks to London, on the pretence that Miss Smith needed to see a dentist. Harriet was eager to leave, and Emma was relieved to avoid a meeting with her. And so, Harriet left for London.

Now Emma could enjoy Mr. Knightley's visits. Now she could talk and listen with true happiness, unchecked by that sense of injustice, of guilt, of something most painful which haunted her when she remembered how disappointed Harriet was.

Emma had only one unfinished task—to tell her father about her engagement. But she would not proceed with that just yet. She had decided to delay the news till Mrs. Weston was safe and well after the birth of her child.

She soon decided, both as a duty and a pleasure, to call on Miss Fairfax. She ought to go, and she was longing to see her.

❧

Emma went, still fearful of being unwelcome. But she was met on the stairs by Jane herself, coming eagerly forward. Emma had never seen her look so well, so lovely, and so engaging.

There was animation and warmth; she came forward with an offered hand and said in a very feeling tone, "This is most kind, indeed! Miss Woodhouse, it is impossible for me to express—I trust you will believe—excuse me for being so entirely without words."

Emma was grateful and would have spoken, but she heard the sound of Mrs. Elton's voice from the sitting room. So Emma simply gave Jane a very sincere handshake. Emma wished Mrs. Elton had not been there, but the woman greeted Emma with unusual graciousness, even thanking Emma for her part in ridding Highbury of the wild vampires.

Mrs. Elton folded up a letter she had been reading to Jane. "We can finish this some other time. I only wanted you to know that *Mrs. S.* is not offended that you will not be going. But not a word more!"

Emma smiled to herself because Mrs. Elton was unaware that Emma knew of the governess position that was no more.

Mrs. Elton began to chatter: "Do you not think, Miss Woodhouse, our saucy little friend here is charmingly recovered? Oh! If you had seen her, as I did, when she was at the worst! I have scarcely had the pleasure of seeing you, Miss Woodhouse, since the party to Box Hill—very pleasant party. But yet there seemed a little cloud upon the spirits of some. We should go again—quite the same party."

Soon after this, Miss Bates came in, and Emma was diverted by her rush of words. "Thank you, dear Miss Woodhouse, you are all kindness to visit. Yes, indeed, dearest Jane is charmingly recovered. And thank you, again as well, for your noble vanquishment of the vicious unnaturals that for so long preyed upon our dear little village!"

Mr. Elton then made his appearance. He was hot and tired and, after paying his respects to the ladies and again thanking Emma for her courage in the famous battle, complained about the heat he suffered from his long walk to visit Mr. Knightley.

"When I got to Donwell Abbey," said he, "Knightley could not be found. Very odd! After the note I sent him this morning and the message he returned that he should certainly be at home till one. Such a dreadful broiling morning! Miss Woodhouse, this is not like our friend Knightley! Can you explain it?"

Emma amused herself by complaining that it was very extraordinary, indeed. She had a feeling that Mr. Knightley was waiting for her at Hartfield.

Emma excused herself and was pleased upon leaving to find Jane Fairfax accompanying her downstairs, giving Emma a chance to have some time alone with her.

"Oh! Miss Woodhouse," cried Jane, with a blush, "in view of my awful behaviour towards you, I am pleased you are not disgusted with me. I want to make my sincere apology to you—"

"You owe me no apology," cried Emma warmly, taking her hand.

"You are very kind, but I know what my manners were to you—so cold and artificial! It was a life of deceit! I know that I must have disgusted you."

"Pray say no more. I feel that all the apologies should be on my side. Let us forgive each other at once."

She thought a moment then said, "I would suppose you will be leaving Highbury, just when we are becoming true friends?"

"You are very right. After three months we shall move to Enscombe, where I shall live with my new husband and his uncle."

"How wonderful," said Emma. "I am so happy for you. I am so happy that everything is settled and decided. Goodbye, dear Jane, goodbye."

CHAPTER 53

Mrs. Weston became the mother of a baby vampire girl named Anna, which pleased Emma greatly. Not because she hoped in future years to match the girl with one of Isabella's sons, but because a girl would be a great comfort to Mr. Weston as he grew older. And Mrs. Weston, being such a wonderful teacher, would be an excellent mother.

"Mrs. Weston has had the advantage, you know, of practising on me," said Emma.

"Mrs. Weston," replied Mr. Knightley, "will surely spoil the child even more than she did you."

"Poor child!" cried Emma. "What will become of her?"

"Nothing very bad. She will be disagreeable in infancy and correct herself as she grows older. I am losing all my bitterness against spoiled children, my dearest Emma."

Emma laughed and replied, "But I had your assistance to counteract the indulgence of other people. I doubt whether my own sense would have corrected me without it."

"Do you? I have no doubt. Nature gave you understanding, Miss Taylor gave you principles. My interference was quite as likely to do harm as good. It was very natural for you to feel that it was done in a disagreeable manner. I doted on you, faults and all, because I have been in love with you ever since you were thirteen at least."

"I am sure you were of use to me," cried Emma. "I was very often influenced rightly by you—more often than I would admit at the time. I am very sure you did me good."

"My dear Emma, you have always called me *Mr. Knightley*. It is so very formal. Can you not call me *George* now?"

"Impossible! I can never call you anything but *Mr. Knightley*. I shall promise not to equal Mrs. Elton by calling you *Mr. K.*, and I shall promise—" She added presently, laughing and blushing, "I shall promise to call you *George* only once—at the altar."

Emma was sad that she could not correct the worst of all her follies—her relationship with Harriet. She realised she should have written more often to Harriet while she was in London.

Isabella's letters kept Emma informed about her friend, who had been in low spirits upon first arriving but soon cheered up and found pleasure playing with Isabella's children. Harriet decided to extend her visit to a month, which pleased Emma.

Soon after, Mr. Knightley produced a letter from his brother John, who responded to the news of their engagement.

"John rejoices in my happiness," said Mr. Knightley, "and has a most brotherly affection for you and great admiration of your courage in battle. He hopes that, in time, you will grow worthy of my affection."

"He is a sensible man," replied Emma. "I honour his sincerity. Had he said anything different, I would not have believed him."

Emma turned her thoughts to the duty of informing her father of their engagement. She must speak cheerfully about it and not make it a subject of misery to him.

With all the courage she could command, she prepared Mr. Woodhouse for something strange. Then she said that if his consent and approval could be obtained, since it was a plan to promote the happiness of all, she and Mr. Knightley meant to marry. Hartfield would receive the addition of Mr. Knightley's company whom he loved, next to his daughters and Mrs. Weston, best in the world.

Poor man! At first it was a considerable shock to him, and he tried earnestly to dissuade Emma from it. She was reminded, more than once, of having always said she would never marry. He assured her that it would be a great deal better for her to remain single and spoke of how Isabella and Miss Taylor had left him.

But it would not do. Emma hung about him affectionately and smiled and said it must be so. She pointed out that, with Isabella and Mrs. Weston, their marriages took them from Hartfield, but Emma was not leaving Hartfield. She would be always there, and her father would be a great deal happier for having Mr. Knightley always at hand.

Emma was assisted in her pleadings by Mr. Knightley, Mrs. Weston, and letters from Isabella—assuring him that it would be for his happiness. He began to think that, perhaps in another year or two, it might not be so very bad if the marriage did take place.

The news of the engagement was a surprise wherever it spread. Mr. Weston went to Highbury the next morning and told Jane Fairfax the news. Was she not to become his eldest daughter? He must tell her. And Miss Bates being present, it passed, of course, to Mrs. Cole, Mrs. Perry, and Mrs. Elton immediately afterwards.

In general, it was a very well-approved match, except in one house—the vicarage. Mr. Elton cared little about it. He only hoped that "the young lady's pride would now be contented" and observed that "she had always meant to catch

Knightley if she could" but admitted that "finally Knightley would have the sustenance he desperately lacked."

But Mrs. Elton very much disapproved.

"Poor Knightley! Poor fellow! Sad business for him. I am extremely concerned, for though he is very eccentric, he has a thousand good qualities. How could he be so taken in? No more outings to Donwell—there would be a Mrs. Knightley to throw cold water on everything. Extremely disagreeable! On the other hand, she may become one of us—there may be hope for her, after all!"

CHAPTER 54

TIME PASSED ON, AND soon Harriet would arrive from London. Emma was worried about her return when, one morning, Mr. Knightley came in and said, "I have something to tell you, Emma—some news."

"Good or bad?" said she quickly, looking at him.

"I do not know whether you will call it good or bad. It is news about Harriet Smith."

Emma's cheeks flushed at the name, and she felt afraid of something, though she knew not what.

"Harriet Smith has accepted Robert Martin's proposal of marriage."

Emma gave a start and her eyes, in eager gaze, said, "No, this is impossible!"

"It is so, indeed," continued Mr. Knightley. "I have it from Robert Martin himself. He left me not half an hour ago."

"I cannot believe it! It seems an impossibility!"

Emma could not conceal all her exquisite feelings of delight. "Well now, tell me everything. I never was more surprised, I assure you. How is it possible?"

"It is a very simple story. Mr. Martin went to London on business three days ago, and I asked him to take some papers to John, who invited him to a family party. Mr. Martin could not resist; he found an opportunity to propose to Harriet. She made him, by her acceptance, as happy as he is deserving.

"He returned by yesterday's coach and was with me this morning. I must say that Robert Martin's heart seemed very overflowing," despite the fact, thought he, that it never beat. And his eyes would soon turn from black to bright red, feasting on Harriet's plumpness.

"I am perfectly excited," replied Emma with the brightest smiles, "and most sincerely wish them happy."

"You have changed greatly since we talked on this subject before."

"I hope so—for at that time I was a fool."

"And I am changed also," admitted Mr. Knightley, "for I am now very willing to acknowledge all Harriet's good qualities. You see, some time ago Robert Martin approached me for my advice: Should he risk asking Miss Smith a second time for her hand in marriage? And so I made an effort to get better acquainted with her. I often talked to her a good deal. You must have seen that I did.

"Sometimes, I thought you suspected that I had affections for Harriet, which was never the case. From all my observations, I was convinced of her being an amiable girl, with very good notions, very good principles, and a wicked swing of her wooden stake. Much of this, I have no doubt, she may thank you for."

"Me!" cried Emma, shaking her head. "Ah! Poor Harriet!" She stopped herself, however, and quietly allowed herself a little more praise than she deserved.

Mr. Knightley added, "And I have abandoned my foolish notion that the wild vampires followed Harriet's scent to our parties. The scent they most likely followed was that of tasty aristocratic blood."

Mr. Woodhouse entered the room and began speaking with Mr. Knightley. Emma left them so she could be alone for a while.

Her spirits were dancing and singing—she talked to herself and laughed and reflected. One could only imagine the joy, the gratitude, the exquisite delight of her feelings. With the news of Harriet's engagement, Emma was really in danger of becoming too happy for words.

What had she to wish for now? Nothing more than to grow more worthy of Mr. Knightley, whose intentions and judgement had always been so superior to her own. Nothing, but that the lessons of her past folly might teach her humility and circumspection in the future.

She was very serious in her thankfulness and in her resolutions, and yet there was no preventing a laugh. She must laugh with joy at the resolution of Harriet's situation. Now there would be pleasure in Harriet's returning. It would be a great pleasure to know Mr. Robert Martin.

∝✦⊃

In high spirits, Emma and Mr. Woodhouse visited the Westons. To their surprise, Frank Churchill and Jane Fairfax arrived to pay a visit also.

Emma was extremely glad to see Frank Churchill, but there was some awkwardness on each side. When Mr. Weston brought baby Anna into the room, there was no longer a lack of animation or of courage and opportunity for Frank Churchill to draw Emma aside and say, "I have to thank you, Miss Woodhouse, for a very kind forgiving message in one of Mrs. Weston's letters. I trust time has not made you less willing to pardon. I trust you do not retract what you said."

"No, indeed," cried Emma, most happy to begin, "not in the least. I am particularly glad to see you and shake hands with you and to give you joy in person."

He thanked her with all his heart and continued some time to speak with serious feeling of his gratitude and happiness.

"Jane is looking well, do you not think?" said he, turning his hungry black eyes towards his fiancée.

Then he returned his attention to Emma. "You truly had no idea about our attachment?"

"I never had the smallest idea, I assure you," replied Emma.

"Ah! By the by," he said, "let me offer you my congratulations. I assure you that I have heard the news of your own attachment to Mr. Knightley with the warmest interest and satisfaction."

Emma added, "We are similar in our engagements—we have each found someone so much superior to ourselves."

"True, true," he answered, warmly. Then he added, "No, not true on your side. You can have no superior, but most true on mine. Is Jane not an angel in every gesture? Observe the turn of her throat." My fangs, he thought, can scarcely wait until our nuptial night.

"Very beautiful, indeed," replied Emma, and she spoke so kindly that Frank gratefully burst out, "How delighted I am to see you again! And to see you in such excellent looks! I would not have missed this meeting for the world."

Emma and Mr. Woodhouse shortly left the Westons and, during the carriage ride home, she felt happy for Frank and Jane. But comparing Mr. Churchill and Mr. Knightley, she felt she was engaged to the gentleman with superior character. Her thoughts regarding his worth completed the happiness of this most happy day.

CHAPTER 55

A FEW DAYS LATER, Harriet returned from London and, within an hour of visiting at Hartfield, convinced Emma that Mr. Robert Martin had thoroughly replaced Mr. Knightley and was now the source of all her happiness.

Emma gave Harriet her most sincere congratulations on her engagement, and Harriet returned her congratulations to Emma.

Harriet admitted that she had been silly, presumptuous, and self-deceived regarding Mr. Knightley. Thus, she was left without a care for the past and with the fullest excitement for the present and future with Robert Martin.

The fact was, as Emma could now acknowledge, that Harriet had always liked Robert Martin and that his continuing to love her had been irresistible.

Harriet's father was revealed to be a tradesman, rich enough to afford his daughter a comfortable life but certainly not the blood of gentility which Emma had formerly imagined! Harriet's father generously approved of his daughter's engagement.

As Emma became acquainted with Robert Martin, who was now introduced at Hartfield, she fully acknowledged his worth for her little friend Harriet.

Emma had no doubt of Harriet's happiness, and in the home he offered there would be security, stability, and improvement. She would be among those who loved her and would be respectable and happy. And Emma admitted that Harriet was the luckiest creature in the world, after herself.

✌

That September, Emma attended the wedding—Harriet's hand bestowed on Robert Martin, with Mr. Elton presiding over the ceremony. Several days later, Emma was pleased to see how happy Robert and Harriet looked—with matching bright red eyes.

Jane Fairfax had left Highbury and was back in the comforts of her beloved home with the Campbells. In November, she and Frank Churchill were to be married.

Emma and Mr. Knightley had decided to marry in October while John and Isabella visited at Hartfield. But Mr. Woodhouse was miserable at the thought of losing Emma. She could not bear to see him suffering and decided to postpone the wedding.

In this state of suspense, a fortunate thing occurred. Mrs. Weston's poultry yard was robbed one night of all her turkeys. Other poultry yards in the neighbourhood also suffered. Clearly, a pilferer was about.

Mr. Woodhouse became very nervous and feared that, without the protection of Mr. Knightley, he would be under wretched alarm every night of his life.

The result of this distress was that, with a much more voluntary, cheerful consent than his daughter had ever hoped for, Emma was able to fix her wedding day—and Mr. Elton was called on to join the hands of Mr. Knightley and Miss Woodhouse.

The wedding was very simple, without finery or parade. Mr. Elton sent shocks of joy through Emma and Mr. Knightley as he joined their hands in holy matrimony.

Mrs. Elton thought the wedding was extremely shabby, very inferior to her own.

But, in spite of these deficiencies, the wishes, the hopes, the confidence, and the predictions of the small band of true friends who witnessed the ceremony were fully answered in the perfect happiness of the union.

As the joyous ceremony concluded, the watchful eyes inside the church were joined by watchful eyes outside—a hundred wild, ragged vampires, some sucking the blood of turkeys while most awaited the more savoury fare of aristocratic blood.

ACKNOWLEDGEMENTS

M Y FIRST THANKS ARE to Jane Austen, who believed she had created, in *Emma*, "a heroine whom no one but myself will much like." It became, instead, a masterpiece. My retelling of *Emma*, aside from the vampire humor, is an attempt to make this delightful novel accessible to modern readers, especially young adults.

I wish to thank my loving wife, Peggy, for her many years of staunch and unwavering support of my effort to launch a second career in writing. I also wish to thank my children—Brad, Seton, and Meg—for their love and faith in me. I especially thank Meg for introducing me to the world of vampires, which helped inspire this book.

I would be nowhere without my glorious agent, Jill Grosjean. Appropriately called the "patron saint of first-time novelists" by one of her New York Times bestselling authors, she believed in me when I did not, and with tireless persistence and encouragement found the very best home for my book.

Sourcebooks Landmark is an extraordinary publishing house with extraordinary people. I wish to thank, above all, my editor, Deb Werksman. She saw the potential in my book and then, with encouragement and compassion, inspired and challenged me to elevate it to its full potential. *Emma and the Vampires* would, quite simply, not be the book it is without her. Thanks as well to my Associate Editor Susie Benton for the time, attention, and care she devoted to my book, my Production Editor Sarah Ryan and her excellent copyediting staff, and my Publicity Manager Liz Kelsch for her exceptional efforts in promoting the book.

ABOUT THE AUTHOR

After a career on Wall Street as a research analyst, Wayne Josephson decided to pursue his long-delayed desire to write. He was a screenwriter for several years before realizing his true passion was fiction. His love of the classics led to the creation of *Emma and the Vampires*. Wayne resides in Virginia with his wife and three children.

MR. DARCY, VAMPYRE
PRIDE AND PREJUDICE CONTINUES...
AMANDA GRANGE

"A seductively gothic tale..." —Romance Buy the Book

A test of love that will take them to hell and back...

My dearest Jane,

My hand is trembling as I write this letter. My nerves are in tatters and I am so altered that I believe you would not recognise me. The past two months have been a nightmarish whirl of strange and disturbing circumstances, and the future...

Jane, I am afraid.

It was all so different a few short months ago. When I awoke on my wedding morning, I thought myself the happiest woman alive...

"Amanda Grange has crafted a clever homage to the Gothic novels that Jane Austen so enjoyed." —*AustenBlog*

"Compelling, heartbreaking, and triumphant all at once."
—*Bloody Bad Books*

978-1-4022-3697-6
$14.99 US/$18.99 CAN/£7.99 UK

"The romance and mystery in this story melded together perfectly... a real page-turner." —*Night Owl Romance*

"Mr. Darcy makes an inordinately attractive vampire.... *Mr. Darcy, Vampyre* delights lovers of Jane Austen that are looking for more." —*Armchair Interviews*

A Certain
Wolfish
Charm

by Lydia Dare

Regency England has
gone to the wolves!

The rules of Society can be beastly...

...especially when you're a werewolf and it's that irritating time of the
month. Simon Westfield, the Duke of Blackmoor, is rich, powerful,
and sinfully handsome, and has spent his entire life creating scandal
and mayhem. It doesn't help his wolfish temper at all that Miss Lily
Rutledge seems to be as untamable as he is. When Lily's beloved
nephew's behavior becomes inexplicably wild, she turns to Simon
for help. But they both may have bitten off more than they can chew
when each begins to discover the other's darkest secrets...

"*A Certain Wolfish Charm* has bite!"

—Sabrina Jeffries, *New York Times* bestselling
author of *Wed Him Before You Bed Him*

978-1-4022-3694-5 • $6.99 U.S./$8.99 CAN/£3.99 UK

TALL, DARK AND WOLFISH

BY LYDIA DARE

REGENCY ENGLAND HAS GONE TO THE WOLVES!

He's lost unless she can heal him

Lord Benjamin Westfield is a powerful werewolf—until one full moon when he doesn't change. His life now shattered, he rushes to Scotland in search of the healer who can restore his inner beast: young, beautiful witch Elspeth Campbell, who will help anyone who calls upon her healing arts. But when Lord Benjamin shows up, everything she thought she knew is put to the test...

Praise for *A Certain Wolfish Charm:*

"Tough, resourceful, charming women battle roguish, secretive, aristocratic men under the watchful eye of society in Dare's delightful Victorian paranormal romance debut."

—*PUBLISHERS WEEKLY* (STARRED REVIEW)

978-1-4022-3695-2 • $6.99 U.S./$8.99 CAN/£3.99 UK

THE WOLF NEXT DOOR

BY LYDIA DARE

REGENCY ENGLAND HAS GONE TO THE WOLVES!

Can she forgive the unforgivable?

Ever since her planned elopement with Lord William Westfield turned to disaster, Prisca Hawthorne has done everything she can to push him away. If only her heart didn't break every time he leaves her. Lord William throws himself into drinking, gambling, and debauchery and pretends not to care about Prisca at all. But when he returns to find a rival werewolf vying for her hand, he'll stop at nothing to claim the woman who should have been his all along, and the moon-crossed lovers are forced into a battle of wills that could be fatal.

"With its sexy hero, engaging heroine, and sizzling sexual tension, you won't want to put it down even when the moon is full."

—SABRINA JEFFRIES, *NEW YORK TIMES* BESTSELLING AUTHOR OF *WED HIM BEFORE YOU BED HIM*

978-1-4022-3696-9 • $6.99 U.S./$8.99 CAN/£3.99 UK